I0733565

# HIGH KING

## A TIME TRAVEL ROMANCE

## BY KATHRYN LE VEQUE

© Copyright 2014, 2023 by Kathryn Le Veque Novels, Inc.
Trade Paperback Edition

Text by Kathryn Le Veque
Cover by Kim Killion

Reproduction of any kind except where it pertains to short quotes in relation to advertising or promotion is strictly prohibited.

All Rights Reserved.

The characters and events portrayed in this book are fictitious. Any similarity to real persons, living or dead, is purely coincidental and not intended by the author.

NOVELS

WWW.KATHRYNLEVEQUE.COM

## ARE YOU SIGNED UP FOR KATHRYN'S BLOG?

You'll get the latest news and information on exclusive giveaways, exclusive excerpts, coming releases, sales, free books, cover reveals, and more.

Kathryn's blog followers get it all first. No spam, no junk.

Get the latest info from the reigning Queen of English Medieval Romance!

**Sign Up Here**

kathrynleveque.com

# AUTHOR'S NOTE

*Finally!*

I know that's what most of you are saying. *Echoes of Ancient Dreams* was the first part of this two-parter and my intentions had always been to finish the second part quickly, but life got in the way. And publishing schedules. My time, as usual, was under such constraint that squeezing in the second part of *Echoes of Ancient Dreams* became increasingly difficult. But—no more. I finally finished it and, holy smokes, what a story it turned out to be!

What can I say? I love Ireland and its rich history!

The first thing I want to be clear on is that I took Part One (*Echoes of Ancient Dreams*) and Part Two (*High King*) and combined them into one book—entitled *High King*. It didn't seem right having the story in two parts sold separately (as you know, I don't serialize or break books up like that), so here's the full novel, both parts, with Part One updated and re-edited. If you already read Part One, you were probably going to buy Part Two, so I just put them together for your convenience.

The second thing I want to mention (and you'll see the family chart) is that the hero of this tale, Conor, is an ancestor of Bric MacRohan from *High Warrior* (and from other Executioner Knight series books). That was always intended—I just had to plot out the actual family lineage. One thing about Irish history (and clan lineage) is that there's a lot of it. And it is very detailed!

There were many kings in Ireland, mostly because there

were many kingdoms in Ireland. There was an overall high king of Ireland since the Dark Ages into the High Middle Ages, but there was so much warring going on that he wasn't recognized by everyone. There were other high kings (for example, a high king of Munster, or of Limerick, etc.). I chose not to get into that history in-depth in this novel simply because it's not a focal point. Frankly, information for high kings comes from many different sources. Suffice it to say that I've done my research, so much of what you read will be historically accurate except for Conor, who is fictional.

Specifically, the kingdom of Ciannachta, the focus of the second part of the tale, is indeed an ancient Irish kingdom and the location is accurate. During this time in which the tale is set, there were no kings, so our hero fit into that line nicely. As an author friend of mine aways says (and she's got a few history degrees), if you can't *prove* it didn't happen, then who's to say it didn't? Meaning that if we can't prove our hero wasn't the king during that period of time, then maybe he was? A stretch, I know, but that's the beauty of fiction.

The usual pronunciation guide:
Ciannachta—Ky-an-ACT-ta
Cian—Ky-an
Bradaigh—Brad-dug, or more like Braddock
Padraigan—Pa-DRAY-gan
Auley—basically, "Ollie"
Anahera—Ah-na-HAIR-uh

All I can say at this point is get ready for a wild ride in Medieval Ireland. I've always loved writing time travel because no rules apply, so this was a fun one to finally finish.

I hope you love it!

Happy Reading,

Kathryn

# LINE OF THE HIGH KINGS OF CIANNACHTA

The Dalcassians, inarguably the greatest tribe in Ireland, has spawned a number of high kings, including the MacRohan line, who were the direct line of the high kings of Ciannachta, later Drogheda.

A man's surname was generally his father's name. In the case of Conor Da Derga, later known as the Traveler/the Wanderer (in a spiritual sense), his eldest son took the name MacRohan, meaning son of the Traveler/Wanderer, which held as part of the firstborn son's name for a few generations until it fell off for a couple of generations because only daughters were born to Berach MacCarthair. She married a man named Braden and through him, the MacRohan line resumed. Rohan MacDurmot picked it up again and his son, Bric, carried the name MacRohan permanently, as did his progeny. Coincidentally, Bric's first son was named Conor.

| |
|---|
| Conor "The Red" Da Derga/Mac Rohan<br>b. 913 |
| Mattock "The Enlightened" MacRohan<br>b. 930 |
| Anrai "The Wise" MacRohan MacMattock<br>b. 960 |
| Cathair "Yellow Beard" MacRohan MacAnrai<br>b. 993 |
| Berach MacRohan MacCathair<br>b. 1020 |
| Caitleen O'Berach, Queen<br>b. 1052 |
| Brien (or Briain) MacBradan<br>b. 1083 |
| Durmot "The Hammer" MacRohan MacBriain<br>b. 1112 |
| Rohan (MacRohan) MacDurmot<br>b. 1148 |
| Bric MacRohan<br>b. 1178 |

# CHAPTER ONE

*Present Day*

"WHAT IN THE hell is that guy doing up there?"

The woman asking the question looked genuinely curious. Her friend, wrapped up against the cold afternoon and kicking at a rock in the middle of the footpath, glanced up to see what the woman was referring to. She could see a man at the top of the green, damp mound, a very big man, speaking with great animation to a group of young people.

"That guy?" She pointed.

"Yes." Her friend nodded. "He's waving his arms around like he's trying to take off."

The friend giggled, looking back to the footpath they were on so she wouldn't trip. "I have no idea what he's doing." She snorted. "These ancient religious places seem to affect people."

The first woman looked around. It was a beautiful afternoon in the lush countryside of Ireland, a color of green she had never seen before. It was so vibrant that it was almost neon in patches. The weather was cool and damp, as it had rained heavily that morning, but now the sun was out and everything just seemed fresh and vivid. A cool breeze blew in from the

Irish Sea to the east, stirring the bushes and branches as the pair walked up the path toward the animated man and his captive audience.

"It's not just these religious sites," the first woman said as she shoved her hands deep into the pockets of her jacket as the wind picked up. "It's the Irish in general."

The friend turned to look at her. "Don't bash my people."

"They're my people, too. I can bash them if I want to."

The two women snorted as they made their way up the muddy, grassy path. They were clearly Americans from their accents, so the talk of bashing the Irish was in a tribute to their heritage, watered down over the generations. They were currently on a tour of the "old country," on a whirlwind holiday that saw them paying a visit to the great Neolithic burial mound of Dowth.

About thirty-two miles north of Dublin, Dowth was a massive Neolithic site that was larger than its better-known counterpart, New Grange. Not many people came to visit Dowth, but Destry Caldbeck and her friend, Aisling Reilly, had made the trip, mostly because Aisling was kicking Destry all the way across Ireland and forcing her to participate in activities when Destry would rather be sitting in a pub drowning her sorrows.

Being jilted at the altar had had that effect on her.

The truth was that Destry and Aisling were enjoying what should have been Destry's honeymoon, but it had been an uphill battle. Constant sightseeing had been Aisling's way of keeping Destry's mind off the situation. Even now, she tried to keep the mood light as they reached the crest of the ancient mound, noting the enormous man with the group around him at closer range. The man was indeed waving his arms around, apparently acting out some kind of scene as the people around him watched intently. Aisling and Destry couldn't help but watch him, too, until Destry finally shook her head and looked away. She pulled a small guidebook out of her pocket and began to read.

"Okay," she said, finding her place in the book. "Let's see what this has to say—Dowth dates from around three thousand BC and has all sorts of underground storage chambers. It's part of the *Brú na Bóinne* monuments."

Aisling looked around the top of the mound where they were standing. "What does that mean?"

Destry continued to read. "Neolithic monuments like New Grange."

"That one is next on our list."

"I know." Destry put the guidebook down and began to look around. "This site is really big."

Aisling began to wander. "Huge," she agreed, wrapping her scarf more tightly about her neck because the wind was blowing. "But why is it so darn cold? You would think it was January and not September. I feel like I'm in the Arctic."

Destry shrugged. "Maybe we should have gone to the Bahamas."

"Maybe."

Aisling continued wandering, looking at their surroundings. Then she came to a halt, cocking her head in the direction of the man and his group. She listened a moment before looking to Destry.

"It sounds like he's giving a tour," she said. "I can hear him."

Destry's gaze lingered on the man several dozen feet away. "Should we go listen?"

Aisling waggled her eyebrows devilishly. "We didn't pay for the tour. Not only that, but we busted through the fence to get up here. I really don't think we're even supposed to be here."

Destry shrugged. "The worst he can do is tell us to go away."

Aisling snorted as Destry began to saunter casually in the direction of the group. The area of the top of the mound was fairly vast and uneven and had been closed off to the public. But Destry and Aisling had climbed through the fence anyway and walked up the narrow path.

As they neared the group, they could hear the man as he continued his story.

And what a story it was.

❧

"...TOMB WAS EMPTIED of its original contents when it was plundered by Viking raiders around 861 AD, who basically plundered all of the tombs in the Boyne Valley," he was saying with great drama. "Much of our Irish heritage ended up on a long boat bound for Scandinavia, where some of it is now in Scandinavian museums."

A young college student with a dirty stocking cap on his head threw up a hand and began to speak. "Dr. Da Derga?" he called. "Haven't we tried to get our treasures back from the Scandinavians?"

Dr. Conor Da Derga turned to look at the young man with a wry smirk on his face. "It's like the British stealing treasures from Egypt and putting them in the British Museum," he said, his Irish brogue heavy and dramatic to the point of barely being understandable. "The British won't give them back to Egypt, and the Viking plunderers won't give us back our treasures, either. They stole our history and claim it as their own."

A question-and-answer session followed as Destry and Aisling stood at the back of the group, listening. Destry's attention was mostly on the teacher and not on the students. Since the group was made up of young adults, she could only assume it was a college class. Dr. Da Derga was, in fact, everything an Irishman should be—he was loud, passionate, animated, handsome, and had a deep red mustache and goatee that stood out against his milky-white skin. Even though the man was bundled up against the cold, she could see that he had red hair beneath his well-worn newsboy cap.

But she noticed more—he was absolutely enormous in both size and height. She was three inches over five feet herself, and the man had to be well over a foot taller than she was, and built like a linebacker. She thought he was very good-looking with his chiseled features and brilliant smile, something that Aisling silently agreed with as she flashed a wicked smile in Destry's direction.

And he was dynamic, too. Great passion came forth as he moved away from plundered Irish history and began to describe the history of Dowth. He waved his arms and bugged his eyes as he described ancient man and their toils on the mound. Then he began to speak of more recent history, of the Dark Age village that had popped up around Dowth, fragments of which had been excavated.

Destry watched the man, finding herself focusing more on his handsome features than what he was actually saying. A couple of times, their eyes met and she felt strangely unsettled as he focused in on her. The man had intense blue eyes, bordering on something magnetic and powerful, and Destry was too fragile to rationally deal with anything intensely male at the moment. She tried to stay and listen, but his gaze kept coming back to her, each look more potent than the last. Disturbed, she broke off from the group as Aisling remained and wandered away.

The grass was thick, wet, and vibrantly green as she made her way down the side of the mound. She lost her footing a couple of times and slid in the grass, eventually ending up at the bottom of the mound.

There was a lot of foliage around the base of the mound, thick brush growing out from the sides. She pulled out her guidebook and began to read again, noting that it said there were three entrances at the base of the mound, all facing southwest. Getting her bearings, she shifted direction and wandered through the brush until she came to the first of the three passages.

The first passage was small, and all she could see was darkness beyond the stone-braced doorway. There was a metal grate covering the entrance that was wobbly in parts, but she didn't feel like pulling it back and charging in to a bottomless black pit. Moreover, she didn't have a flashlight, and the sun was beginning to set, so it was difficult to see more than just a few feet inside. Still, she could smell wet earth and mold coming forth, invisible wisps of ancient times that were reaching out for her. She wasn't superstitious by nature, and she wasn't easily spooked, but something about the dark bowels of the ancient burial mound made her shiver. Maybe it was just the coldness of the air coming forth. Whatever it was, she shrugged it off and moved to the next entrance.

She could see more through this entrance, but it wasn't any grander than the last. It was just old and creepy, covered with another gate. On to the third entrance, she moved in and out of the heavy growth, trying not to get wet from the moisture that still lingered.

Over to the southwest, the sun was sitting on the horizon as night began to approach, and Destry was beginning to think that they should head back to the car. She was looking forward to a hot meal and a hot bath, in that order. Maybe they would also hit a few of the pubs, seeking some solace and distraction in the Irish pastime. Not that she wanted to get drunk. Well, maybe. It seemed to be the only thing that made her forget about the hell of the past two weeks.

Of the anguish she'd been put through.

The third passage was taller than the other two, with the same black-hole entrance. Oddly, the gate was ajar. Destry couldn't see more than a few feet inside of it, and wished she had brought a flashlight. She could feel the dampness from this hole reaching out to her again, caressing her face with cold fingers. It also smelled strange, like the dank depths of a grave, which it essentially was. The guidebook said that Medieval people used the mound to store food and that there was a storage chamber inside.

Peering into the blackness, Destry noticed the weak rays of the setting sun were shining on this side of the mound. A few streamed through the bushes and fell upon the peripheral of the ancient doorway. She stood there for a moment, hoping if she waited long enough that the sun would act as a flashlight and shine down into the tunnel.

It was growing colder as the sun was lowering in the sky, and she tightened up her scarf and shoved her hands into her pockets, waiting for the sun to shine its dying rays into the ancient tunnel. The breeze had picked up, too, filtering through the bushes around her. The wind whipped into the passageway and found its way out again. The first couple of times, it whipped around her, and she shivered against the iciness. Then came a particularly strong gust of wind that soared through the other tunnels, and then blasted out of the tunnel where Destry was standing. She turned her back on it as it swirled around her, whistling through the stone and earth with an odd hum. At the height of the gust, she thought she heard something whispered upon the wind.

*Etain!*

Startled, Destry turned to see if someone was standing behind her. It sounded as if someone had whispered in her ear, a breathy gasp that was quickly gone. But the tunnel was dark, the wind brisk, and she shook her head, thinking that it had only been the wind. Clearly, it couldn't have been anything else.

Yawning, she watched the sun set lower on the horizon, turning to see that some of the weak rays had invaded the tunnel. She was looking forward to seeing what was deep down inside the hill. But another gust of wind whipped through the mound, and she turned away from the tunnel as bits of rock and loose earth kicked up at her. She closed her eyes against the flying dust, and the whisper on the wind filled her ears again.

*Etain!*

Destry jumped at the sound, turning back to the dark opening now that the sun was just beginning to fall upon it. She gazed at it suspiciously, thinking that someone was playing tricks on her.

"Hello?" she called. "Who's in there? Come out of there or I'm coming in."

Nothing but the wind answered. Levelheaded and brutally practical, Destry waited for a few red-headed Irish kids to come running out to scare her. But no one emerged from the tunnel, and as she moved in to get a closer look, the sun's rays hit the ancient entrance, reflecting on stone and earth that had seen five hundred centuries of such events. The sun reached the rock, cut by the ancients, and the cold, porous blocks roared to life.

Abruptly, it was very bright in the entrance, and Destry could see all the way back to the end of the tunnel. The walls were lined with stone, great carved slabs that held back the tons of earth surrounding it. The sun gave the stone a strange yellow glow, reflecting the brilliance of the setting rays. But as Destry studied the tunnel with interest, the yellow glow took on an even brighter countenance.

It wasn't so much the stone, as something else seemed to be creating a light of its own. The great yellow glow became brighter and brighter until it was nearly white. Destry put a hand up to shield her eyes from the glare, and as she did so, something in the midst of the great white glow reached toward her.

*"Etain!"*

It wasn't one whisper; it was several. It was like hundreds of children whispering as one, a chorus of angels that breathed life upon the earth. Destry felt a great rush of air as the whisper burst forth like a thousand shooting stars, reaching out to touch her. It all happened so fast that she didn't have time to be startled; as she stood there, something brushed against her hand, and she heard the chorus of whispers once more.

*"Fanacht, morrigan, gnáthlá agus oiche og ceanna; tar ar cúl do sinne."*

Destry didn't even remember running away until she was halfway up the hill. Her heart was pounding and her head swimming, and she was so frightened that she could hardly think straight. But she was walking very quickly up the hill, anxious to put space in between her and the mysterious tunnel. She had no idea what those odd whispers were, but it was the touch that had sent her scurrying.

For several long moments, disorientation consumed her. There was no way that whatever had happened was real, she told herself firmly. She forced herself to calm, taking deep breaths, struggling with her equilibrium and her composure. It hadn't been real; it *couldn't* have been. The sunlight, the wind, had been playing tricks on her.

She kept telling herself that, over and over.

By the time she reached the top of the mound, Destry was slightly less frazzled, but only barely. At least she wasn't gasping for air any longer. On the crest of the mound, the students had disbanded and were walking around the ancient hill in small clusters, inspecting it, and she could see Aisling standing with the tall and imposing figure of Dr. Da Derga. She was talking to him about something, her hands flying all around, as they usually did when she talked.

Taking another deep breath, and with a glance over her shoulder, Destry made her way over to Aisling and Dr. Da Derga.

But she swore that the whispers were following.

# CHAPTER TWO

C ONOR SAW HER coming.

He saw her the moment she crested the top of the hill, the very moment her gaze turned in his direction. He'd noticed her the first time she and her friend had joined his class, a woman of unearthly beauty and brilliant blue eyes. He couldn't seem to stop staring at her, like she was a magnet and his eyes were steel. The two kept coming together, and he could feel the sparks fly every time. Something about that woman leapt out at him like nothing he had ever experienced before. It was a strange and alluring sensation, and one not easily discarded.

Her friend, a nice young lady with the good Irish name of Aisling, had engaged him in conversation when his class broke up. As his students went about on exploration before the sun sank too low, the young woman with curly brown hair and brown eyes had approached him with a smile. She wanted to know if he had any information about the great burial mound at Dowth and whether or not the legends were true about it being a portal into the Underworld.

Conor had responded politely to her foolish question, mostly because she was American and he knew she was only repeating what she had heard or seen in movies. Most Americans viewed the world the way their movies portrayed it. But he was also courteous because of the fair-skinned goddess that had accompanied her, on the off chance that he might actually get to speak with her.

Now, she was heading right for him.

His hopes were about to be fulfilled. He couldn't help but stare at the woman as she approached; she was short in stature, clad in a sweater and jeans, but there was no mistaking her curvy figure. Her light brown hair was long, with streaks of blonde in it, and cut into one of those layered styles that could be very sexy with a toss of the head.

As the woman came upon them, he was struck by the porcelain beauty of her face and eyes so bright that they were nearly glowing. He'd never seen such a brilliant shade of blue.

When their eyes finally met, he felt his heart flutter in his chest. He stared at her with a dumb grin on his face as Aisling spoke.

"Where did you wander off to?" she asked her friend.

The woman threw a thumb over her shoulder. "Down the hill," she said in a sweet, sultry voice. "There are passages down there."

"Passages?" Aisling was curious but remembered her manners, indicating the big Irishman standing next to her. "This is Dr. Da Derga. He's a professor over at Trinity College in Dublin. We apparently invaded his class."

The woman turned to him, her bright blue eyes swallowing him up. She extended a hand. "Nice to meet you, Dr. Da Derga," she said. "Destry Caldbeck."

Conor was stupefied as he shook her soft, warm hand, feeling rather overwhelmed with such beauty. He felt like an idiot just staring at her and realized he should probably say something in return.

*Where have you been all my life, gorgeous?*

"Nice to meet you," he replied in his heavy Irish accent. "You're American also?"

Destry nodded. "I am," she replied. "California."

"Where in California?"

"San Diego." She pulled her hand discreetly from his grip because he hadn't let her go yet. He'd just stood there holding her hand. There was something very big and virile and overwhelming about him. "Thank you for letting us infiltrate your class. You looked like you were having a lot of fun."

He smiled at her. In fact, he couldn't seem to stop smiling at her. "I was," he replied. "This is one of my ancient Irish history classes. We've toured three of the major sites today, this one being our last. It's going to get dark quickly, so they're taking a few moments to explore the site before we buzz off."

Destry nodded, glancing around at the students who were spread out over the top of the mound, poking around.

"You certainly had their attention with your stories," she said. "It sounds like you have a pretty cool class."

His grin grew. "They're not stories," he corrected her. "They're Irish history."

She laughed softly, displaying her beautiful smile and the big dimple in her left cheek. "I believe you," she said. "In fact, it wouldn't hurt Aisling or me to learn a little Irish history. Aisling's parents were born in Ireland, and my mother's parents were both born here before immigrating to the States back in the nineteen fifties. That's sort of why we're here; to get back in touch with our roots."

Conor was completely focused on Destry, the shape of her

face and the soft curve of her lips. He couldn't seem to look at anything else. "Welcome back."

Destry grinned at him, giving him a quirky lift of the shoulder. "Thank you," she said. "It's good to be back."

He laughed softly, shoving his hands in his pockets as the wind picked up. "There's a problem, though."

"What?"

"You're lacking a good Irish name like your friend. I'm surprised they let you into the country."

In spite of herself, Destry was finding herself swept up in his charm. There was something very magnetic about him. "My middle name is Kenna," she offered, putting up her hand as if swearing in court. "I promise; my mother named me after my grandmother, so there really is Irish in me."

"Kenna." He rolled it off his tongue with his Irish brogue. "It means ancient one. But I have no idea what Destry means."

"It's of French origin. It means desired," she said. "My entire name means desired ancient one."

He grinned from ear to ear. "Then I approve," he said. "It suits you perfectly."

Destry laughed, feeling rather giddy for a woman who had been wallowing in rejected misery for the past two weeks. Dr. Da Derga's compliments were doing something to ease that great big hole in her chest where her heart had once been. In fact, his presence had an odd effect on her, making her feel light and happy like she hadn't been in a very long time. She had seriously wondered over the past several days if she would ever be happy again.

"Thank you very much, Dr. Da Derga," she said graciously, distracted when a big gust of wind whipped around her and reminded her of the bizarre experience she'd had a few moments before. She couldn't help but think of the whispers, of the word she'd heard more than once from that dark, unnatural tunnel.

Since Da Derga seemed to be an expert on the site, she decided to probe him a little to see if she'd really been imagining things. "Do you mind giving us a crash course in this site? Anything interesting that the guidebook doesn't tell us?"

He looked around, watching his students wander around the slick green hill. "It's a Neolithic burial mound," he said. "During the Dark Ages, the indigenous population used to say that the gods lived under mounds like this. It was their way of explaining away what Stone Age man had built."

Destry thought of the howling passage, of her experience, and began to get creeped out again.

"Have you ever heard the word 'Etain'?" she asked, out of the blue.

Conor turned to look at her. "Of course," he said. "She's a heroine in Irish mythology."

A bolt of shock ran through Destry, and she glanced uneasily down the hill where the dark passages loomed. All of the effort she had taken to convince herself that the experience had been in her imagination was torpedoed by those eight little words.

"Seriously?" she asked, feeling somewhat sick. "It's a woman?"

"Absolutely."

Destry's sense of uneasiness increased. "Is she evil?" she asked, then quickly clarified because she didn't want him to think she was some oddball. "I mean, what was her story? Did she live underneath one of these mounds?"

He shook his head. "No," he replied. "She's a heroine in

some of the earliest Irish mythology cycles. She appears a few times in a few different stories. Why do you ask?"

There was no way Destry was going to tell him the reason behind her questions. She shook her head, almost too quickly.

"No reason," she replied. "Just curious. I heard the name somewhere, and I was just… curious."

He bought her explanation. "I'd be happy to refer you to some books on Irish mythology that recite Etain's tales," he said. "Or I could tell you the stories myself. Sometime. If you're not too busy."

The man didn't waste any time. He had known her all of two minutes and was already asking her on a date without really asking. As much as he had charmed her, Destry wasn't ready to interact with a man one on one, no matter how attracted she was to him. Too much about her personal life was painful and unsettled, and she didn't want to complicate things.

Problem was, she couldn't bring herself to flatly turn him down.

"You know all of the Irish mythology stories by heart?" she asked with incredulity.

He shrugged. "It's my job to know them," he said. "Plus, they're very exciting. Better than the movies."

"I saw you reciting something to your students earlier, flapping your arms around. Were you telling them some of the stories?"

"Of course." His grin broadened. "What else would I be doing?"

A sharp whistle pierced the air, and they turned to see one of the male students rounding the group up. Aisling, having been largely ignored throughout the conversation between Destry and Dr. Da Derga, tugged on her friend's arm.

"Come on," she said. "It's getting dark, and we need to head back. I'm not comfortable driving on the right side of the car on these small roads after dark."

Destry followed as Aisling began to walk, turning to thank Dr. Da Derga for his time but seeing that he was trailing after them. Everyone was traveling in herds toward the slope that led down to the car park on the north side of the mound as the world around them began to dim with the coming night.

"How long are you both here?" Conor strolled up beside Destry. "Are you doing any tours or just winging it?"

Destry glanced up at him. "We're here for another five days and then we head to Paris," she told him. "We took a tour yesterday in Dublin, and tomorrow we're doing a tour of ancient religious sites on the outskirts."

He nodded casually at the information as his students milled around and behind them, all trudging to the car park.

"So you're staying in Dublin?" he asked.

She nodded. "We're staying at the O'Callaghan Davenport," she told him. "It's by the National Gallery."

He bobbed his head quickly. "I know exactly where it is," he said. "You're not far from the college."

"I didn't know that."

"That's a fairly nice hotel. It's famous for its honeymoon suite, you know. It's supposed to be very romantic."

Destry was staring at the ground as she spoke. "It is," she said softly, then turned to look at him with a forced smile. "It was very nice to meet you, Dr. Da Derga. Good luck with your class."

Conor watched her quickly make her way down the footpath toward the darkening car park. Aisling was still walking a few feet away from him, her brown eyes focused sorrowfully on her friend. She cast an apologetic glance at Conor.

"Thanks again," she said. "It was very nice to meet you."

Before she could scoot after Destry, he reached out and stopped her.

"I'm sorry if I said something offensive," he said, his eyes lingering on Destry at the base of the mound. "I think I upset your friend. I didn't mean to."

Aisling gazed down the hill, watching Destry squeeze through the fence and head toward the car. It wasn't like they were ever going to see Da Derga again, so she just told him the truth.

"Don't worry about it," she said. "You didn't know. The O'Callaghan really does have a hell of a honeymoon suite, and I was supposed to be her husband."

"Come again?"

"She was supposed to be on her honeymoon right now. But I came instead of her groom."

Conor got it, sort of. He watched Aisling skip down the trail, watching the woman slide through the fence in pursuit of her friend. *She was supposed to be on her honeymoon.* He rolled the words over in his head. It was a sad tale, but he couldn't honestly believe that an idiot would refuse to marry that woman.

She was absolutely perfect, and then some.

While he felt some sympathy for her, the larger part of him was glad that she didn't get married. He had her name and the place she was staying at. Right or wrong, like it or not, he intended to do something about it.

# CHAPTER THREE

CONOR GOT THE shock of his life the next morning.

It was around six thirty a.m., a full hour and a half before his eight o'clock class on early Irish Gaelic. He had some papers to grade and some other work to attend to, so he had come in early. The building his office was housed in was the West Theater, an old building on the campus of Trinity College that was well over one hundred years old. It was built of brick and solid masonry, able to withstand the test of time, and always smelled like musty old stone.

Conor had his arms full of his briefcase, laptop, and lunch bag as he entered his office suite. The door was unlocked and his secretary's desk empty; she didn't arrive for another hour. Even so, there was someone sitting in her office.

Destry stood up from the chair she had been patiently planted in as Conor entered the office. His gaze fell on her, and he came to a halt, startled. The lunch bag fell to the ground, and Destry bent down to retrieve it.

"Hi." She smiled weakly at him, propping the lunch bag back on top of his briefcase.

He stared at her a moment as if hardly believing what he

was seeing. "Hi yourself," he replied, a baffled but delighted expression coming to his handsome features. "Uh… what are you doing here?"

Destry's weak smile became genuine. "That's a very good question," she said, suddenly putting her hands up. "Don't worry, I'm not stalking you."

His gaze lingered on her as he moved for his office door. "I'm disappointed," he teased. "Are you sure?"

She giggled. "Pretty sure."

"Can I talk you into it?"

Her laughter grew. "Probably not."

He opened his door. "Truly unfortunate," he said, bobbing his head in the direction of his now-open office. "Care to come in so we can discuss it further?"

Smirking, Destry preceded him into his office, standing near his cluttered desk as he dumped the contents in his arms onto the desktop. She watched him unload, noting he looked distinctly different than he had yesterday—the newsboy cap had concealed flaming red hair, which he had spiked this morning so that it was standing straight up in the air. It was the tallest flat-top she had ever seen, increasing his already substantial height. Given his red goatee and mustache, he looked like a pirate. But his skin was beautiful and pale, and his eyes a clear blue. He was a unique-looking man but absolutely and powerfully handsome.

He pulled off his jacket—he was wearing a worn collared shirt beneath—and when it came off completely, Destry's eyebrows lifted at the size of the man's arms and chest; she had noticed yesterday that he was a big boy, but she had no idea just how big.

The most obvious physical attribute was that he was exceptionally tall; he had to be at least six and a half feet in height. But he was also enormous in breadth, powerfully built like a weightlifter, with a massive upper body and a chiseled torso. He also had very big legs—she could see them through the jeans he wore. His shirt was rather formfitting in displaying his powerful physique. In fact, it made her a little hot to gaze at those beautifully massive biceps, so she tried not to stare as she spoke.

"I'm really sorry to intrude on you so early," she said as he hung up his coat. "I was wondering if you could give me a couple of minutes of your time. I won't take long, I promise."

He turned around from the coatrack and faced her. "I can give you all the time you need until my eight o'clock class," he said. "How'd you find me, by the way?"

She shrugged. "You said you worked at Trinity College. I looked you up in the directory and followed the map."

He nodded faintly, eyeing the woman who only seemed to grow more beautiful with each passing second. Her hair was pulled into a ponytail, revealing the beautiful shape of her face, and she was dressed in a sweater and jeans that accentuated a figure he had only seen on the pages of men's magazines. The sweater gave a tantalizing peek of spectacular cleavage, but he tried not to let his eyes wander down there. He could have stared at that for the rest of his life.

But as he looked at her face, he noticed that she looked exhausted. Her bright blue eyes were somewhat dim. Curious, he indicated the seat in front of his desk.

"Then I'm honored," he said as he took a seat; his old chair creaked and groaned under his considerable weight. "Are you here to take me up on my offer of telling you more glorious Celtic legends?"

Her weak smile returned, and she glanced around his office;

artwork of Celtic crosses lined the walls, as did replicas and images of swords and other battle instruments. There was also a big cape that had some kind of Celtic knot sewn into it, matted to the biggest shadowbox she had ever seen. All in all, it was an office full of rich Celtic relics, something he displayed proudly as a man dedicated to the history of his people.

"Sort of," she replied, suddenly looking uncomfortable. "I didn't know who else to ask about this."

He sat forward, folding his hands on his desk. "Ask what?"

Destry took a deep breath, trying to figure out how to start this conversation. She'd been trying to figure out how to start it for the past two hours, ever since she decided to seek out Dr. Da Derga. She'd been up all night with the dilemma, and now, she hardly knew where to begin. But she had to start somewhere.

She could only hope she didn't come across like a mad-woman.

"Okay, here goes." She puffed out her cheeks and fixed him in the eye. "Dr. Da Derga, I know you don't know me, but I want to assure you that I'm not an idiot or a drama queen. I'm actually quite normal. I have a master's degree in nursing, and I'm a shift supervisor in the coronary care unit at the University of San Diego Medical Center. I come from a nice, normal family with a mom and a dad and a younger sister. I don't drink and I don't do drugs. I was a cheerleader for the San Diego Chargers for a couple of years, and I also do charity work, if that makes any difference. Anyway, I'm a normal girl. But I really need to ask you a question."

His gaze was glittering at her over the top of his desk. "Ask away. I'm all yours."

She stared at him a moment before finally shaking her head. "Please don't think I'm nuts, but I've been up all night with terrible nightmares. I haven't been able to sleep at all. Ever since I left that mound yesterday, I've been having all sorts of… well, crazy thoughts. Really crazy things."

He sat back in his chair. "Like what?"

She threw up her hands, and he could see how exasperated she was, bordering on tears. "All night, every time I fell asleep, I'd have these dreams that I was back at the mound and people inside of it were talking to me."

His brow furrowed. "People *inside* of it?"

She nodded vigorously. "Yes," she insisted. "It was like they were ghosts or something, and I could hear them whispering. They kept trying to talk to me and reach out to me. But I couldn't understand what they were saying."

He was trying not to grin at her, thinking that her problem was more than likely just an overactive imagination. Ancient tales and an ancient site could do that to people who were not accustomed to such things. Personally, he didn't really care why she was here, crazy stories notwithstanding, because it gave him an excuse to see her again.

He remained casual in his reply. "So you've come to me to interpret your nightmares?" he said. "That's really not in my scope of work, but I'll give it a try. What did they say?"

Destry thought a moment, terrified that if she closed her eyes again to remember the words, then she would start having those visions again. They'd swamped her all night, faceless wraiths that invaded her dreams and whispered mysterious words to her. Even thinking about them again made her heart pound. She had been so scared that she had sat up most of the night in the bathroom with the light on. She just couldn't face the dark again.

She gazed at Conor with some pain in her expression. "I

hope you can figure it out," she said, "because I've never had anything like this happen to me, ever, and you were the only person I could think of that might know."

"Like I said, I'll give it a go. What were the words?"

"I don't even know what language they were. They sounded like gibberish to me."

"More than likely, since it was a dream. Do you remember them?

She took a deep breath before haltingly spitting them out. "*Fanacht, morrigan, gnáthlá agus oiche og ceanna; tar ar cúl do sinne.*"

Conor's smile vanished with unnatural rapidity. He stared at her, sitting forward in his chair as a queer expression crossed his features.

"What?" he said, as if he couldn't think of anything else to say. "Where did you hear that?"

She looked sick and scared. "I told you," she said wearily. "That's what those… those ghosts said to me in my dreams. Do you know what language it is? Is it even a language?"

The longer he looked at her, the more confused he became.

He stood up, moving his big body around the side of the desk, all the while seemingly thoughtful. But his expression was full of confusion.

Destry watched him anxiously.

"Do those words mean anything to you?" she asked again.

He looked at her. Then he plopped his buttocks on the edge of his desk and reached out, taking her hands. Flesh met flesh, and the heat from his enormous hands seared her skin. He ended up pulling her off the chair and holding her hands against his broad chest as he looked at her with the most confused expression Destry had ever seen.

"You'd better start from the beginning, sweetheart," he said with a mixture of confusion and patience. "Where did you hear those words?"

She was starting to become frightened. "I told you," she said. "Those ghosts said them to me. But… but I didn't tell you all of it."

"Then tell me all of it."

She hung her head miserably. "Oh, God," she whispered. "You're going to think I'm crazy."

He squeezed her hands, still clutched against his enormous chest. "No, I'm not. Tell me."

"But even I think I'm crazy," she insisted, her eyes coming up to meet his. "Yesterday when you were talking to your students, I walked around the mound."

"I know. I saw you."

"I went down to where the passages were," she said. "I was looking in one of the passages when this wind blew up around me and then I heard someone whisper 'Etain.'"

His eyebrows lifted. "Etain?" he repeated. "Is that why you asked me if I'd ever heard the name?"

She nodded. "Yes," she said. "And… and right at sunset, right when the sun's rays hit the stone slabs of the passage where I was standing, something really weird happened."

"What?"

"I'm not lying about this."

"I know. Tell me what happened."

She took a breath for courage, trying to ignore the fact that he was caressing the fingers he was holding so tightly against his muscular chest. "The passageway got really bright," she said. "And as it brightened, the wind kicked up, blowing out of the tunnel. Not into the tunnel, but out of it. I could hear these whispers coming from inside the mound, like hundreds of people whispering at me. They said, '*Fanacht, morrigan, gnáthlá agus oiche og ceanna; tar ar cúl do sinne.*'"

He gazed steadily at her. "The same thing they said to you in your dream."

"Exactly." She looked imploringly at him. "But what does it mean?"

He continued rubbing her hands, clutched against his chest, as he thought a moment. "Well," he said slowly. "The literal translation is *Be still, fair queen, as day and night become the same. Come back to us.*"

She stared at him, digesting his words, and her eyes suddenly widened. "You… you understood that?"

"I did," he said. "It's an old dialect of Gaelic."

She sighed heavily and pulled away from him, a hand to her head as if to hold in her brain. She stumbled back, sitting heavily on a small couch he had against the wall.

"But that's impossible," she finally said, looking up at him. "I don't even know Gaelic. I don't know anything about it. How could I dream something like that?"

He stood up from his desk, moving slowly in her direction. "You've been in Ireland for a few days," he said. "Maybe you inadvertently heard something like that. Who knows how the mind works?"

She shook her head, baffled. "But that's a full phrase," she said. "More than that, I swear to you that something from that mound touched me yesterday. I could feel it brush against my hand. And I kept hearing 'Etain.' I didn't even know who that was until you told me. How could I imagine that?"

He drew in a long, thoughtful breath before lowering himself next to her on the couch; she was such a little thing compared to his enormous size, and he resisted the urge to put his arm around her to comfort her. She seemed like she needed it, and he would have very much liked to. Instead, he rested his elbows on his knees, folding his hands to keep them from reaching out to her.

"Who knows?" he said quietly. "I wish I could tell you, but that kind of thing is out of my line of work. I wouldn't get so upset about it; it was probably just a fleeting thing."

She looked at him, as close to him as she had ever been. She could see the smoothness of his pale skin and his long white eyelashes.

"So you don't think I'm crazy?" she asked softly.

He smiled faintly. "No," he said. "I think you've got some jet lag and an exhausted mind playing tricks on you."

"I hope so."

"I think I might be able to help, though."

"How?"

"Dinner and drinks. I'd like to show you a little of Dublin and take your mind off your troubles."

A small but genuine smile spread over her lips. "I'm not a charity case, doctor. You don't need to take me on a pity date because deep down, you really think I'm crazy."

He laughed, displaying his big white teeth and slightly prominent canines. He had a magnificent smile.

"Are you joking?" He snorted. "If anything, people will think you're doing me a favor simply by going out with me. In case you haven't realized it, you're an incredibly beautiful woman. I realize that you're way out of my league, but I'd be honored if you would at least consider the dinner and drinks."

Destry was appalled to realize that she was actually considering it. But there was a larger part of her that was bent on self-protection, given what she had just gone through. It was enough to make her greatly indecisive.

"I'd like to," she said honestly. "But… well, it's just not a good idea for me right now. But thank you for the offer."

Based on what her friend Aisling had told him yesterday, he had a pretty good idea why she was rejecting him, and he wasn't the least bit offended. Nor was he deterred.

"I'm really a cad, you know," he said softly.

"Why?"

He waggled his red eyebrows. "Because I'm going to stalk you until you agree to go out with me." As she started to laugh, he grew more animated; he started throwing his big arms around for emphasis. "I'm going to hang out in your hotel lobby and plead my case every time you come out of your room. I may even latch on to your leg and refuse to let go. And if you don't go out with me, I'll… I'll throw myself from the roof, and then you'll be sorry."

She shook her head, still snorting with laughter. "Don't do that," she told him. "I'm not worth it."

His eyes glimmered with humor, with warmth. "Yes, you are," he insisted, his voice softening. "I know this is supposed to be your honeymoon. I may not be your groom, but I'd certainly like to treat you like a very special lady once or twice while you're here. Please don't turn me down."

Destry stared at him, her smile fading. "Did Aisling tell you that?"

He nodded. "When you walked away from me so quickly yesterday, I thought I had offended you. I told Aisling to apologize to you on my behalf, but she said that I hadn't done anything wrong. She told me that you were supposed to be in Dublin on your honeymoon but that it hadn't worked out. So, I apologize if I upset you yesterday commenting about the Davenport's grand honeymoon suite."

Destry averted her gaze from his handsome face and probing eyes. "You didn't," she said. "I guess I'm just going to have to get used to the idea."

"What happened?"

She looked at him sharply, preparing to tell him it was none of his business, but she could see that he wasn't trying to invade her privacy. His gentle question felt caring and sincere. She found herself answering him before she really thought about it.

"I was stupid, I guess." She shrugged. "We had been dating about a year. He was a professional athlete, and I'd heard rumors of him having other women, but I guess I just didn't want to believe it. I thought I could be everything to him. We had this big wedding planned, and on the day of the wedding, I'm all dressed up at the church and his best man came in with a note. The note said that he was sorry but he just couldn't go through with the wedding. So I put away my wedding dress and brought Aisling along with me on what was supposed to be my honeymoon. And here I am."

Conor gazed at her, shaking his head with great regret when their eyes met. "Can I say something, please?" he asked softly.

"Sure."

"He is the stupidest man who has ever walked this earth. What fool would turn down a chance to spend the rest of his life with you?"

"You don't really know me; for all you know, I could be a major pain in the ass."

He laughed. "If you were, I would have already seen the signs by now."

"The nightmares aren't enough of a sign?"

He shrugged. "Maybe a sign that you're a future mental patient, but not a sign that you're a pain in the arse. Your fiancé is a moron, and you're better off without him."

She smiled faintly; somehow, telling him had eased her damaged heart a little. His words made her feel comforted, supported.

She shrugged again, looking at her hands. "I guess I would rather have him back out before the wedding than after," she said. "The main thing is that I'm going to enjoy this trip if it kills me. But this thing with the nightmares is really getting to me. I'm afraid to go back to the hotel and try to sleep, even though I'm exhausted."

His gaze drifted over her face. "You look exhausted," he agreed. Then he suddenly looked around, grabbing a pillow from behind him. He wedged it against the arm of the couch where Destry was sitting. "You can lie down here. I've got some work to do at my desk, and I'll sit with you for a while. If the nightmares come back, I'll chase them away."

She smiled gratefully. "You really don't have to do that," she said. "I've already taken enough of your time."

He waved her off and began shoving her sideways so she would lie down on the couch. "Don't fight with me," he said. "Just lie down. I'll be at my desk if you need me."

"But I can't."

"Why not?"

"Because… well, because we just met each other. This is really strange."

"If you won't go out with me, then at least lie on my couch. It's the least you can do, since you're going to break my heart."

She snorted. But the thought of trying to sleep with his enormous, protective presence just a few feet away admittedly brought her comfort. She could feel herself relenting as she lifted an eyebrow at him.

"Well…" she said reluctantly. "You're not going to try anything funny, are you?"

His brow furrowed. "Like what? Whisper old Irish phrases in your ear while you're sleeping?"

"You'd better not."

He grinned. "I won't, I promise."

They smiled at each other for a few moments, the first true genuinely warm moment they had shared. He was breaking Destry down with his chivalry and kindness, something she very much needed. She finally lowered herself onto the couch as he stood up, taking her legs and putting them up on the couch.

He stood over her a moment, watching her get comfortable. "Are you cozy now?" he asked.

She snuggled down against the pillow, already feeling sleepy. "Fine," she said. "Thanks, Dr. Da Derga. I really appreciate your kindness."

He watched her, realizing he'd probably give everything he owned at the moment for the chance to lie down next to her. He couldn't explain the strong attraction to her or the fact that he wanted to take her into his arms and never let her go. He'd known a lot of attractive women in his life, but he'd never known a pull as strong as this one. It was unsettling but marvelous.

"Please call me Conor," he said softly. "And it's my pleasure."

Destry smiled at him as he winked at her and turned back for his desk. She didn't even remember him sitting down behind it before she was fast asleep.

Destry was screaming again before she realized it.

# CHAPTER FOUR

DESTRY WAS GASPING with panic that was squeezing the breath out of her. Along with the gasping came the tears, and it took her a full minute to realize she was wrapped up tightly in someone's arms. Her face was pressed into a warm, broad chest, and a deep, soothing voice was speaking softly to her. She could smell fabric softener and deodorant.

"It's all right." Conor was sitting on the couch with Destry smothered in his big, warm embrace. A big hand cradled her head against his chest, fingers in her hair. "Quiet, now. You're all right. Everything is all right."

Destry's panicked gasps slowed, and she began to cry as if her heart was broken. "They… they… they came back."

His cheek was against the top of her head as he rocked her gently. "I know," he murmured. "I heard."

His voice was so sweet, so soothing. Destry forgot about her heartbreak, her sorrows, and allowed herself to feel his comfort. She pressed against him, disoriented, exhausted, and half-asleep. It was heavenly.

Eventually, her sobs lessened and she shifted so that her right cheek was against his chest. She could hear his heart beating strongly and steadily, and found more comfort than she had ever known in the arms of a stranger.

Before she realized it, she was asleep again.

Her next awareness was of Conor speaking softly into the top of her head. He was telling her to wake up, and Destry did, gradually, feeling groggy and exhausted. Becoming more oriented, she realized that she was lying against Conor's chest as he sat back against the couch. His big hand was on her head, caressing it, as his soft voice gently brought her around.

"Destry?" he murmured. "Are you awake?"

She sighed heavily, not wanting to move. He was warm and comfortable. "Yes," she whispered.

She swore she felt him kiss the top of her head before speaking. "I'm truly sorry to have to wake you, but I have a class in a few minutes."

"That's okay," she said, forcing herself to wake up. "Oh my God… that was insane."

His mouth was against the top of her head. "What was?"

His hot breath sent shivers down her spine. "The dreams." She finally lifted her head, looking up at him. He was so close that she could have licked him had she stuck out her tongue. "Why in the hell would they come back again? Have you ever heard of recurring dreams like that?"

He shook his head, realizing he wanted nothing more at that moment than to kiss her. It was a badly misplaced impulse that he struggled against. But to have her in his arms wiped out the memory of every other woman he had ever known. No one had ever been so sweet or soft or warm.

No one had ever come close.

He had been sitting at his desk when she first started to whimper in her sleep. By the time he looked up to see what the trouble was, she had been in full-blown hysteria. The only thing he could think to do was to throw his arms around her and hold her tightly, hoping that would give her enough comfort to chase the nightmares away. It had worked, at least for the half-hour he sat with her in his arms. It had been the best half-hour of his life.

"No," he said honestly. "But like I said, this is out of my scope of expertise. Did they repeat that phrase again?"

She shook her head, exhausted, and collapsed back against him. Conor gladly wrapped her up in his enormous arms.

"It wasn't the same one." She huddled against his broad chest. "They said… I think they said something like, '*Tagtha go sinne, morrigan. Naofa… naofa doras uair an grian codail.*' Do you know what it means?"

She felt him sigh before speaking. "'Come to us, fair queen, to the holy door when the sun sleeps.'"

Destry lifted her head, focusing on him again. "Really?"

"Really."

"What in the hell does that mean?"

He gazed at her, reaching up to push a stray strand of hair out of her eyes. "I have no idea," he murmured, his eyes inspecting every inch of her lovely face. "But for your dreams to say something different every time… that's pretty strange."

Destry almost forgot about the dream as she stared at him. She could feel the pull between them, lusty and magnetic, that frightened and enticed her at the same time. There was something overwhelming about the man, growing stronger by the moment.

"I know," she replied softly, knowing she should probably put some distance between them but unwilling to move. "I've been trying to tell myself since yesterday that all of this is in my mind, but I'm starting to think that it's not. Maybe someone is trying to tell me something."

"Like what?"

"I wish I knew," she said. "You're the expert in Irish myths and legends. What do you think?"

He lifted a thoughtful eyebrow as she stared up at him, as if he held all the answers. After a moment, he simply pulled her back against his chest and rested his chin on the top of her head.

"Well," he said, thinking. "The first phrase they spoke was *fanacht, morrigan, gnáthlá agus oiche og ceanna; tar ar cúl do sinne.*"

"Say it again."

"*Fanacht, morrigan, gnáthlá agus oiche og ceanna; tar ar cúl do sinne.*"

"Again."

He grinned. "Why?"

"Because I like hearing you say it."

He laughed softly. "'Be still, fair queen, as day and night become the same. Come back to us,'" he said. "Then the next one was 'Come to us, fair queen, to the holy door when the sun sleeps.'"

"What does it all mean?" she asked.

He thought a moment. Conor had a doctorate in Celtic and Irish history, plus a second doctorate in anthropology—he was a man of reason. He was a great teller of stories, myths, and legends, but the truth was that he didn't believe in ghosts or spirits or prophetic dreams. He had to believe there was a rational explanation for such things.

"Do you honestly want to know?" he replied.

"Of course."

He sighed faintly. "I think that you're in a new place, seeing new things, and that you're exhausted and emotional from what happened to you. I think that you're having nutty dreams because your senses have been weakened by everything going on around you. I further think that somewhere, somehow, you either read or heard those phrases and your subconscious is playing tricks on your tired mind."

Destry looked at him with some disappointment. "You think I made this all up?"

"No," he said firmly. "I think your subconscious did."

As he feared, she pulled out of his arms and stood up, unsteadily, her expression both exhausted and accusing.

"So you really *do* think I'm crazy," she said, jabbing a finger at him. "Look, Dr. Da Derga, I told you I wasn't crazy. I told you I really heard this stuff, and right now, I really dreamed it. I'm not making it up."

He stood up, holding his hands up to soothe her. "I believe that you didn't make it up," he insisted. "But you asked me what I think, and I'm telling you. I think you must have heard these phases some time in your life, maybe so long ago that you don't even consciously remember it, and now they're coming back to you in dreams."

She stared up at him, just looking hurt at this point. After a moment, she lowered her gaze and reached down to collect her purse.

"I am really sorry to have bothered you," she said, putting her purse on her shoulder. "Thanks for... well, not calling me crazy in the beginning. At least you waited a little while."

He moved so that he was standing between her and the door. "Please don't leave," he implored softly. "I didn't call you crazy. And I didn't mean to upset you. I really didn't."

She waved him off, but she couldn't help but notice he was creating a very big barrier between her and the exit. "You didn't upset me," she said. "But I know I didn't imagine being touched out there at Dowth. I know something touched my hand."

He gazed at her a moment. "You said it was very windy," he reminded her quietly. "It could have been the wind."

She lifted an eyebrow. "You don't think I know the difference between a wind gust and a touch?" She went to him and grabbed one of his gigantic hands, holding it up in her warm fingers. "This is a touch, Dr. Da Derga. I know what this feels like. What I felt yesterday felt just like this, only there wasn't anyone there."

He could only concede that he understood what she was saying. Whether or not he believed it was another matter.

"I don't have any explanation for that," he said, holding her hand. "Look, I have a class in a few minutes. Why don't you go back to the hotel and try to get some sleep? I'll ring you around noon to see how you are. If the dreams won't go away, then maybe we need to figure something else out."

She smiled weakly, pulling her hand from his grip when he wouldn't let her go. "I appreciate your offer," she said, "but this isn't your problem. I just wanted to know if you could figure out what those phrases meant. Whatever is going on with me, I'll take care of it."

He regarded her carefully. "You really aren't going to let me take you out, are you?"

Destry could read the disappointment in his face. In fact, she was starting to feel some disappointment, too, at never seeing the man again. He had been a spot of brightness and comfort in her darkened world.

With a heavy sigh, she moved to him, stood on her tiptoes,

and put her soft hand around his thick neck. Pulling his face down to her level, she kissed him gently on the right cheek and quickly stepped back.

"You've been really sweet and incredibly accommodating," she said quietly. "You don't know how much it means to me. Right now, I'm going to take your advice and go back to the hotel and see if I can sleep a little. This whole thing has me kind of rattled."

The kiss to his cheek left Conor with a pounding heart. Had she not moved away from him so quickly, he would have taken her in his arms and kissed her with something more than just a gentle peck. That was kids' stuff. He wanted to kiss her like a man kissed a woman, deeply and passionately, so much so that his hands were beginning to sweat. He wanted to grab her in the worst way.

"You didn't answer my question," he murmured.

"That's because I don't really have an answer for you."

"So there's hope?"

"Maybe." She sighed again, slapping a hand against her thigh in a helpless gesture. "Probably."

His grin returned, as did his complete and utter joy. "To-night?"

She laughed at his enthusiasm. "Hold on," she said. "I don't know about tonight. Let me sleep a little and recover, and we'll go from there."

"That's fair. But I'm still going to ring the hotel later on to see how you are."

Her smile was genuine. "I'd appreciate that."

Since he knew there was hope he'd be seeing her again on a social—and perhaps romantic—level, he stopped blocking the path to the door and escorted her out of his office.

"Is there anything else you want to see that hasn't been included on any of your tours?" he said hopefully. "I'd be happy to be your personal tour guide this weekend."

She laughed softly. "It's not just me—it's Aisling, too."

"She can tag along."

Destry grinned at him. "That's very generous." She sobered as they came to the door that led from his offices out into the main corridor beyond. She paused, gazing up into his pale, handsome face. "Seriously, you've been extremely kind. I can't thank you enough."

He dipped his head graciously. "The pleasure has been all mine, Destry Kenna Caldbeck." He cocked his head. "How'd you get that name, anyway?"

She lifted her eyebrows. "My dad's an old movie buff. I was named after the James Stewart movie of the same name." When he grinned, she shrugged lamely. "Hey; it could have been worse. My younger sister's name is Angel after the John Wayne movie *Angel and the Badman*. Mom threw in the good Irish names; Angel's middle name is Caitlin. That's what she goes by."

He snorted. "I'm the last one to laugh at names," he said. "My birth name isn't Conor Da Derga. It's Conor Peter O'Farrelly. I legally changed it when I got into college and became obsessed with Celtic mythology. I've always felt so misplaced, as if I was born in the wrong time, as if I belonged back in the days when Cuculainn roamed the earth. I wanted to pattern myself after the Irish high warriors, so I adopted a true Irish name."

"And O'Farrelly isn't?"

He shrugged. "It is, but there's an old Irish tale called *Togail Bruidne Dá Derga*, or the Destruction of Da Derga's Hostel—a tale, I might add, that involves the lovely Etain. I changed my name after reading that tragedy because even as I read the words, it was as if I could picture myself right in the middle of the story. It changed my life and focused me on the true value and richness of my Irish heritage."

He was very passionate in his speech, an animated man with a gift for storytelling. She appreciated that quality, something rarely seen where she came from. Conor was a true anomaly in the world, something she was increasingly coming to appreciate.

"You're the most authentic Irishman I've ever met, that's for sure," she said with a twinkle in her eye, extending her hand to him. "Thanks again for everything."

He took her hand, dwarfing it, his eyes never leaving her beautiful face. "*Slán*, sweetheart."

She cocked her head. "What does that mean?"

"Farewell. At least until I ring you later on."

She smiled, almost shyly. "Thanks again."

He should have let her go; he really should have. But he couldn't; impulsively, he grasped her face with his enormous hands and slanted his lips hungrily over hers. He could feel her pulling away out of shock, but very quickly, she stopped pulling. The harder he kissed her, the weaker her resistance. He could feel her caving against him, her soft body melding to his.

Conor's hands left her face as he wrapped his enormous arms around her body, pulling her tightly against him. What was meant to be a short, sweet kiss turned into something heated and sexual very quickly, broken up by the sounds of students entering the corridor for morning classes.

Before they realized it, they were standing about three feet apart. Conor had no idea how they got so far apart; last thing he remembered, he was tasting her sweet, musky flavor with a hint of cherry lip gloss and loving it. Now they were staring at each other as students began to walk by, filling the old corridor as classes prepared to commence.

Conor looked at her apprehensively. "Should I apologize for that?" he whispered.

Destry stared at him a moment, nodding, then shaking her head. She threw up her hands. "I have no idea."

"I don't want to apologize for something that good."

Destry licked her lips, tasting him on her flesh, unbalanced by the entire circumstance. She averted her gaze as she began to walk away.

"Have a good day, Dr. Da Derga," she said as she passed him.

He reached out and grasped her arm, forcing her to stop. She wouldn't look at him as he spoke. "I probably shouldn't have done that, but I'm not sorry I did, if that makes any sense. I don't want to make you uncomfortable."

"You didn't."

From her stiff stance, he wasn't buying it. "I… I don't know what came over me," he insisted softly. "It's just that you're so… I'm so attracted to you that… Destry, I'm sorry. I'm truly sorry if I offended or upset you. I swear to God I'm not trying to get you into bed. I just wanted to kiss you. I've never wanted to do anything so badly in my life."

She did look at him then, forcing a weak smile. "Don't worry about it." She patted the hand on her arm, and he reluctantly let her go. "I'll talk to you later."

"Really?"

"Really."

She took a few steps away before coming to a halt, turning

to see if he was still standing there. He was, looking at her, anxious and distressed. Destry could feel herself easing.

"If it makes any difference, I liked it too."

With that, she turned and continued down the hall.

Conor stood there, watching her perfect butt in her tight jeans and the sexy slope of her torso. He could have watched that woman's butt for the rest of his life. But she eventually disappeared from view, and he went back into his office, struggling to compose himself before his class. Try as he might, he just couldn't shake her. It made for an interesting class when his students couldn't figure out why the normally unflappable Dr. Da Derga seemed so scatterbrained.

Promptly at noon, he rang the hotel, only to find out that she had gone missing.

# CHAPTER FIVE

"I WENT ON that tour this morning of religious sites around Dublin," Aisling said. "She was supposed to come with me but said she wasn't feeling well. And you said that she came to see you this morning?"

Conor and Aisling were in Conor's ten-year-old Vauxhall wagon that had seen better days, tearing north on the M1 motorway from Dublin to Drogheda in the midst of a pouring rainstorm. Dowth was a few miles to the east of the city.

"She did." Conor held tight to the steering wheel as the rain pounded. "Like I said earlier, she told me that spirits or ghosts talked to her when she was out here yesterday, and she had bad dreams about it all night. She came to see me because these ghosts, or whatever they were, were speaking to her in a language she didn't understand. She thought I might. She was upset about it, and something tells me that she might have come back out here again."

Aisling watched the weather ominously. "But why?"

He shook his head, concerned. "She seemed to think her nightmares centered around Dowth because that's where everything started," he said. "Since you have no idea where she is, and she doesn't know the city very well, I just have this odd feeling that she's come back out here to figure out why she seems to be having these nightmares."

"But what if she's been kidnapped? Don't you think we should call the cops?"

"If she's not at Dowth, then we will."

Aisling looked at him, feeling rather guilty about the whole thing. "I know she didn't sleep last night because I woke up in the middle of the night and could see the bathroom light on," she said. "When I got up and knocked on the door, she said she was reading in the bathroom because she couldn't sleep and didn't want to wake me up. Then, this morning, she said she didn't feel well, so I went on the tour without her. But I shouldn't have left her. I should have stayed with her."

Conor could see their exit coming up, the roundabout to the N51 highway east. His sense of urgency was so great that he was flooring the car when he thought he could get away with it.

"You couldn't have known," he replied, though he was feeling some guilt as well. "Maybe I'm the one to blame for this. When she came to see me this morning, she repeated the phrases she had heard in her dreams. I could see how upset she was about it. Maybe… maybe I just should have stayed with her until she calmed down."

Aisling shook her head again, gazing out at the driving rain. "Why?" she said. "She's not your responsibility. But you were able to make sense out of those phrases from her dreams?"

He nodded. "Indeed I was," he replied. "They were a form of Old Gaelic. I told her that somehow, she must have heard the phrases and tucked them into her subconscious. She thought that ghosts were talking to her, and I told her that there had to be a rational explanation."

Aisling just shook her head, baffled by the entire event. "I can't believe she didn't say anything to me about it," she said. "I've known her since we were ten years old, and she tells me absolutely everything."

Conor thought about the implications of that; his growing interest and concern in Destry prompted him to ask questions he hoped Aisling didn't consider probing. He tried to be cool about it.

"Has she ever pulled anything like this before?" he asked.

Aisling shook her head. "No way," she said firmly. "Not Des. It's not like her to leave and not tell anyone. She's one of the most normal, down-to-earth people I know. She's the most perfect person you'll ever meet. She doesn't smoke or drink—she even flosses her teeth every night. Did she tell you that she's a nurse?"

"She did."

Aisling turned to him. "She's not just any nurse—she volunteers her skills to Doctors Without Borders, and she's gone to Haiti twice to give free medical care to refugees. She's like a modern-day Florence Nightingale." She shook her head again, looking back to the window. "What that jerk did to her on her wedding day… I swear, so many people want to kill him. Her dad probably put a contract out on him already."

Conor was forced to slow down in order to take the roundabout. "How did she meet him?"

Aisling held on to the door handle as they took the circular turn. "He's a wide receiver for the San Diego Chargers," she said, looking at him. "Do you know who they are?"

For the first time since getting into the car, he grinned. "Yes, I know who they are," he said, changing lanes as they entered the N51 motorway. "I'm a fan of American football."

"Oh." Aisling continued with her story, gazing out over the new highway. "Anyway, she was one of the Charger Girls, their cheerleading squad. She only tried out for the squad because some of her friends dared her to, but she ended up making it. Boy, was she hot in that little Charger outfit. She got a boob job, and she looked like… Uh, that was probably too much information, right?"

Conor fought off a broader grin. "Not at all. It explains why I… Well, that *would* be too much information, so forget it."

Aisling snorted. "Well, she was the hottest cheerleader they had, at any rate. She was even on the cover of their calendar last year. She was smoking."

"What do you mean 'was'? She still is."

"I saw that you noticed," Aisling teased him. He just waggled his eyebrows, and she continued. "Anyway, I guess he saw her on the sidelines and found out who she was. The cheer squad isn't supposed to fraternize with the players, but he really pursued her heavily. He was a nice guy in the beginning but really full of himself. It was clear that he put himself before her, in almost everything. I got to the point where I just kind of tolerated him because she was so in love with him, but when he left her at the altar… Well, that went beyond even what I thought he was capable of. What an ass."

Conor didn't say anything as he read the motorway signs that were coming into view. "Is she into professional athletes, then?"

Aisling gazed out of the window at the wet green countryside. "No," she said. "She's dated cops, firemen, salesmen… She even dated an actor once. But she always says it doesn't matter what he is but who he is on the inside. But after this debacle, I'm sure she's sworn men off forever."

Conor changed lanes again as their exit approached. "That would be a real tragedy."

Aisling grinned, turning to look at him. "I don't think she's dated a college professor before," she said. "Do you want me to put a good word in for you, Dr. Da Derga?"

He grinned but wouldn't look at her. "To a woman like that? Only in my dreams."

"Oh, I don't know." Aisling's brown eyes twinkled. "She seemed to enjoy the conversation with you yesterday. I think she kind of liked you."

He looked at her, hardly daring to hope. "Do you really think so?"

Grinning, Aisling pointed at the highway sign coming up. "There's our exit."

Conor refocused on the road, taking the off-ramp and then a left onto Littlegrange Road. The rain was coming down in sheets as they headed south. The road eventually turned into Dowth Road as they neared the mound. They could see it in the distance, a great green loaf rising above the flat countryside, and he sped up.

When they finally pulled into the small car park, water and mud sprayed as he came to an abrupt halt. He threw the car into park and turned to Aisling.

"You stay here," he told her. "If she doesn't want to be found, she might run from me. I need you to stay here in case she runs. You can see the entire mound from here, so if she takes off and you see her, I want you to honk the horn like crazy. All right?"

Aisling nodded, watching him get out of the car. "Do you want an umbrella?"

He shook his head, pulling his crumpled Drogheda United

baseball-style hat out of the back seat and pulling it onto his spiked hair. After slamming the car door, he zipped up his raincoat and began to walk around the base of the mound, heading toward the southern tunnels.

The rain was letting up somewhat as he made his way around the east side of the mound. It was heavy with wet foliage from the light rain now falling. The clouds above were even starting to clear, and patches of blue appeared. Moving through the dripping brush, he came upon the first of the three tunnels. Pulling out his torch, he flashed it down into the tunnel but saw nothing.

It was dark and cold.

He moved on to the second tunnel and shined his torch in that one, but it was black and empty. The third tunnel was several feet away, and he prepared to shine his torch into it. But as he took a step into the dark archway, he immediately spied a lump on the ground just a few feet from the door.

Startled, he flashed his torch downward and saw Destry sitting with her back against the wall, huddled in a ball. Her knees were up, her arms embracing them and her face buried in the top of her knees. When the flashlight fell on her, she yelped in fright, her head swiftly coming up. Conor jumped too. He snapped off the torch so it wouldn't blind her.

"Destry?" He went into a crouch in the small tunnel, moving toward her in the wet earth. "What are you doing here, sweetheart? You scared Aisling to death when she couldn't find you."

Destry looked at him; she was pale, her beautiful face streaked where she had wept and wiped her face with dirty hands. She was also wet, shivering in the darkness.

"How did you find me?" she asked.

He could see how cold she was, and he knelt beside her, taking her hands into his warm palms and feeling that they were like ice. "I took a wild guess when Aisling said you were missing," he told her. "How did you get here?"

His hands felt so good. She looked down at his massive mitts as they closed around her small ones, and fat tears began to roll down her cheeks.

"I took a taxi," she whispered. "It cost me a fortune."

He caressed her cold hands, trying to rub some warmth back into her fingers. "Why did you do it?"

She wiped at her cheeks. "I tried to go back to sleep this morning when I went back to the hotel. Every time I closed my eyes, those whispers came back. And there were faces—white faces, scary faces. I couldn't really see them clearly, but they were there, trying to talk to me. Then I'd wake up scared, fall back asleep again, and then wake up screaming all over again. It happened four times. I know you told me that it was my subconscious mind playing tricks on me, but I just don't think it is. Nothing like this has ever happened to me before."

He put a big hand on her head. "Oh, sweetheart," he murmured. "I'm so sorry. But it still doesn't explain why you came back here."

"Because," she said, sounding frustrated, "I figured if I couldn't get away from the whispers, then I'd at least try to make friends with them. Maybe they'd leave me alone then. So I came out here, and I've been talking to them all afternoon."

"Have they talked back?"

She looked at him reluctantly. "No," she said, glancing around the dark tunnel and sighing heavily. "It's been quiet and still, just like this. Oh, hell; maybe I *am* crazy. I just don't know anymore."

She hung her head again and started to cry. He sat down beside her and opened up his jacket, putting it around her as he pulled her against his big torso. She wept softly, and he hugged her, his cheek against the top of her head.

"Don't cry," he murmured. "I'm sure whatever this is, it will pass. If it doesn't, I'll volunteer to spend the nights with you and chase the bad dreams away. They wouldn't dare tangle with me."

Her face was against his chest, a warm and comforting thing. After a moment, she lifted her head, and he looked down at her, realizing she was smiling. The wet, bright blue eyes gazed up at him.

"You *are* pretty scary," she agreed. "You're a big guy."

He lifted a red eyebrow at her. "Big and skilled in the art of warfare from the time of the Romans up until the end of the Medieval period. I can fight with clubs, swords, fists, feet, spears, knives, and anything else that can even remotely be used as a weapon. If those ghosts know what's good for them, they'll leave you the hell alone."

Her tears were forgotten at his chivalrous declaration. "You can really fight like that?"

He nodded firmly. "I teach a Medieval warfare class," he said. "I get my students out in the cricket field to the north of the campus, and we learn the art of real war, not this sophisticated stuff that we do nowadays. Back in the day, men fought hand to hand, and only the strongest survived."

She smiled faintly. "I saw all of the weapons you had on the wall of your office."

"I'm very proud of my collection."

"Ever use them on anybody?"

"Not yet. But if the university is attacked by barbarian

hordes, I'm ready."

She was feeling better with him around. She had spent the past several hours sitting in the tunnel, watching it rain outside and inviting the ghosts to talk to her again.

Once he put his big arms around her and his warmth began to envelop her, she began to realize how exhausted she really was and how foolish it had been to come all the way out here just because of some bad dreams. Maybe she really *was* losing her mind. A botched wedding, grief, and exhaustion could do strange things to even the strongest person.

"Well," she said after a moment. "Now that you're here, I feel like an idiot for coming out here. You didn't have to come after me."

He waggled his eyebrows dramatically. "Yes, I did."

She chuckled softly. "I was just sure that… Oh, I don't know. I guess I was just sure that I would experience something again."

He leaned down and whispered hotly in her ear, his lips against her flesh, "*In am, sárálainn bean.*"

She turned to look at him, feeling more than the heat from his body. She was feeling the heat from his gaze and from his words. She found herself watching his full, soft lips, remembering how they tasted.

"What does that mean?" she asked breathlessly.

"It means, 'You will in time, beautiful girl.'"

"Will what?"

"Experience something again. Maybe better than before."

She felt giddy and tremulous against him. He had that effect on her. But her self-defense was kicking in, the last shred of protection between her broken heart and the outside world. She looked away from him, but there was a smile on her lips.

"You're sweet, Dr. Da Derga," she said. "And I'm wet and freezing. I assume you brought a car so I don't have to take out a loan to pay for a taxi back to Dublin?"

He nodded, disappointed that she'd pulled away. "Aisling is waiting for us in my car," he said. "We should probably head back before she comes looking for us."

Destry nodded, but looked around the tunnel one last time as if hoping the ghosts would come forth, just once, so she could prove to Conor that she wasn't insane. As nice as he was, she knew that he must have some doubt.

As she turned to him, she caught a glimpse of the clouds clearing outside the mound. The sun was sitting low on the horizon, creating brilliant orange and yellow rays that warmed the wet countryside.

She nodded in the direction of the sun. "Look," she said. "Another beautiful Irish sunset."

He turned to look at the sun even though his attention was on the feeling of her in his arms. As he watched it set, he realized that he didn't want this time with her to end, this magic that he was feeling every time he looked at her. It was an odd sensation, something between adoration and excitement. From the moment he first saw her, he had experienced sensations that he had never experienced before, with anyone.

As the sunset deepened, he pulled her more tightly against him, watching the dying rays. "I'm glad I found you out here today," he said quietly.

She looked at him, at his strong profile warmed by the orange rays. "What do you mean?"

He turned to look at her, very close to her face. "Other than the relief that you are in one piece, I'm glad I got to share the sunset with you."

She looked at him, at his intense blue eyes, and felt as if they had reached some sort of pinnacle. Whatever she was feeling for the man, whatever anticipation or excitement he represented, the truth was that she wasn't emotionally strong enough for it at the moment.

It was time for some honesty.

"And I'm glad I got to share it with you," she said softly. "But… I'm not sure this can go any further."

"What can't go any further?"

She lifted her eyebrows. "I know it's presumptive of me to anticipate what you may or may not be thinking, but you and me… I mean, not that there is a you and me, but—"

He cut her off. "I wish there was. I'd give my right arm for it."

She grew serious. "Aisling told you why I'm here, right?"

"She did."

"Then you know the last thing on my mind is a hookup. I'm not emotionally ready for anything close to that."

He knew that. But he wasn't going to give up hope. "I'm a patient man," he told her. "When you're ready, I'll be here."

Her brow furrowed. "Are you crazy? I live in California."

"It's only a plane ride away."

She shook her head at him as he tried to make the situation seem simpler than it was. "It's six thousand miles away."

He shifted his big body, tightening his enormous arms around her. Destry felt his heat, his power, and it began to weaken her resolve. His handsome face loomed in front of her, half of it illuminated by the sunset.

"I'm going to try to explain this, so listen closely," he said, his tone a gentle growl. "When I saw you yesterday, no one I had ever seen in my life caught my eye like you did. Here I was, teaching a class, and an angel walked right into my midst. I don't know how else to describe it. Then when you came to my office today, it was like my prayers had been answered. And the kiss… Destry, I don't know if I can ever kiss another woman again, because you've ruined them all for me. No other kiss will ever come close. If I died tomorrow, I would die a happy man. Therefore, a six-thousand-mile plane ride doesn't concern me. I'd go to the Arctic if that's where you were. Anywhere you are, I'll follow."

She gazed at him with an expression between disbelief and pleasure. "Nobody talks like that, Conor."

"Like what?"

"Like something out of a romance novel. You sound like Prince Charming."

He grinned. "I hope so," he said, his eyes glittering. "Is it working?"

She laughed. "I don't know. Maybe."

"I'm willing to live the rest of my life on a maybe."

She was incredulous. "Just for me?"

His smile faded as his gaze grew intense. "Only for you."

Destry wasn't sure what more she could say. She had stated her case, sort of, and he was making his desire plain. She stared at him, trying to figure out his true motivation—infatuation? Insanity? She wondered.

"But you don't even know me," she said. "You just met me."

He unwound a big arm from around her torso, taking her chin between his thumb and forefinger. Turning her head slightly, he kissed her gently on the cheek.

"I know enough," he whispered, turning her face again and kissing her nose delicately. "What I don't know, I can learn. What I can't learn, I can feel."

She closed her eyes as he moved his mouth to the other cheek, kissing her with great tenderness. "Oh my God," she breathed. "Are you for real?"

Conor's eyes were closed as well. He didn't miss a beat as he swooped in for her lips. "Very real," he murmured as his mouth clamped down over hers.

As Conor and Destry lost themselves in a deeply passionate kiss, the rays from the setting sun were beginning to fall on the entrance of ancient stone. Just as they had yesterday, the soft yellow rays hit the porous slabs, warming them, creating the same odd glow as they had yesterday—only tonight the glow was stronger and more potent. An odd hum was also beginning to churn as the rock heated up, reverberating through the slab with an ancient song.

Had Conor not been so consumed with Destry in his arms, he might have noticed that the sunlight was now streaming in through the tunnel, hitting the back of the chamber as it had done for every spring and fall equinox for five thousand years. The old stones were positioned just so, creating the right conditions for worlds to collide at just this place, just this time.

There was something his educated mind didn't know.

The old mound of Dowth had never been a burial chamber. It had been a chamber where ancient man moved through times and worlds as easily as moving from one field to the other. But only under the correct conditions, when the days and nights were of the same length, and the stars were aligned just so. When the sun was at the right angle and its magic light started the ancient portal, like the snap of a spark plug. This was one of those times. Those caught within the mound would walk between worlds in echoes of ancient dreams.

One moment, Conor had Destry trapped firmly in his arms,

and in the next, a brilliant flash of light blinded him. It was enough to pull his attention from Destry, who gasped with fright at the blinding white light. But her gasp was the last thing he heard before the light drowned out every conscious thought, every waking awareness.

And then… there was darkness.

# CHAPTER SIX

THERE WAS A soft wind blowing gently about her. Destry was half-conscious, feeling the breeze. Something cold was tickling her face, but she wasn't lucid enough to brush it away. She was in a dreamy daze, somewhere between light and dark, and the only sound that met her ears was that of birds singing overhead.

Consciousness came and went. She drifted into darkness again, a sweet and blissful place, until warm hands touched her and she gradually became aware that someone had lifted her up. She felt a gentle touch on her cheeks, stroking her.

"Destry?" She could hear the distinctly male voice. "Can you hear me, sweetheart? Open your eyes. Look at me."

Destry was trying. In fact, she was trying very hard, but she just couldn't seem to open her eyes. When she was able to marginally crack them open, the light was so bright that she closed them again. The darkness swarmed around her, and she drifted off.

Conor could see that she had passed out again. He was fairly woozy himself, but he fought it. Looking around, he saw they were in heavy foliage, remarkably dry, as the weak sunlight beat down through the tree canopy overhead. Were he not feeling so ill, it would have been a lovely sight. But all he could manage to feel at the moment was disorientation, confusion, and nausea.

Everything was a fog.

His last memory had been of kissing Destry in the dank, cold tunnel. The kiss had been hot and delicious, everything he could have imagined it would be. Then he had awoken in the overgrown grass, staring straight up at the sky, wondering what in the hell had happened.

He felt as if he'd been on the losing end of a fight as he struggled to clear his head, sitting up slowly as the world rocked. He had no idea what had happened. Over to his left, he could see Destry crumpled on her side like a rag doll.

Heart in his throat, he forgot about his spinning head as he struggled to Destry's side. Carefully, he rolled her onto her back, very carefully inspecting her to see if he could see any visible damage. At this point, not knowing what had happened, he ran his hands down her arms and legs, feeling for broken bones, but she was intact. Then he carefully scooped her into his arms and tried to rouse her.

Destry was struggling to come around, but she was still fairly out of it. Conor wasn't feeling much better, but at least he was upright. He held her against his broad chest, watching her sigh and twitch, before taking a look back up at the mound. He expected to see it exploded outward at the very least, because something had thrown them clear. They were at least twelve feet away from it. But it took him a moment to realize that the mound was very much intact and extremely overgrown. In fact, he could barely see the tunnel they had been huddled in for all of the growth around it. His gaze drifted over the lines of the mound, something he knew very well, but it just didn't look the same as it had a few minutes earlier.

Puzzlement began to sprout.

"What the…?" he muttered.

His brow furrowed in confusion, and he began to look around—nothing was as he remembered it. No fences, no farmhouses, no neatly tended fields. It was wild meadow as far as he could see. It was all very weird, but he shoved his bewilderment aside. He had no idea what had happened to them, other than some kind of natural explosion, and decided the best course of action would be to return to his car and get Destry to a hospital. Then maybe he needed to get his head checked, too, because things didn't look the same as they had just a few minutes earlier. Maybe the explosion had given him a concussion or something.

He certainly felt like it.

Conor gently scooped Destry into his arms, cradling her carefully as he made his way around the east side of the mound. Here, too, it looked extremely overgrown, and the entrance tunnels on this side were nearly blocked off with fallen stone and bramble. He rounded the side of the mound with the expectation of finding the car park dead ahead, but he came to a halt when he realized there was nothing there but open, green field.

Everything was gone.

Conor stared at the area where his car should have been, starting to wonder if he hadn't lost his mind. Nothing was as it should be or where he'd left it, and he was struggling against an increasingly strong sense of dread. As he stood there with Destry cradled in his arms, trying to figure out what he should do next, the bramble off to his left suddenly rattled.

Startled, he whirled around in time to see a very small, willowy woman push through the trees with three small children at her side. His brow furrowed as he realized the woman was wearing a nightgown. At least, he thought it was a nightgown, because it was as white as she was, the color blending into her skin, all wispy and flowing. She also had a walking stick in her hand, a stick that was twice her height.

As the trees parted and the woman drew closer, he could see that she was a young woman, her white hair long and straight, and the children with her weren't so much children as they were dwarves. He truly had no idea what they were, because they had big hands and big heads, and they were dressed in raggedy pajamas as they suddenly rushed at him. Startled, and at a disadvantage with an unconscious woman in his arms, Conor backed off.

The woman in the nightgown lifted a hand to him in greeting. "*Mo Thiarna,*" she said. "*Dia bheannaithe linn ar an lá seo de laethanta le do thuairisceán. Táimid ag guí ar an lá seo.*"

Conor stared at her. It was an extremely archaic form of Irish Gaelic, something odd and out of place in this modern world. Although he understood her, her words had no meaning to him. *Great lord, God has blessed us on this day of days with your return. We have prayed for this.*

"*Dia,*" he replied. "*Duit go bhfuil an bhean bhí gortaithe. An féidir leat glaoch ar chabhair leighis?*"

*This woman is injured. Can you call for medical assistance?* He tried not to sound too panicked or too bewildered as he asked. Getting help for Destry was all he could think about at the moment, so everything else, all of the weirdness and disorientation, would have to wait.

But the woman smiled faintly at him. "You do not remember me, do you?" she said in her heavy Gaelic. "'Tis of no concern, great lord. You will remember in time."

Conor regarded her, shaking his head after a moment and replying in her dialect, "I'm sorry, I don't know who you are. Do you have a mobile phone with you?"

There was no word for "phone" in Gaelic, so he had to go with the best translation he could. The woman cocked her head, looking rather amused. "I am Padraigan the White," she said. "Your memory will return. But you must come with me now, quickly. They must not find you here."

Conor had no idea what she was talking about. He thought the woman was a little crazy, so he started to walk away, thinking it would be best to put distance between them, but she trailed after him.

"Please, great lord," she said with growing insistence. "You must not go that way. You must come with me. You must—"

He came to a halt, whirling on her. "Stop," he cut her off, a distinct look of agitation on his face. "This lady is injured. She needs a doctor. Can you at least call for a taxi so I can get her to a hospital?"

The little people collected at Conor's feet and began to tug at him, inspecting his jeans. He actually kicked one of them away when the man got too close to his crotch.

Padraigan put her stick out and tapped one of the little folk on the shoulder, causing all of them to look at her. "Quickly," she commanded softly. "Get the horses. We must return them swiftly or all will be lost."

"What are you talking about?" Conor asked, growing more distressed. "Can you even understand what I'm saying? I need to get this woman to a hospital."

For the first time, Padraigan's gaze moved to Destry, who

was lying still and pale in Conor's enormous arms. Her gaze softened as she studied the lovely face, and brought a hand up as if to touch Destry, but just as quickly pulled away.

There was reverence in her expression, in her tone, as she spoke.

"*Fanacht, morrigan,*" she whispered. "*Gnáthlá agus oiche og ceanna; tar ar cúl do sinne.*"

Conor's eyes narrowed, and he took a step back as if to protect Destry from this strange and mysterious woman. He was becoming upset by all of this, the strange people, the odd land, and the fact that he didn't feel well. Something terrible had happened, but it was like living a nightmare, because he couldn't seem to get any help. No one understood what he needed. Short of walking to Drogheda, which was just a few miles to the east, he wasn't sure what more he could say or do to stress his urgency. Now, with this bizarre woman repeating the very words that Destry had sworn she had heard in her dreams, he was at his limit of patience.

"Where in the hell did you hear that?" he asked.

Padraigan looked at him, not at all offended by his tone. "I called to her and she heard me," she replied. "That is why you are here, great lord. She brought you here. You *must* come with me. Please."

Conor's fury was being overwhelmed by confusion and, if he were to admit it, some fear. "What are you talking about?" he demanded. "Who in the hell are you? And no more of this bullshit you've been feeding me. What is going on here?"

Sounds of horses could be heard, and they both turned to see the little people returning with four of them. But these weren't just any horses—they were shaggy and fat, with short legs.

Padraigan motioned toward the beasts. "Come, great lord," she said, her calm tone now having a sense of urgency to it. "We must hurry if you are to survive."

Conor stood his ground. "Hurry where? I'm not going anywhere until you tell me who you are."

Padraigan remained calm. "I told you, great lord," she said, "I am Padraigan the White. I am your *litrithe*. You do not remember now, but you will in time. You must trust me and come with me; otherwise, your life is in great danger."

Conor just stared at the woman, the sense of dread that had been gnawing at him sprouting wings and taking flight. "My sorceress?" he repeated, translating her word. "What is—"

"There is no time, great lord," she said, cutting him off. "You must come now. I will explain everything when we are safe."

Conor pulled Destry tighter, glancing around to the overgrown mound, the heavy foliage, the fields that were wild and untamed. Overhead, clouds skipped across the blue sky. It all looked fairly normal to him, but something was different, something he couldn't put his finger on.

His defiance began to slip in favor of genuine fear.

"What in the hell is going on?" he finally pleaded.

Padraigan sensed his despair; she had known this would be his reaction, and struggled to get the man moving without sitting down and telling him the entire story of why he was here. At this moment, they needed to leave. The urgency was growing.

"Please," Padraigan begged. "I will tell you everything once we reach safety. Will you please trust me?"

Conor wasn't sure he had a choice, but he really didn't want to go with her. He wanted to find his car, but his car wasn't there, and nor was the car park, or Aisling, or the small farm that sat just to the west of the mound. Nothing was as he remembered it.

It began to occur to him that the blast that threw him and Destry clear of the mound had done something else. He wasn't sure what yet, but *something* had happened.

Something he couldn't explain.

But one thing was certain—he had to find help for Destry. With no car and no phone on him, since he had left it in his car, he thought that perhaps he should go with the woman who called herself a sorceress. Once they were at her house, maybe she had a landline phone that he could use. Furthermore, he reckoned that if he didn't feel comfortable, he could just leave. Drogheda was about a five-mile walk to the east. He'd carry Destry all the way to Dublin to find help for her if he had to.

He was pretty sure one small woman and three dwarves wouldn't pose much of a threat.

Without another word, he began to walk toward the horses. Padraigan softly commanded her three little friends to give the fastest horse for Conor, and a shaggy, cream-colored horse was produced. But there was no saddle, at least not like one he had ever seen. It was a series of heavy blankets held together with a frame of wood for the seat of the saddle.

"Oh, God," he muttered. "A horse? I haven't ridden a horse in years."

"Mount your steed, great lord."

He shook his head, looking at Destry, wondering how he was going to mount the horse and hold her at the same time. After a moment, he sighed heavily.

"How in the hell am I going to do this?" he asked.

In his arms, Destry stirred at the sound of his voice. She

threw up a hand, which ended up thumping him on the cheek. He gazed down at her, seeing that her eyes were marginally open. The hand that had smacked him in the cheek went to her head as if to block out a throbbing headache, and her eyes closed again.

"Destry?" he said softly. "Can you hear me?"

This time, she responded. "Yes," she whispered, the bright blue eyes slowly opening again. "What's going on?"

"I'm not sure yet," he said. "How do you feel?"

She was quiet a moment. So far, she hadn't tried to move anything but her hand, and she remained tucked against his chest, her open eyes staring into his shirt. He could feel her great, heavy sigh.

"Like I've been thrown off a building." She stirred again, this time lifting her head and squinting in the light. "What happened?"

"I don't know," he said quietly. "One minute I was in the tunnel with you, and in the next, we were both lying on the grass."

She gazed up at him. "Are you okay?"

He smiled faintly. "I'm fine," he said. "I'm more worried about you."

She reached up and wound her arms around his neck, pulling herself up so that she was sitting up somewhat. But as she struggled to settle herself, she caught movement out of the corner of her eye.

Padraigan came into view, an unfamiliar and somewhat odd sight, and Destry startled with fright.

"Oh, God," she gasped, suddenly pressed up against Conor as close as she could without actually crawling inside the man. "Who's that?"

Conor looked at the small, thin woman clad in the dirty, pale nightgown. "She says her name is Padraigan," he said quietly. "She says… Well, she says a hell of a lot of weird things, but she mostly says we need to get out of here because we're in danger."

Destry's head came up, eyes wide with fear and disorientation. "What danger?"

He shook his head, his gaze on the strange woman and her three companions. "I don't know," he murmured. "They won't say, but they want us to come with them."

Destry looked over her shoulder at the very small woman with the pale face before turning back to Conor, throwing her arms around his neck and burying her face against his shoulder.

"I just want to go back to the hotel," she muttered. "I need to lie down. Please take me back."

He sighed. "I would, except the car is gone."

Her head came up, her face within inches of his as she fixed him in the eye. "Where did it go?" she said. Then she frowned. "Did Aisling take it? Where in the hell did she go? Oh my God, my head is killing me."

Her head flopped back down on his shoulder, and Conor laid his cheek against the top of her head, rocking her gently. In spite of the bizarre and concerning circumstances, he had her just where he wanted her. He could have stayed like this forever.

But Padraigan approached the pair timidly, rattling him out of his fantasy world.

"Please, great lord," she said. "We must leave immediately."

"What did she say?" Destry hissed. "What kind of language is that?"

Conor pursed his lips; he didn't particularly want to tell her, fearful that it might set her off. But he had no choice.

"Very old Gaelic," he said quietly.

Her face screwed up in confusion. "Doesn't she speak English?"

Conor looked at the tiny wisp of a woman. "Do you understand English?"

Padraigan stared at him, having no idea what he had said. After a moment of confusion, she pointed to the horses again.

"Please, great lord," she begged. "Please ride with me to safety. Time grows short, and your children await."

Conor's eyebrows lifted. "Children?" he repeated. "What children?"

Padraigan's gaze moved between Conor and Destry as a faint smile graced her lips. "Your sons," she said. "Perhaps they will help you remember."

Destry was looking at Conor as the woman spoke her bizarre language. It was clear that he was communicating with her, but Destry couldn't understand a word. She felt like she was on another planet. Her head was killing her and her body ached terribly, and she was feeling woozy and weary.

With a big surge of strength, she suddenly pushed herself out of Conor's enormous arms and almost fell to the ground.

Conor steadied her as she gained her feet and her balance, but she shrugged him off. Looking around, she spied the mound several yards away, and her eyebrows rose at the sight. It was lumpy and overgrown with foliage. It didn't look anything like the well-manicured mound she had arrived at a few hours earlier. It didn't even look like the same relic, in any way.

An odd sense of foreboding swept her.

"What happened to the mound?" she asked, pointing.

He turned to look at it. "I have no idea," he said. "It doesn't look like it did just a few minutes ago."

Destry's hand went to her head in a gesture of confusion as she started to walk in the direction of the mound. "It's all covered with bushes and grass," she said. She turned to Conor. "You said we were thrown out of the tunnel?"

He was walking after her. "Yes," he replied. "When I woke up, we were about three or four meters from the tunnel entrance."

Destry wasn't feeling at all well, but her sense of curiosity and fear were taking over. "Then there must have been an explosion." She was trying to be logical about it. "Is it possible that the explosion threw us out and made it look like this? It looks like some of the tunnels are collapsed."

He just shook his head. "I doubt it," he said. "Whatever damage you see looks as if it has been that way for years. Plus, none of the overgrowth has been disturbed, as it would have been by an explosion."

She couldn't wrap her mind around his assertion. "But there *had* to have been an explosion," she insisted. "How else would we have been blown out of the tunnel?"

Conor was feeling just as much trepidation as she was, but he was more in control of it. "I have no idea," he replied. "But it happened."

She looked at him, her bright blue eyes pleading. "But how?" she demanded softly, then her eyes grew suspicious. "Were we gassed? Maybe someone gassed us and then dragged us outside to rob us."

He almost laughed but couldn't quite bring himself to do it because she was serious, and so was he. It was a serious situation.

"We would have seen someone, or heard them," he said,

taking a few steps closer to her. "Even though my attention was on you, I'm sure I would have heard someone sneaking up to gas us."

"Did you check your pockets? Is your wallet still there?"

"I left my wallet in the car."

She pursed her lips as if he had just made an awful mistake. "Now Aisling has it and is probably charging up all of your credit cards."

He grinned. "If she does, I'll take it out on you."

"Oh, yeah? And how are you going to do that?"

"Do you really want to know?"

"Yes. No. Well, maybe."

Conor laughed softly. They had come to a halt about twenty feet from the mound, facing each other, when an object suddenly zinged past Conor's head. He turned, startled, in time to see several creatures in the trees to the north side of the mound.

"Creatures" was the only way to describe them, because they were green and brown, blending in with the foliage like wraiths. They whooped and yelled and threw things, and then started dropping out of the trees. When they began to run, Conor could see that they were human—naked human men smeared in mud and leaves.

They clutched crude bows in their hands made of thin, stripped branches and animal sinew. Conor could hardly believe what he was seeing. It was like watching an ancient reenactment, only this one had the distinct element of danger. People didn't launch arrows because they wanted to be friendly. They launched them because they wanted to kill.

One of the group launched a very crude arrow again, and it weakly sailed off to the left.

As they drew closer, Conor knew they meant to attack him and Destry, but he still couldn't believe it. He just stood there and observed, like an anthropologist would.

Beside him, Destry let out a shriek. "Holy crap!" she yelped.

Her cry startled him from clinically evaluating the situation. Although he was an expert in ancient warfare, he'd never really had cause, other than an occasional bar fight, to use his skills. As big as he was, he'd never really been called upon to use his hand-to-hand combat skills in a mortal situation, and, truth be told, he was a little apprehensive.

But he could see that all of that was about to change. He was about to put his money where his mouth was. Something in his gut told him that these men were not the reasoning type. They looked like wild animals, and he responded in kind.

He sent a fist the size of a ten-pound ham flying at the first man, delivering a crushing blow that sent him to the ground. Conor grabbed the second man by the neck and tossed him off into the trees. Two others descended on him, and he found himself in a vicious fight, tossing men to the ground only to have them jump up and try to strike him. One man had a crude bronze knife blade, and he swiped it at Conor, catching him in the arm and drawing blood. Furious, Conor drove his fist into the man's head.

Destry had darted away when Conor threw the first punch, but she had nowhere to go, no place to hide, and she didn't want to get clobbered in the fight. She'd never heard of gangs hanging out in the countryside of Ireland, beating up tourists. But there were at least six of them—though three of them were already out cold thanks to Conor's crushing blows. The man could deliver a punch like nothing she had ever seen this side of a movie screen.

But as she watched him, she began to realize that he might need help. She'd never been in a fight in her life, but that was about to change.

She had to help him.

Over to her left, the strange woman was trying to get her attention, beckoning her to come, but Destry had no intention of going with the woman or leaving Conor alone. Forgetting her splitting headache and nausea, she looked around for anything she could use as a weapon. Rocks would do—but she quickly spied a fairly thick branch on the ground about four feet long and with leaves and smaller branches still growing out of it. Swiftly she retrieved it, and the next time one of the skinny, naked men came around, she whacked him over the head with it.

He fell like a stone.

This left two men going after Conor; he had one of them in a headlock and the other one by the throat. Destry rushed up with her branch and cracked the guy in the headlock on the back of the head.

Surprised, Conor looked up just in time to see Destry brain the last man in his grip; she took a swing at his head like a baseball player swinging a bat and knocked the guy out of the park. But he was tough, and she had to whack him twice.

When the man fell to the ground, unconscious, Conor let out a roar and beat at his chest, kicking at the men on the ground. It was a release of fear, the expending of testosterone, on the most basic primal level.

Destry, sickened by the fight, dropped her branch and staggered back, tripping over a rock and ending up on her bum. There she sat as Conor bellowed his victory.

He was hyped up on adrenalin, the primordial surge of

battle in his veins. He was a strong personality as it was, demonstrative, but his victory yell was truly something to behold. For a man who had never truly been in a battle situation, he had taken to it with frightening ease.

Still riding the adrenalin high, he looked up from their six victims to see Destry sitting on the ground looking horribly pale. He forgot his testosterone seizures and rushed to her.

"Are you all right?" He reached down to pick her up off the grass. "Did you get hurt?"

She shook her head, weakly trying to pull away from him and struggling to hold back the tears. But the tears came, and she broke down.

"I'm fine," she said as she sobbed softly. "I just want to get out of here."

He put his arms around her, pulling her against him. "I'm so sorry," he murmured, giving her a gentle squeeze. He pulled her away from the pile of bodies. "Come on—we'll get out of here right now."

"Who were those guys?" she asked.

He hugged her again. "I don't know, sweetheart," he said. "A group of ruffians, I suppose. Who knows?"

"They don't have any clothes on."

"A group of insane nudists, then. I don't know who they are."

Destry was torn between giggling at his humor and her tears, and the tears won out as he began to walk her in the direction of the car park. Or where the car park had once been. He didn't know what else to do.

But Padraigan was still lingering behind him with her three little helpers, leading the shaggy horses with them.

"Wait," she called. "Please, great lord, not that way. We must go this way."

Conor turned to look at the woman, exhaustion evident on his face now that the adrenalin rush was gone. "I'm not going to—"

Destry cut him off. "What does she want?"

"She wants us to go with her. She insists."

"Maybe we should," she said, turning toward the north. "There's no car out there, and now that I look at it, no road. There's no farmhouse or cars driving by, or anything else that moves. There's nothing at all. We just got attacked by crazy, dirty, naked guys who tried to shoot arrows at us. What in the hell is going on here?"

His focus was moving with hers, and he saw the same sights, felt the same dread.

"I don't know," he said quietly.

"Maybe *she* does."

Conor didn't say anything for a moment. But he came to a stop, his hands still on Destry as he turned for Padraigan. Considering the circumstances, he figured that he didn't have much choice.

"We will go with you," he told her in her language.

Padraigan smiled timidly, encouraging her little helpers to provide horses to Conor and Destry.

Destry had ridden a great deal, and mounted easily when Conor gave her a leg up. He, however, took a bit longer; throwing his big body over the back of the horse, he finally swung a leg over and sat up somewhat uncertainly. He didn't look particularly comfortable. But as storm clouds began to gather again overhead, he followed Padraigan and her little group off to the east, heading into a massive forest he had never even noticed before, and they lost themselves in the dark and musty depths of the thickening trees.

# CHAPTER SEVEN

T HE SENSE OF urgency followed them for a few miles.
As they were fearful that they were perhaps being followed by whatever dangers Padraigan had alluded to, there was a sense of apprehension. Through the trees they moved, sometimes traveling through bramble so thick that the horses had a difficult time getting through it. Padraigan urged them onward, and the little people swatted the horses with switches to get them going. The forest around them was thick and still, the canopy dense, and the feeling of unease pervasive. It was like an impenetrable cloak that they couldn't shake, this odd feeling of disorientation and apprehension that seemed to blanket them.

Follow them.

Conor felt it, but he didn't say anything to Destry, who finally seemed to be feeling better after their rough experience. She was actually enjoying the horse ride, patting the animal on the neck or stroking its mane.

Not being used to horses, however, Conor had been more than ready to get off the animal since shortly after they started. His bum was killing him, as well as something else a bit more tender, so when they eventually entered a clearing deep in the thick wood and Padraigan dismounted from her small white pony, Conor slid off his shaggy horse and started walking. He just couldn't ride anymore, and rubbed at his backside to bring some circulation into it. He swore it was numb.

Beside him and still astride her fat gray beast, Destry grinned at him.

"Hurt yourself, Dr. Da Derga?" she asked.

He gave her his best scowl. "Mind your own business."

For the first time since he'd met her, Destry burst into unrestrained laughter. It was a wonderful sound. "Poor baby," she said. "Not much of a cowboy, are you?"

He cast her a long look. "I have it on good authority that you're about to be spanked if you don't zip your lips."

She giggled and steered her horse so there was a big gap between them. "I'm sorry," she said, although she didn't mean a word of it. She was leaning back to get a good look at his butt beneath the baggy jeans. "I hate to tell you this, but your ass is flat. You must have damaged it riding on the horse."

He just shook his head as he walked, a smile playing on his lips. "Great," he said sarcastically, heightening his Irish brogue. "Now my arse is damaged. If I had trouble getting you to go out with me before, now I've just lost one of the biggest guns in my arsenal. What else can I attract you with if not my fantastic, now flattened, arse?"

Destry snorted as the horses plodded along. "How about those fabulous biceps?"

He looked at her very hopefully. "You like my biceps?"

Her laughter faded and her eyes twinkled at him. "I do," she admitted. "You must work out diligently."

"Religiously," he said. "My father was an amateur bodybuilder, and he started me when I was in my teens. If I don't maintain this bulk, it turns to fat, and then I'll look just like Dowth mound—a big, round blob. So I go to the gym four times a week."

"Did you compete as a bodybuilder?"

He shook his head. "No," he said. "I was more interested in school. My dad was disappointed, too; he doesn't have nearly my height or build and always wished he had. He used to give me grief about not reaching my potential."

She watched him walk and continue rubbing his bum. "You reached your potential academically," she said. "You're a Ph.D., for heaven's sake. Wasn't he proud of you about that?"

He nodded, now watching the ground as it passed beneath his feet. "Sure," he said. "I have a double doctorate in Celtic and Irish history as well as anthropology, but he would have been proud of me if I ended up working at a petrol station."

She smiled, looking away flirtatiously when he glanced over at her. Conor was so smitten with her that it was all he could think about, even though they had bigger problems at hand. For the moment, she was responding to him as she never had before, and he wanted to enjoy every minute of it. Finally, her walls of defense were cracking, and he was banging away at them with a sledgehammer.

"Do you have brothers?" she asked.

He nodded. "One," he replied. "Garrett is eighteen months younger than I am."

"Any sisters?"

"None." He looked over at her, and their eyes met. "You have a sister, right?"

She nodded. "Caitlin."

"Does she look anything like you?"

Her smile was back. "A little," she said. "She's taller than I am. She teaches high school."

"Is she married?"

She laughed softly. "No," she said. "Why? Are you looking for a wife?"

He lifted a red eyebrow. "I've already found one; she just doesn't know it yet."

Destry's smile faded as she stared at him, knowing he meant her. She looked away, and Conor could feel the mood plummet. He scrambled to get it back on track.

"Did I do it again?" he asked.

She was looking off into the woods. "Do what?"

"Offend you."

She didn't say anything for a moment. Then she sighed and shook her head. "No," she said. "It's just that I don't know what to say when you say things like that."

Conor watched her carefully, watched her body language. He wasn't very good at reading women, but he was trying very hard.

"I guess I shouldn't say them at all," he said. "But I can't help myself. Destry, if you're not interested in me in a romantic sense, just say so. I don't want to make you uncomfortable by telling you what's on my mind if it's not something you want to hear."

She looked at him. "That's not the case at all," she said, averting her gaze and looking back to the horse. "Maybe that's the problem. I just feel… confused."

"Why?"

She lifted her shoulders. "Because I was supposed to be married two weeks ago," she said. "You know something? I've done a lot of thinking in that time, and I came to realize that

I'm really not all that upset about losing Jake. If I really think hard about it, he was a jerk—self-absorbed, mean at times, critical. He was hard to be around. So I guess in that sense I really don't miss the guy. I don't miss the pressure I felt every time he came around me. It seems to me that what I'm most upset about is being humiliated. And that's selfish."

He gradually walked in her direction and closed the gap between them. "No, it's not," he said. "It's perfectly natural to be upset at being dumped on your wedding day. Don't you love the guy?"

She thought a moment—hard. Then she started to shake her head. "I guess I really don't," she admitted. "Sure, I thought I did at first, but then the infidelity rumors started. Hell, I don't know… When we got engaged, it all happened so fast. He's a fairly popular sports figure in the States, and I guess I just got swept up in it. I think I was more in love with the idea of getting married than with who I was actually marrying. In hindsight, being left at the altar was probably the best thing that happened to me. I just didn't see our marriage lasting."

He stared up at her, finding her confession both interesting and oddly encouraging. "Aisling said he wasn't very nice to you," he said.

Destry smiled ironically. "He wasn't," she agreed. "Just little things—you know, not opening a door for me, or pulling out my chair, or telling me he loved me or that I was beautiful. But there were bigger things, too; he'd be out on the road for weeks, come home and spend the night at my house and then take off again for weeks. He rarely called me from the road, and when he did, it was always really hurried, as if he had better things to do. I think… I think he just used me for sex and the fact that his friends really liked me. I heard his friends say that I made him look good."

She trailed off, falling silent, and Conor noticed that they were coming upon an extremely rustic structure up ahead. In this day and age, he'd never seen or heard of people still living like this in Ireland, not in the farthest reaches of the isle, and his anthropologist's brain started kicking in. He was starting to wonder if he hadn't discovered an entirely new Irish culture, something primal and crude right in the midst of modern-day Ireland.

His attention was becoming diverted by the new scenery, but he retained enough focus to answer her.

"Well," he finally said, "like I said before, the guy was a moron. You're the most beautiful woman in the world, and never under any circumstances would I not pull out a chair for you, or open a door, or tell you every day that I loved you. That's what you deserve. You deserve to be treated like a queen, Destry."

Destry glanced at him, feeling her heart race a little at his declaration, but she was prevented from replying, as Padraigan suddenly headed in their direction, speaking to Conor in that odd dialect. The woman might as well have been speaking Martian for all Destry understood it, so she remained silent while the tiny white woman addressed Conor.

"*An mbeidh tú féin agus an banríon teacht taobh istigh le do thoil?*" she asked. "*Beidh mo sheirbhísigh a réiteach na capaill.*"

"What did she say?" Destry whispered to him.

He handed over the reins to one of the poorly dressed dwarves and then went over to Destry, reaching up to help her off the horse. "She asked you and me to go inside," he replied. "Her little friends will tend the horses."

Destry slid into his arms, and he lowered her to the ground.

Padraigan was already up ahead, heading toward the primitive cottage, and Conor took Destry's hand in his and began to follow. Destry rather liked the feel of his big, warm hand around hers, and she didn't pull away. They made their way across the heavy, wet grass toward the structure almost hidden within a cluster of trees.

Conor looked around the compound with interest; there was a ragged-looking barn for the horses flanked by a giant pile of dried grass. Next to that was a pile of wood, and behind that he could see a crudely fashioned corral that contained two sheep, a goat, and a shaggy cow. Everything was run-down, cluttered, and rough. As they drew closer to the cottage, he could see that it was entirely of sod, built in between two trees that protected it from the elements and also provided a great deal of camouflage. The ceiling was low enough that when Padraigan opened the door, he had to fold himself over in order to enter.

Once he was inside, the home smelled of earth and dampness. It was three rooms wide; a main room in the middle flanked by two smaller rooms, all uneven and asymmetrical. The floor was dirt and pitted with small divots. A badly made table sat in the center of the room along with four stools.

Padraigan indicated the stools. "Sit," she invited. "I will start a fire."

Conor still had hold of Destry's hand as he bent over and pulled out a stool for her. She grinned at him as she took it, and he pulled out the next and picked it up to look at it with a critical eye.

"This thing will never hold me," he growled.

Destry grinned, shaking her head. "How much to you weigh?"

He cocked an eyebrow at her. "A lot."

She giggled. "You can't be more than three hundred pounds."

He made a face at her and set the stool down. "About twenty stone, so don't be so smug."

"Convert that into pounds for your American friend."

"About two hundred and seventy pounds."

He was carefully lowering himself onto the stool as she watched. "Well," she said, "if it breaks, at least you don't have far to fall to the floor."

"Very funny."

He sat, and the stool held, at least for the moment. He was seated right up against Destry, his left thigh and arm against her. She was looking at the stool, grinning at him when she abruptly noticed the blood on his arm. His jacket was torn, and she began to peel it back to get a better look.

"What happened here?" she asked, peeling back the material and noting the big gash on his left forearm. "Ouch. How did you get that?"

He looked down at it. "When those naked guys attacked us," he replied. "One of them had a knife."

She clucked regretfully as she took a closer look. "That may need stitches, Conor. We should get you to an emergency room."

"I'll get it looked at when we get you looked at. How are you feeling?

"Better," she said. "But my head is killing me. I wouldn't be surprised if I have a mild concussion."

"Then we need to get out of here."

She couldn't disagree with him, looking around the dark cottage, her gaze falling on the small woman lighting the fire in the hearth.

She leaned into Conor as her eyes remained on Padraigan. "I don't see a phone here," she muttered. "What do we do?"

He wiped at his goatee in a thoughtful, if not nervous, gesture. His eyes were on Padraigan, too.

"I'm not sure we can do anything right now." He leaned over, his lips on her ear. "Just sit tight and we'll figure it out."

There wasn't much more they could do. Sitting silently, Destry felt Conor's arm go around her waist, his hand coming to rest gently on the curve of her torso. Just like the handholding a few moments earlier, she didn't try to pull away. He was trying to be casual about it, but there was nothing casual about the man's touch. It was like fire. She let go of her resistance and allowed herself to enjoy it. Feeling his enormous body next to her, warm and protective, brought her tremendous comfort.

When Padraigan finally stood up from the hearth, she turned to the pair with a gentle smile on her face. Behind her, the hearth was sparking, and then the entry door opened, emitting one of the little people with wood in his arms. As he fussed with the growing fire, Padraigan went into one of the small adjoining rooms and banged about. Conor and Destry looked at each other, curiously, before the woman emerged with three wooden cups and a pitcher made from clay.

It was very primitive, and Conor's scientist brain kicked in again as he visually examined it. Padraigan set the cups down and poured a dark liquid into each of the cups before putting the full vessels in front of Destry and Conor. Then she sat on one of the stools and faced them.

"I realize this is all very strange to you," she said in her dialect to Conor. "But you must know the truth."

Conor relayed the words to Destry before replying. "What

truth?" he asked.

Padraigan lifted her cup, encouraging Destry and Conor to do the same. Conor picked his up immediately, but Destry was more hesitant. When he took a big gulp of the liquid, she took a timid sip and nearly choked; it was very strong alcohol, and she sputtered as she set the cup down, wiping the burning liquid from her lips.

Conor looked at her and grinned. "Are you all right?" he asked.

She had her hands around her throat as if she was choking. "Fine," she rasped.

He laughed softly, the hand on her waist moving to pat her on the back gently as she sputtered. He was about to say something more to her when Padraigan interrupted.

"Although you do not remember now, in time, it will come to you," she said to Conor. Then her gaze traveled back and forth between the pair. "I knew this day would come. May I explain what has occurred?"

Conor nodded. "I wish you would."

Padraigan commenced. "Your name is *Conor mac Aonghusa, oidhre chun an throne ard*," she said. "You are a great king, great lord, *Conor ard rí Ciannachta*—so great that your legacy is already established and you are much admired and much feared throughout Ireland. The woman at your side is Etain, your queen, and the two of you have three sons together—Mattock, Devlin, and Slane."

Conor stared at the woman, hearing her words but not comprehending much. He was still fixated on the first sentence of her story.

"Conor, son of Aengus, heir to the high throne?" he said incredulously, translating. "Where did you get that? What in the hell is that?"

Padraigan remained calm. "Please, great lord, hear me," she begged. "Your legacy as a ruler and warrior is so great that your brother, a vain and jealous man, began to want for the throne himself. He made a few attempts on your life, but you were too clever for him. You evaded him at every turn, and eventually, you banished him from your kingdom. But your brother dabbles in the dark arts, great lord. He lured you to a conference under the guise of peace and commanded his sorcerer, Olc of the Eye, to exile you into the dark mists of the nether realm. As soon as we realized this had happened, your wife sent your children into hiding with me. Then she took your army and went to your brother to demand your safe return, but your brother tricked her into a private meeting, and his sorcerer exiled her as well. You were both sent through the *doras na gréine*, to the same nether region. But your brother, fearful that you would someday return to kill him, cast a curse upon you— you and your wife would have no memory of each other and no memory of the life you shared. You would wander in the nether region forever, ignorant of who you really were and of your mighty kingdom."

Conor gaped at the woman as if she had lost her mind. After several moments of staring, he wiped at his goatee again in a nervous gesture and shook his head.

"That's madness," he said. "You're out of your mind."

Padraigan shook her head. "Nay, great lord, on either account," she said. "I knew what Olc had done to you—he had sent you and your wife through the *doras na gréine* at a time where the day and night are of the same. At the moment where day turns into night, the door opens to the nether realm, and for a brief moment, we may see both worlds through the swirling mists. I traveled to the sacred mound when I knew this time was approaching, many times since Olc banished you both, and was able to see your wife at my most recent visit. I spoke to her, hoping she would return, and she did. She heard me and she returned. *Fanacht, morrigan, gnáthlá agus oiche og ceanna; tar ar cúl do sinne.*"

As Conor sat dumbfounded, Destry finally spoke up. She put her hand on his thigh to get his attention. "There's that phrase again," she said, squeezing his leg until he looked at her. She looked rather frightened. "That's the woman who spoke to me from the tunnels, isn't it?"

He stared at her, hardly believing what he was hearing. But as he gazed into her bright blue eyes, Padraigan's bizarre story suddenly started making some sense. He remembered the first time he had seen Destry, how he couldn't take his eyes off her. He said once that an angel had walked into his midst, and that was exactly what it had felt like. Her allure had almost been magnetic because it was so strong. It was the most natural of things being with her, as if they were meant to be together in every way.

He couldn't explain it better than that.

But what the pale woman was telling him was pure fantasy… wasn't it?

Conor exhaled heavily, rubbing at his forehead as his brain tried to process what he was being told. At some point, Destry was going to want to know what Padraigan was telling him. He didn't want to answer her now because he didn't have any answers himself.

His gaze moved back to the tiny, wispy woman. "Those mounds are burial chambers from long ago," he told her. "They're not doorways to the nether region."

Padraigan lifted an eyebrow. "They were not built by men," she said. "They were built by gods. When the sun is just so, the doorway opens. It opened today when you and your queen stepped through. I called to you, and you came."

Destry squeezed his thigh again, but he put a big hand over hers, stilling it. He wanted to make sure he was absolutely clear on things before he started translating because, quite honestly, he was rather overwhelmed by it all. It was crazy, interesting, and oddly believable all at the same time.

He looked at Padraigan with a mixture of suspicion, disbelief and fear. "None of that makes any sense," he told her. "Destry is not my wife. I only just met her. And we have lives; I remember where I was born and I know my parents. How do you explain that?"

Padraigan lifted her slender shoulders. "Rebirth."

His brow furrowed. "Rebirth? What does that mean?"

"It means that your transition into the nether region saw you reborn," she murmured. "You returned as an infant and grew into the man you are today. That is why you only remember your life in the nether region. But you are still our king; you are still *Conor ard rí Ciannachta,* and we need you here."

He stared at her. "Conor, High King of Ciannachta," he translated softly. He had to admit, he liked the ring of it. But that didn't dispel the fact that it was nonsense; his logical mind just couldn't give in, not yet. "I'm not a high king. I'm not anything. You must have me mixed up with someone else."

She smiled faintly. "May I ask a question, great lord?"

"Go ahead."

"How do you explain your appearance outside of the *doras na gréine*?" she asked. "You said yourself that nothing looks as you remember it. Would the nether region change so much in the blink of an eye that you would not recognize it?"

He sat back, trying to come up with an answer that would satisfy them both, mostly because he was feeling a great deal of horror in the realization that any answer he could come up with lent credence to her story. But something in his brain, some small and tucked-away place, was telling him that what the woman said just might be true. It was more a feeling than anything else, and he was resistant to it.

But that resistance was fading.

"It's a great story, I'll give you that," he said. "I appreciate your hospitality. But Destry and I need to get to a hospital. If you don't have a phone we can use, do you have any neighbors with phones?"

Padraigan's gaze was steady. "If I can prove to you that what I say is true, will you believe?"

He lifted his eyebrows and scratched at his head, showing signs of restlessness and exasperation. "Sure," he said. "Go ahead. Do your worst."

Padraigan stood up and disappeared into the small room from where she had retrieved the cups and pitcher. When she vanished from view, Destry turned to Conor and squeezed his thigh again.

"Now will you tell me what she said?" she hissed.

He nodded, putting his arm around her shoulders to calm her down. "I think she's nuts," he said.

"Really? Why?"

He looked her in the eye, trying to summarize what he was told and not flip her out in the process. "Well…" He scratched at his goatee. "She says that Dowth is apparently not so much a Neolithic burial chamber as it is some kind of time-travel device. She says that I am really some kind of high king and you are my wife. Evidently I have a jealous brother who had his wicked sorcerer banish us into whatever doorway opens up in Dowth, sending us into the nether region with no memory of our former life or of each other. She further says that she called to you and that you heeded her call. That was the voice you heard calling to you in your dreams."

Destry stared at him as he finished his tale. He could see the thought processes in her expression—interest to incredulity to disbelief. By the time he was finished, however, her cheeks were growing pink and he could see tears in her eyes.

"I *did* hear her voice," she said, leaping up from the stool. "I told you I heard her voice. But she must have been lying in wait for me somehow, hiding in those old tunnels."

"What about the dreams?"

She looked increasingly upset. "She must have freaked me out so bad with her whispers in the tunnel that I just dreamed of them," she said. "Maybe she hypnotized me. How else can you explain something like that?"

"You heard two complete phrases."

"Whose side are you on?"

He could see how upset she was becoming and grasped her hands to keep her from panicking. "Your side," he insisted softly. "I'm always on your side."

"Let's get out of here before something awful happens."

He nodded patiently. "We'll leave," he assured her. "But I need you to calm down, sweetheart. There's no reason to get so upset."

"So upset?" she repeated, her voice rising in pitch. "That woman is telling you crazy stories, and you just sit here calmly listening to them."

"You're the one that said we needed to come with her."

She shook her head so hard that her long hair flopped in her eyes. "I've changed my mind," she said. "We need to leave before she murders us. I want to go back to the hotel now."

He put up a hand to soothe her before she went wild. "We'll go," he murmured, trying to steer her back onto her stool. "Just calm down. Please."

She'd opened her mouth to argue with him when Padraigan entered the room again, followed by her three little helpers. Her gaze moved between Destry standing up and looking at her with some fear, and Conor as he held on to Destry's hands. Padraigan could guess what had happened by the skittish look on Destry's face. When she spoke, it was mostly directed at Destry.

"My great and noble queen," she said. "Do you not recognize my face? You and I were as sisters, once."

Conor looked up to Destry and quietly relayed the question. Destry shook her head fearfully in response, and Padraigan continued.

"Your love for your husband was great." She told the story with a delicate lilt. "So strong it was said that it could move mountains. You and the king loved each other from times of old, from times before this, passing through the centuries in different forms but with the same strong love for one another. Somehow, you always found each other no matter what. And it is your love for your husband, and for your family, that gives you your strength. It binds you, protects you, and guides you. It is that love that has guided you here today."

Conor whispered Padraigan's words to Destry verbatim. Confused and frightened, Destry didn't have any reply other than to burst into quiet tears. Conor gently pulled her down onto his lap, wrapping his arms around her and hugging her. He didn't know what else to do.

Padraigan took a few timid steps toward the couple, her focus on Destry. "When Olc of the Eye exiled your husband through the *doras na gréine*, you came to me with one request," she whispered. "You wanted me to protect your sons, three fine and strong lads in the image of their father. Of course I agreed, and it is since that time that I have lived out here in the wilds, concealing the lads from those who would harm them. Today I will give them back to you, and then you will understand the truth of my words."

Conor's gaze lingered on Padraigan a moment before he reluctantly relayed the statement to Destry. Her weeping grew stronger, and she wrapped her arms around his neck, burying her face against his shoulder. Conor held her tightly, his gaze riveted to Padraigan, as he wondered with some trepidation what she was going to do next.

The woman met Conor's gaze strongly before turning to the hearth. There was a clutter of containers and other miscellaneous vials near one corner of the hearth, lined up against the stone of the wall, and she began rummaging about in the clutter. Pulling forth a wooden vessel, she blew the dust out of it and began to pour various ingredients into it.

"When you brought your sons to me for safekeeping, I knew that it would be a difficult task to hide them against those who would seek to harm them," she said, pouring another measure of something mysterious into the cup and swirling the contents. "I also knew that I could not keep them locked in a hole until your return, so the most logical conclusion I could reach was to hide them in plain sight. And they have been hidden, in full view, since your exile."

She poured a final ingredient into the cup and watched it smoke. By this time, Destry had calmed her tears and was watching the woman mix the concoction. But her arms were still wrapped around Conor's neck, holding on to him tightly.

"What's she saying?" she said, sniffling.

He turned to look at her, his face right up against hers. He couldn't help himself from kissing her on the cheek.

"She says that when you brought our sons to her for safekeeping, she had to hide them in plain sight," he said softly.

Destry turned to look at him, realizing she was literally right up against his face. She loosened her grip on his neck slightly, just enough so there were a few inches of space between them. But she found herself giving in to the closeness, feeling the heat from his body and loving it. He was so powerful, so sweet and compassionate, and she could feel herself succumbing to it.

Truth be told, she really didn't care any longer. She didn't care that she'd had a broken engagement two weeks ago, or her confusion about her love life and her future. There was something about Conor Da Derga that broke down her walls and touched her deeply.

She lifted an eyebrow at him.

"You know," she murmured thoughtfully, "if you and I had… well, you know… *that*… I think I would have remembered it."

He smiled. "I know for a fact that I would have."

"She says we have children together?"

"That's what she says."

"I think I would have remembered giving birth, too."

He laughed. "I would remember that also. It wouldn't be like me to forget my baby's mama."

She started laughing. "You sound like you've had experience with that kind of thing."

He snorted. "Thank God, no," he said. "I'm just saying that I think I would have remembered the woman who gave birth to my children."

Destry gazed into his eyes, permitting herself for the first time to feel the pull between them. She didn't resist. "I don't think it would be such a bad thing to give birth to your children," she said. "I'll bet you'd make a great dad."

Conor couldn't help it. He leaned forward and slanted his lips over hers, kissing her gently and passionately. Destry wrapped her arms tightly around his neck and kissed him in return, the first time she voluntarily did so. It was warm, gentle, but full of promise. A thrilled Conor was preparing to deliver a more powerful kiss in response, but Padraigan's voice interrupted his intentions.

"Mattock is your eldest and a very good lad." She stood up from her makeshift laboratory. "He took the potion first. When Devlin and Slane saw Mattock drink it, they took it as well. The spell transformed the boys into dwarves so they would not be suspected by those intent on harming them."

The three dwarves stood expectantly behind her. She handed the cup to the first little man, and he took two big, healthy swallows. Then she passed it to the other two, who drained it between them. Setting the cup down, Padraigan stood back and watched.

Conor and Destry were watching, too. The three little men seemed to stand there for a small eternity, looking at each other, inspecting their hands, touching their faces. Then the first dwarf who had drunk the potion suddenly coughed loudly and fell back onto his bum. He groaned and flipped over onto his belly, kicking his legs and mumbling unintelligible words.

Concerned and curious, Destry and Conor had strained to catch a glimpse of what was going on when the other two little men went down.

Being a nurse, Destry's first instinct was to help. She stood up from Conor's lap, trying to get a better look at the writhing men.

"What did she give them?" she demanded, looking at Conor. "Ask her what she gave them."

Conor said something to Padraigan, who merely turned to smile at him. Destry, increasingly concerned as the three little men rolled around on the dirt floor and grunted, tried to move toward them, but Conor stopped her. He had hold of her hand, pulling her back to him.

"Wait a minute," he said. "I doubt she's poisoned them right in front of us. Just wait and see what happens."

Destry still wasn't convinced. "But they're obviously in distress," she said. "At least let me take a look at them and make sure their vital signs are stable."

He could see the feet of the little men as they rolled around, the backsides of their bodies, but not much else. He finally shook his head. "If something is going on, I don't want you to get caught up in it," he said. "You've already got a mild concussion, and I don't want to see something worse happen to you. Just… give this a moment to see what happens, okay? If it looks like they're getting worse, then you can take a look."

Torn, concerned, Destry did as he asked, although she wasn't completely comfortable with it. She let him pull her back down onto his lap and wind his arms around her torso again. But as she watched, something strange began to happen.

First, she thought it was a trick of the light. She began to see an odd aura around the men, something that looked slightly purple. She blinked, but it didn't go away. Then she rubbed at her eyes, but it still didn't go away. As she watched, the first little man pushed himself to his knees. The purple light around him undulated, seemingly transforming him like a hand would transform clay. The man's body moved strangely, elongating, working with the tricks of the light to transform him into something taller and more slender. By the time he stood up, he wasn't anything as he had been. Whatever magic the light accomplished was evident in the younger, taller, and skinnier figure. He was no longer writhing or grunting, now completely calm as the purple aura faded. Then he turned around.

The man was no longer a man; he was a boy, perhaps ten years of age, with auburn hair and bright blue eyes. He was a handsome child with beautiful features, and his gaze moved immediately to Destry and Conor. Suddenly, he was bolting across the floor and throwing himself into Destry's lap.

She shrieked when the boy landed on her and wrapped his arms around her and Conor, his little face pressed into her belly.

"*Máthair, athair!*" the child cried. "*Tá mé caillte agat!*"

Destry had her hands full of little boy. "What did he say?" she asked Conor.

He, too, was looking with astonishment at the boy on Destry's lap. "He called us mother and father," he said. "He said that he has missed us."

Destry looked at Conor, her eyes wide with bewilderment. "He thinks we're his—"

She didn't get a chance to finish her sentence. Suddenly, two more boys were rushing at them, both with light brown hair, about six and four years of age, respectively. They threw themselves on top of the other boy, and now all three young lads squirmed in Destry's lap. They were weeping with joy, especially the youngest one; he was an adorable little boy with light brown hair and blue eyes. When he gazed up at Destry, tears running down his face, she felt the overwhelming need to pick him up and hold him. She had no idea who the kid was, but that didn't matter. He was distressed and she wanted to comfort him.

The child wrapped himself around her, holding her tightly, as she looked at Conor.

There were tears in her eyes. "These poor little boys," she whispered. "They're so… sad."

Conor had his lap full with Destry and the other two boys. He, too, felt the instinct to comfort them. It was true that they were distraught, but there was also something else deep in his heart that cried out to these children. The sensation confused and distressed him as a big hand found its way onto the oldest boy, still weeping in his lap. The child's head came up, and he threw his arms around Conor's neck, holding him tightly.

"*Athair.*" he squeezed Conor's neck. "You have come home. You have come back!"

Conor hesitantly hugged the boy, not knowing what else to do. He looked at Destry over the top of the auburn head; their eyes met and silent words of bewilderment and compassion passed between them. It would seem that neither one of them knew what to do about these children. But Destry seemed a little edgier, more fearful.

"Those… those midgets were really these children," she said.

Conor lifted his eyebrows. "I suppose so," he muttered. "I just don't know. There has to be a logical explanation for it."

"Like what?" she asked. "You saw them turn into these kids

just like I did. What's logical about that?"

She was growing agitated, even with the small child wrapped up around her. Conor simply didn't have an answer for her. "I don't know." He wouldn't look at her. "But there has to be some kind of explanation."

Destry's gaze drifted to the biggest lad, the one with his face pressed into Conor's neck. She studied the child, the shape of his head, and began to feel the faint wafts of déjà vu clutching at her. The feeling got stronger the more she stared at the child; more than that, the feel of the little one in her arms was vaguely familiar, as if she had known it once before. It was the sweetest thing she could have imagined.

Her gaze found Conor once again.

"Did you see his face?" she whispered. "Conor, he looks just like you."

Conor hadn't gotten a good look; now he wasn't sure he wanted to. So much of this situation was now becoming unbearably real to him, and he felt like he was losing his grip on reality. After a moment, he held the boy back, at arm's length, and studied his handsome little face. He found himself inspecting bright blue eyes that looked just like Destry's, and a mouth, nose, and jaw line that looked just like his. It was the weirdest thing he had ever seen.

"*Cad é do ainm, buachaill?*" he asked softly. *What's your name, boy?*

The lad looked as if he was about to weep with joy. "Mattock," he responded. "I love you, Dada. I missed you."

Conor didn't know what to say. The little boy was so sad, so pathetic, that he couldn't help but hug the child. He looked over at Destry, who had her face buried in the top of the smallest child's head. As he watched, the middle boy cuddled up against her, and she opened one of her arms for him before holding him tightly. Conor had to admit, as he watched the scene, that something inside him felt whole and settled. It was the most overwhelmingly comforting feeling he had ever known, as if now he was suddenly and finally complete.

As he watched Destry with the other two boys, pictures began to flash in his mind, like snippets of a movie reel. He saw himself with his hand on a pregnant belly, with a baby in his arms, and then flashes of more children at his feet. He blinked his eyes, shaking his head, thinking he was having hallucinations, but more visions flashed in front of him, this time of Destry. He had visions of kissing her, of making love to her, and he suddenly felt as if his heart was going to explode from his chest from the love he felt for her. He couldn't breathe. All he could feel was adoration that went beyond words, beyond time. He couldn't seem to think or feel anything else.

As Conor struggled through intense visions, Destry was quickly succumbing to something even more intense. The feel and smell of the boys in her arms was doing something to her. Somehow, she knew these children. She could feel them deep down in her heart, and as she hugged the littlest one, she, too, began to have flashbacks of something fluid and dreamlike. She saw Conor in a way she'd never seen him before—dressed in leather, with primitive weapons—and began to feel such love and affection for the man that she audibly gasped. Then she saw him making love to her, and she could feel her limbs grow warm and weak as she tasted his kisses and felt the emotion that he stirred within her.

Flashes of a rounded belly came to her mind, startling her, then finally the last few moments of childbirth as pain surged and she pushed out a male child, who was immediately handed over to a weeping Conor. Tears came to her eyes as she saw these things and the powerful emotions they created.

But another vision came along, more powerful than the rest, and she was lying on a bed struggling to give birth to another child, pain as she had never experienced surging through her body. It was enough to cause her to release the youngest child and set him down with shaky arms as she stood up, hand to her head as if to forcibly wipe away the visions that were now slamming into her with painful force.

She stood up, hand to her belly, hearing Conor's voice ringing in her head, calling to her, but unable to discern if he was really speaking to her or if it was the odd hallucinations calling out. The vision of childbirth had not gone away; it was more intense now as she envisioned herself pushing out a dead child, hearing someone say that the daughter was not meant to be.

Grief, the depths of which she could have never imagined, swept her, and she began crying. She felt pain such as she had never known, and her head began to swim. She tried to turn around, to say something to Conor, but she couldn't seem to manage it.

Blackness closed in over her before she realized it.

# CHAPTER EIGHT

CONOR SAT AT the table and watched the boys as they moved around the small mud cottage at Padraigan's direction. They had brought him a cup of strong, tart wine, some kind of rustic soda bread, and big hunks of white cheese. The two older boys were obedient and intelligent from what he could see, but the youngest didn't want to work. He remained by Destry as she lay passed out on a small bed in the next room. The little one hadn't moved from her side.

Conor had carried Destry into the room when she fainted. Laying her upon the misshapen bed made from branches covered over with a rough blanket, he could only feel confusion and remorse as he gazed at her. Her pulse was strong and her breathing regular, so he could only assume that the stress of the situation must have somehow pushed her beyond her endurance. Coupled with everything else she'd gone through over the past two weeks, unconsciousness was her body's way of coping with the stress.

So he kissed her forehead and returned to the bigger room when Padraigan insisted there was nothing they could do for the lady that rest would not more ably accomplish. He sat where he could watch Destry and the youngest boy as he sat by her side, holding her hand and speaking to her in his soft Gaelic lilt.

The more he observed, the stronger the sense of déjà vu he felt.

Every time he looked at the three boys, it was as if something deep inside was struggling to burst forth with recollections. He couldn't quite put his finger on how he knew these children, only that, for some reason, he knew he did. And the fact that they looked like him and Destry only fed his sense of confusion. Something was happening here that he had yet to fully figure out. But, given time, he knew he would. It would come to him.

He hoped.

Padraigan had seemed to steer clear of him since her initial tales of his true identity. She sent the boys to gather wood as she went outside and killed a chicken herself. Conor sat in relative silence, watching Destry in one room while inevitably finding interest in Padraigan and her archaic ways. Her cottage was incredibly primitive, with no running water, no bathroom that he could see, and its dirt floor and crude furniture.

But there was a clue in that.

More and more, he was coming to realize that perhaps there was something to what she had told him. Perhaps a door really had opened into the past, and he and Destry had really stepped through. He was starting to feel as if there was no other possible explanation for what had happened.

Still, there was a part of his brain, the logical part, that resisted. As the sun began to set and darkness settled over the land, he was starting to feel a new sense of disorientation. To see this primitive land in the daylight was one thing, but when night settled, it was as if someone had thrown a black curtain. He'd never seen such darkness. But, taking a few steps outside to gaze up at the sky, he couldn't ever remember seeing such a clear dusting of stars. In all his years in Dublin, he'd never seen such a crystalline night sky. It was quite beautiful.

Standing just outside the door, he could smell something cooking. Padraigan was making something with the chicken she had killed, and he could see the boys off in the crude barn tending to the animals for the night. He was coming to suspect that Padraigan must have said something to the boys about him and Destry, because after their initial display of affection, they had kept a distance. All except for the littlest one; he was still inside seated on the floor next to Destry.

Conor turned to catch a glimpse of her as she lay inside on the small bed. She was still on her side, still passed out. The little boy with the light brown hair was also sleeping now, his head on the bed next to Destry while his body remained on the floor. It was rather touching, and Conor smiled at the sight. The little one was a cute kid, no doubt. He couldn't help but warm to the boy.

As he gazed into the warm, fragrant cottage, he realized he had company. He turned to see the two older boys standing next to him, one with a pony on a lead. They gazed up at him timidly.

"Dada," the oldest boy said. "Would you like to see my horse?"

"You're Mattock, right?" Conor asked, watching the boy nod. Then he looked to the middle boy. "What's your name, lad?"

The boy cocked his head as if hurt by the question. "Devlin," he said. "I'm your Devlin."

Conor nodded, realizing that the boy looked a great deal like Destry. He had her bright blue eyes and the shape of her mouth. It was such an odd realization, but not an unpleasant one. He had seen the transformation this afternoon just as Destry did, when the dwarves had somehow turned into these young boys. That event, more than anything else, was breaking down his resistance. Something like that just couldn't be explained, even to a man as logical as he was.

The longer he looked at the boys, the more he realized that they looked vaguely familiar to him. He felt something for them, kindness and warmth and something else he couldn't put his finger on. He realized that the idea of these children as his sons didn't distress him in the least.

He crouched down in front of the boys so he could be more at their level. The two little faces gazed back at him eagerly. Conor looked between them, his gaze both friendly and curious.

"You say that you're my Devlin?" he asked the lad with the beautiful auburn hair. "How old are you?"

"I have seen eight years," the boy replied. "I was only seven years when last you saw me. I have grown a whole year."

He said it proudly, and Conor fought off a smile. "Then maybe that's why I didn't recognize you," he said, watching the boy beam from ear to ear. He turned to Mattock. "And you— how old are you?"

Mattock would not be outdone by his brother. "I am eleven years, Dada," he said. "I was only ten years when last you saw me. Have I grown much as well?"

Conor's smile broke through. "You're the biggest boy I've ever seen," he said, watching Mattock grin. "I would never have known you. And… and your little brother in there. What's his name?"

Mattock and Devlin looked into the open doorway of the cottage. "That is Slane," Mattock replied. "He is just a baby. He was only three when you last saw him. He has cried for Mother every day."

Conor's smile faded as he, too, looked inside to see the little boy sleeping next to Destry. It was touching and sad, and the sight tugged at his heart.

With a sigh, Conor rose to his full height, towering over the boys, looking between them and feeling his sense of déjà vu grow stronger. He swore he knew these kids. More and more, he could feel it.

Moving toward Mattock, he clapped the lad on the shoulder as he pretended to inspect the pony. "So this is your horse, is it?" he asked. "He's good-looking. What's his name?"

"Deneb," Mattock said proudly. "I can ride him like a warrior."

"How is that?"

Before Mattock could reply, Devlin shoved him. "He still falls off," he announced.

Mattock came back with a balled fist, but Conor stopped the slugging before it could start. "Tell me about home, Mattock," he said to divert their attention. "When did you last see me?"

As he hoped, the boys were sidetracked. "At Cian," Mattock said. "You were off to fight Geric, and Mother begged you not to go. But you did, and… well, we did not see you again. Padraigan came for us and brought us here. She made magic upon us, and we became *daoine*."

Conor cocked his head. "Little people? Dwarfs?"

Mattock nodded solemnly. "So Geric could not find us."

Conor shook his head in puzzlement. "Who's Geric?"

"Your brother." Padraigan approached; she had been listening just inside the doorway and thought perhaps that now was the time to continue their conversation from earlier in the day. "Geric is your younger brother, great lord. He is the one who ordered Olc of the Eye to banish you and your wife to the nether realm."

Conor focused on the woman, realizing he wanted to know all of it. Too much about this situation was bizarre; bizarre enough that he was just coming to believe it. It was time he heard everything.

"All right." He rested his fists on his hips, a gesture of resignation. "So I have a brother who had me banished into some magical other-region. If that's true, why did he do it?"

Padraigan's pale eyes were intense. "Your brother is wicked, great lord," she told him. "He has always coveted your kingdom and your abilities as a powerful warrior and a good king. He is an immoral and bitter man and managed to raise a small army to challenge you. You were able to quash him quite easily, but he continued to make trouble for you. Then, one day, he asked you to attend a private peace conference, and you agreed. When you arrived, without your warrior trappings or your guards, he set Olc upon you and banished you through the *doras na gréine.* Then he came to your wife to claim her as his own, but she escaped him and came to me, begging me to protect your children. As I escaped with the young ones and your court fled for their lives, your brother found your wife again and gave her a choice—either marry him and retain her life as a trusted queen or be banished to the nether region with you. She chose to go with you."

By this time, Conor was feeling a good deal of sorrow. He couldn't explain the feeling, only that it was very real. It was as if everything she was telling him was saturating his heart, his mind, and he was feeling the story as well as hearing it. It sounded familiar.

It felt real.

"So she made the choice to come with me rather than stay with him?" he asked. "If that's true and that woman in there is my wife, then why don't I know her?"

Padraigan emphasized her words with her tiny hands. "It was part of the curse that Olc of the Eye cast upon you," she said. "Your curse was to walk the nether world with no knowledge of who you are or who she is. I was able to coax you back to the *doras na gréine* and bring you back where you belong. Now you must remember your place, great lord, and assume your destiny as a mighty king for the sake of your family and your kingdom. We have waited a long time for your return. You must try hard to remember who you are."

Conor stared at the woman, thinking on her words. He did as she asked—he was trying hard to remember. As crazy as her story sounded, he was aware that he could easily believe it.

Something deep inside of him very much wanted to.

"Tell me about my kingdom," he said. "Maybe that will help."

Padraigan complied. "You are Conor, High King of Ciannachta, and your fortress is Cashel Cian along the River Boyne," she said. "You have a mighty army that is loyal to you; they hate your brother because he has formed an unholy alliance with the Northmen who raid this coast. They give him power and money, and in return he allows them access to a great part of Ireland through the river and harbor. The Northmen have killed and plundered many towns because of your brother's alliance with them. For many years, the Northmen would not dare attack Ciannachta because they feared you. You kept our land safe. But your brother has turned all of Ciannachta into a whore for the Northmen, to appease their lust for our riches."

Conor stared at her, digesting what he had been told. Ciannachta. He knew that name, that kingdom. It was the ancient name for Drogheda. Torn between shock, disbelief, and something that felt like excitement, he turned his focus to the gist of her distress, something that had plagued Ireland, England, and Scotland for hundreds of years.

"Northmen?" he repeated. "Viking raiders?"

"Aye, great lord."

"What year is this?"

He didn't really expect that she would know, but he asked anyway. Whatever year it was, it had to be well before the Norman conquest of England and the subsequent conquest of Ireland. The Viking raids on Ireland had gone on for hundreds of years, so he wasn't sure he could pinpoint when, exactly, this was. But he was determined to try.

Padraigan replied without hesitation, "The year of the brown rabbit."

Conor thought hard on that, knowing that the ancient Irish would measure their time by events, animals, or even kings. Try as he might, however, he couldn't seem to remember anything about the year of the brown rabbit that seemed to be significant. So he tried again.

"Who is the king of Dublin?" he asked.

"Gofraid, great lord."

Now, things became a little clearer. It was a name he knew and a history he knew all too well.

As he struggled to wrap his mind around the possibility,

Padraigan interrupted his turbulent thoughts.

"Please," she said. "We need you, great lord. The army hates Geric, but they have no choice but to serve him because he is king. But let them see their true king and you shall once again have their support and rule of Ciannachta. The army will follow you to the depths of hell if you wish it, great lord. We need you to make us whole and strong again."

Conor felt overwhelmed by her tale. But, oddly enough, he didn't resist it. Even as she told him, he felt as if he already knew the details. It was the strangest thing he had ever experienced, but even as he rolled the tale over in his mind, the details seemed to make him feel whole.

He began to feel strong again.

Behind him, he heard a noise and turned to see Destry standing in the open doorway. She stood there backlit in the light from the cottage, creating an ethereal vision as the darkness of the night enfolded everything it touched. Destry had little Slane with her, and held the child's hand as her gaze lingered on Conor.

She looked weary and pale, but in spite of that, Conor had never seen such a beautiful woman. Every time he looked at her, he felt more strongly about her.

He began to walk toward her. "You're awake," he said. "How do you feel?"

She watched him approach. "Better," she said. "What was she telling you?"

He stopped when he came upon her, standing just a few inches from her. His gaze was soft as he looked into her lovely face.

"About my brother and my kingdom," he said quietly. "Or at least what she believes is my brother and my kingdom."

Destry's gaze drifted to Padraigan and then to Slane, who was still holding her hand. "This is just a wild stab in the dark," she said, "but I'm guessing that we aren't going back to the hotel."

He wasn't sure how to answer her except with what he believed to be the truth. "No," he murmured. "I don't think there is a hotel."

"Then you really think we passed through some kind of time portal?"

He put a hand on her head, pulling her forehead to his lips for a gentle kiss.

"Something happened," he said. "Until we can figure out what it is, then all we can do is go on the assumption that somehow, someway, we have moved back in time."

She looked up at him, her gaze lingering on his handsome face. "So you're supposed to be some sort of king?"

He shrugged. "That's what I'm told. And you're my queen."

She waggled her eyebrows. "We have three boys."

His eyes twinkled. "That means that we've…"

She fought off a grin. "I still don't remember that part of it, but I did have weird dreams about giving birth." She looked down at Slane, who was gazing up at her adoringly. Then she looked to Padraigan. "I had a dream about giving birth to a girl."

Padraigan didn't understand her words, so Conor relayed the statement. Padraigan's features gentled. "You did," the sorceress said. "Between Devlin and Slane, you gave birth to a daughter who was born dead. You named her Angel because you said she was an angel on earth."

Conor whispered the translation, and Destry's heart started to beat faster. Powerful emotions she didn't recognize, yet somehow remembered, flooded her. She blinked rapidly, chasing away the tears.

"I have a sister named Angel," she whispered.

With Conor translating, Padraigan smiled. "Your Angel found you in the nether region and was reborn as your sister," she said. "It is the way of the Life Cycle. Our souls find one another in both life and death. Dying never truly separates us from those we love. We all find one another again, eventually."

Conor repeated her answer verbatim, and Destry struggled not to burst into tears at the thought. Her dreams were very vivid about giving birth to her children, including her dead daughter. She had visions of Conor weeping over the dead child, distraught by the passing.

More than anything, her visions and dreams had conveyed to her the compassion and caring of Conor, a man she had only just met but whom she apparently knew very well. Every moment that passed, she came to know him even better. She was starting to understand just how deeply he was ingrained within her.

Gazing down at Slane, she squeezed the child's hand before looking back at Conor. "These children are ours, Conor," she whispered. "I don't have any recollection of being a queen, or of this life we had together, but I can tell you for a fact that these children are ours. I know my children."

He could see that she was serious. He moved closer to her so their bodies were touching, gently resting his hand on her back, pulling her a little closer.

"You don't remember me?" he whispered. "I'm told you gave up everything to follow me when I was exiled. I'm told you loved me very much."

The heat from his body was making it difficult for her to

breathe. Her head hurt and her stomach was uneasy, but Conor's touch and closeness seemed to make her forget everything. She snaked her free hand around his slender waist, feeling his warmth and power against the palm. Her heart began to race again, now for an entirely different reason.

"That's possible," she said, laying her cheek against his warm, broad chest. He felt incredibly good. "I'm sure you're going to do your best to remind me."

He grinned and pulled her closer. "Absolutely."

She couldn't help but grin at the enthusiastic way in which he said it. She lifted her head to look at him, flicking her eyes leadingly in the direction of the four-year-old at her side. "Everything? Even…?"

He laughed softly. "Especially that."

She joined in his laughter. "I'm not sure what to say."

"Say you'll at least give me the chance."

Her laughter faded as she gazed steadily at him. His power, his handsome face, and his decent character had her spellbound. She could no longer resist him.

She stopped trying.

"I'll give you the chance," she whispered.

His smile faded, and his eyes blazed with interest and adoration and passion. He didn't miss the fact that she had just given him the green light to pursue her, and he was thrilled beyond words.

Just as he lost himself in her eyes, preparing to swoop in for a deep and luscious kiss, Mattock's pony suddenly let out a chilling scream.

Everyone jumped at the sound, turning to see the pony being dragged off in the darkness by one leg. Conor's shock only lasted a split second before he rushed forward to grab

Mattock and Devlin, who were rooted to the spot, yelling in fright at the top of their lungs. He thrust the boys in the direction of the cottage, then moved to shove Destry as well before realizing she already had Slane in hand and was running toward the door. Padraigan bolted, but Conor couldn't worry about her; he was more concerned with getting Destry and the boys to safety.

Destry couldn't see what had the pony in its grip, but she could hear growling and snorting, which scared her to death. Instinct had her practically tossing Slane into the cottage and then pausing at the door as Mattock, Devlin, and Conor brought up the rear. She grabbed hold of Mattock and Devlin as they rushed into the shelter, shoving them back into the room and away from the door, because she truly had no idea what was happening. All she knew was that the horse was being dragged off into the darkness, the kids were screaming, and she was terrified.

Conor, however, hadn't come into the cottage. He was standing in the doorway, watching the pony as it struggled against whatever had it. It was so dark that he couldn't see whatever had the horse in its grip. Mattock was weeping hysterically because his pony was being attacked, and Destry found herself comforting the boy, watching Conor with a terrified expression as he watched the horse struggling in the darkness.

"What is it?" Destry asked him, her voice shaking. "Can you see anything?"

Conor's eyes were riveted to the movement in the darkness; it was over by the makeshift barn now, and he could see that the pony's struggles were lessening. The animal was losing the fight. He could hear the growling and snorting, as something horrific and terrible was lingering in the shadows. As he opened his mouth, Padraigan appeared, rushing at him from the direction of the crude corral. She had a flaming torch in her hand and was dragging something with her. She rushed at Conor, struggling with both the weight of the torch and whatever she was dragging.

"Great lord," she said breathlessly. "Your weapon."

Conor was surprised. "Weapon?" he repeated. "What—"

Padraigan tried to lift it, but she wasn't strong enough, not with one arm. Conor saw her struggles and took it from her. The little sorceress held the torch high in the direction of the struggling pony.

"I will blind it with the light," she said. "You must kill it."

"Kill what?" he demanded, frustrated and a little scared. "I can't even see it."

"You must, great lord. Kill it now!"

Conor's gaze lingered on her before he took a look at the weapon he now held in his hand. It was heavy, and as he lifted it into the light, he could see that it was a gloriously crafted broadsword. The magnificent piece was massive, at least four feet long, with a thick, sharp blade etched with crosses and other Celtic designs. The hilt was forged from a solid piece of steel, and as he put his hand around the leather pommel, he realized that it fit his grip perfectly. He was quickly becoming enamored with the beauty and craftsmanship of the blade— until Padraigan hissed at him.

"Great lord!" she said, motioning for him to follow her. "We must kill it because it will come for us when it finishes with the pony. Hurry!"

Conor didn't like the sound of that at all, but he still couldn't see what had the horse. "What is it?"

Padraigan's features were filled with anxiety. "*Uafásach.*"

His brow furrowed. "Terror? What terror?"

"Please," Padraigan urged. "You are a great warrior, great lord. You have killed many *fiacla nathair*. Hurry!"

*Snake teeth,* Conor translated. It sounded too weird to adequately comprehend. But he was urged on by her words and the pony's screaming. He could no longer stand idle.

He glanced at Destry before he charged on, seeing fear and trust in her eyes, and it fed him like nothing else he had ever known. As Padraigan ran toward the barn with the torch held high, he charged after her.

He could see the pony in the darkness, lying on its side as something chomped on its leg. Conor was a man trained in the art of Medieval warfare. He'd trained ten years' worth of students in the same thing and considered himself an expert. He knew tactics, weapons, and psychology.

But nothing had prepared him for the sight of the creature when he finally beheld it.

Padraigan rushed forward with the torch, and the thing screamed, releasing the pony and recoiling in fear of the fire. Conor could see that it was some kind of enormous lizard with great, jagged teeth—he couldn't describe it any other way. But it was terrifying, like something out of a horror movie, and for a moment he was actually stunned into inaction. As Padraigan thrust the torch at it, Conor just stood there with his jaw slack, drinking in something he could have never imagined in his wildest dreams.

But he was spurred into action by Padraigan's howl when the beast suddenly reared back and spat at her. Something horrible smelling and steamy hit the ground, scorching all it touched.

"I will distract it, great lord!" Padraigan called to him, her voice tense. "Kill it!"

Conor could feel his heart pounding in his chest, and was both terrified and strangely excited. This was something new, horrifying, and weirdly brilliant. He was in the middle of something he couldn't quite comprehend, like a dream, but in spite of that, he knew what he had to do. He needed to call upon his classic weapons training and carve into a beast he'd never even heard of, much less seen. He had no idea what it was, but he knew he had to kill it. He couldn't chance that the thing would go after Destry or the children. He was the only defense they had, and he was going to kill it before it killed them.

The first test of the high king had begun.

Conor took a deep breath and cleared his mind, thinking logically on how to approach the hissing creature as Padraigan bravely thrust the torch at it, using the fire to distract it. But as Conor got a good grip on the enormous broadsword and circled to the left of the animal, moving out of its line of sight, he could hear Padraigan uttering faint, mysterious words.

"*A gheobhaidh tú ar ais leis an dorchadas,*" she hissed. "*Chréatúr de, fiacla olc dubh an bháis, ar ais chuig an dorchadais ó áit a tháinig tú.*"

*She's casting a spell,* Conor thought as he moved with stealth to the left, translating Padraigan's words as he went—*To the darkness you will return. Creature of evil, black teeth of death, return to the darkness from where you came.* It all seemed surreal as he got a good look at the animal, something scaly and prehistoric-looking. He couldn't even be clinical as he studied it, because the thing went beyond what his scientific mind was capable of analyzing. He tightened his grip on the sword, watching the thing spit some kind of secretion that sizzled and burned at the foliage beneath its feet. It was horrible and terrifying.

And he could waste no more time.

He charged forward, holding the blade aloft in both hands as he aimed for the torso where the front legs joined with the chest. He fell upon the cold and scaly beast, ramming the sword into its body as hard as he could.

The creature screamed, sounding very much like a human cry, and fell over onto its left side. Conor withdrew the sword and plunged it in again and again. As the beast went through its death throes, a claw caught Conor on the right shoulder blade, and he fell back, rolling away from the creature that was thrashing about violently. Somehow, he ended up about twenty feet away, watching the beast die. He didn't even remember how he got there. He just stood there and watched the animal as its thrashing grew less and less until finally, the beast gave one huge shudder and suddenly lay still.

The air was abruptly quiet, the only sounds those of distant night birds or an occasional forest creature. Conor felt as if he couldn't breathe. It was as if the silence had sucked the air right out of his lungs. When he finally resumed breathing, it sounded as if he was gasping. He just couldn't believe what had happened, or what he had done, but the proof was dead and bleeding in front of him.

Padraigan leaned over the beast, jabbing it with her torch to make sure it was dead. As Conor stood there, stunned, she turned to the pony, who was still on the ground with a mauled rear leg. The pony nickered softly in pain, and Padraigan called to Conor.

"Great lord," she said, her voice quivering from the stress and fear she had so recently endured. "The pony is injured. You must ease him into the next world."

Conor was still staring at the dead beast, but he managed to get his legs moving and made his way over to the little white pony. By this time, Destry and the boys had spilled out from the cottage, timidly making their way toward Conor and the dead creature. Destry had Slane by the hand, but Mattock broke loose and ran to his pony. When he saw the state of the animal's leg, the tears began to flow.

"Deneb," he said as he fell to his knees, stroking the soft white fur. "'Twill be all right, boy."

Conor stood over the pony, seeing the mangled leg and knowing that it was unsalvageable. His heart went out to the boy as Destry walked up beside him. Her soft, warm hand touched his wrist.

"Are you all right?" she whispered.

He nodded, still staring at the boy. "I'm fine."

"What in the hell was that?"

Conor tore his focus away from the pony and looked down at her. The impulse to pull her into his arms was very real, because he needed that reassuring warmth. He needed to draw upon that strength. Therefore, he put his arms around her and held her tightly. Suddenly, he felt shaken and frightened now that it was all over, and was looking to Destry as his source of strength. He really needed to hold her, just for a moment. He'd never been so scared in his entire life.

Destry could feel him shaking, and she let go of Slane's hand, putting her arms around Conor and hugging him tightly. He seemed shaken up, and she found herself in the role of giving comfort.

"It's all right," she murmured to him, caressing his broad back. "It's all over now. Everything is all right."

He just stood there and trembled. Destry unwound her arms from his waist and pulled back to look him in the face, moving her hands to his cheeks. She looked him in the eye.

"Do you hear me?" she whispered, smiling encouragingly. "It's all over and you did fine. We're all fine."

He just looked at her, his pale face even paler. He couldn't even speak. Clucking with sympathy, she threw her arms around his neck and kissed his cheeks, whispering words of comfort. As Conor wrapped her up in his enormous arms again, they heard soft sobs off to the left and turned to see Mattock weeping quietly over his pony. The boy was broken up, and Conor wasn't so shaken that he didn't know what needed to be done. Taking a deep breath, he steadied himself.

"Take the boys inside," he told Destry. "I need to… take care of the pony."

Destry looked up at him. "What are you going to do?"

He looked at her, and she got the hint. "Just… take them inside," he said softly.

Destry let go of Conor and went to Mattock, timidly putting her hands on the boy's shoulders. The lad began to weep harder when he realized that they were trying to separate him from his beloved pony.

"Conor?" Destry looked up at him, desperate. "I don't speak his language. Tell him to come with me."

Conor leaned over, putting his hand on the boy's auburn head. "Mattock," he said in Gaelic. "Go with… with your mother now."

Mattock shook his head, weeping pitifully. Destry felt so sorry for the boy; she hugged him gently, trying to pull him away from the pony.

"How can I tell him that everything will be okay?" she asked

Conor.

Conor helped her pull the boy up. "*Beidh gach rud ceart go leor.*"

Destry put her arms around the child, her head against his. "*Beidh gach rud ceart go leor,*" she repeated softly. "Everything will be all right, Mattock. Come inside."

She managed to pull him away from the bleeding animal. Conor took hold of Devlin and Slane, directing them to follow. He stood there and watched as Destry escorted the boys back inside the cottage, his gaze lingering on the gently glowing open door even after they had disappeared through it.

It had been an extremely eventful night in a day that had been full of such monumental events, and he still wasn't quite sure how he felt about it. But he was glad for one thing—Destry was with him. All of the craziness and bizarre happenings aside, he could handle anything that was thrown at him as long as she was with him.

Already, he could feel that bond.

He needed it.

With a sigh, he turned back to the dead creature several feet away with the sword still stuck in its belly. Conor went to retrieve the sword, feeling a little squeamish about what he needed to do with the pony. He went to the little horse, gazing down into its big brown eyes as Padraigan began to throw wood all around the dead beast. As Conor reluctantly took care of the horse, quickly and painlessly, Padraigan made a neat bonfire around the lizard beast and lit it with the torch in her hand.

With the inky darkness surrounding them, Conor went to stand next to Padraigan as she murmured spells into the night that would cast the creature's soul deep into the underworld. As an anthropologist, he found it extremely interesting and curious, but as a man who had just killed some mythical beast, he was willing to believe that that science wasn't all it was cracked up to be.

Maybe a little magic was something to put some faith in.

# CHAPTER NINE

BY THE TIME Conor and Padraigan entered the cottage, the fire was burning low in the hearth and everything was quiet. Poking his head into the smaller room that contained the small bed, he found Destry and the boys asleep.

"Eat something, great lord," Padraigan whispered, indicating for him to sit at the table.

Conor was exhausted, but he realized that he was also very hungry. With everything that had happened, it hadn't even occurred to him until now. He pulled up one of the little stools and sat heavily, watching Padraigan bring bread, cheese, and a big, steaming bowl of something to the table. She had dished it out from a big iron pot that sat tucked back in the hearth, and he smelled it suspiciously, trying to figure out what it was.

Padraigan watched him anxiously. "Is it not to your satisfaction, great lord?"

He half shrugged, half nodded. "What is it?"

"Fowl," she told him. "It is cooked with grains and greens."

Conor figured he had nothing to lose by trying it. He tore off a big hunk of the rustic, very brown bread and dipped it into the stew. He didn't count on it being delicious. It was basically a thick chicken and barley stew with peas and something white, which he thought might be turnips. He couldn't really tell. But it was hearty and tasty, and very salty, and he ended up eating about a half-gallon of the stuff.

Padraigan also produced boiled eggs, smaller and denser than modern eggs, and he ate a dozen of those as well. Along with the loaf of dark bread and half-pound of cheese, Conor polished off a significant meal. He washed it all down with a very tart wine that gave him a pretty decent buzz.

Exhausted, and full, he sat at the table and burped as Padraigan cleared away the remainders of his meal.

"Go and sleep tonight, great lord," she told him, pointing to the room where Destry and the boys were. "We will speak again in the morning."

Conor didn't argue. His mind was muddled and he couldn't think any longer. He just wanted to sleep for a while and forget all of this madness. Maybe it would all be gone when he woke up in the morning.

But as he rose from the stool and stood in the doorway of the smaller bedchamber, he sincerely wished that he wasn't dreaming. He didn't want to wake up and find Destry a figment of his imagination.

It was dark in the room, but he could see the layout of the group—Destry was on the bed with the mattress of leaves and branches, sleeping on her left side and turned away from him. Mattock was curled up at her feet, while Slane and Devlin were sleeping on her left. She was lying so that her right arm was protectively around both boys.

Conor stood there a moment, watching the tender scene, feeling warmth and contentment in his veins. What was it Destry had said to him? *I know my children.* Apparently, she did. It was obvious in everything about her. He knew his children, too.

He also knew his wife.

He was dressed in jeans and the heavy shirt and jacket. He quietly pulled the jacket off and laid it on the ground near the bed, then pulled off the shirt as well. It landed on top of the jacket. Lowering himself to the floor, he removed his shoes, his socks, and finally his belt. They all ended up with the jacket and shirt. Quietly, he lay down beside Destry in a moment he would remember for the rest of his life.

She had taken off the jacket and sweater she had been wearing earlier, and was now clad only in her jeans and a lightweight long-sleeved shirt. The moment he lay down next to her, she took her arm off the boys and turned around to face him. Conor wrapped his arms around her and pulled her close against his naked chest. He could feel her face against his skin, her breath hot on his chest, and his physical reaction was almost instantaneous. He wanted to bury himself in her softness and never let go.

He pulled her closer.

"Are you sure you're okay after all of that?" Destry whispered.

"I'm fine," he murmured.

She pulled her face out of his chest and gazed up at him in the muted light. "I saw that scratch on your back," she whispered. "I should probably take a look at it."

He looked into her sleepy face, wanting very much to kiss her. He was buzzed from the wine, that was true, but his feelings for her had nothing to do with alcohol. He was in love with her. He'd always been in love with her. It was something that grew stronger by the minute.

"It's nothing," he assured her. "I can't even feel it. You can look at it in the morning if it'll make you happy."

"You don't know for sure that it's nothing," she countered. "What the hell was that thing, anyway?"

He shook his head. "I have no idea," he said. "Padraigan called it a snake with teeth. It looked like something prehistoric to me."

Destry's eyes were fixed on him. "Is that even possible?" she asked. "A dinosaur?"

He shrugged. "Legends abound from this time in history," he murmured, caressing her back, feeling the texture of her hair. "There were all sorts of legends of creatures. It's possible that there was some basis for that, creatures that somehow survived millions of years only to be made extinct by Dark Age Man."

She pursed her lips. "You saw the proof with your own eyes," she hissed. "You killed the damn thing. What if there are more of them?"

He sighed faintly. "Then I'll be killing a lot of lizards, I suppose." He winked at her when she frowned. "Right now, I don't want to think about it. I just want to sleep."

She let him pull her back against him, cuddled up against his enormous chest. But her eyes were open, staring into the darkness as she felt his warmth wrap all around her.

"Do we even know what time period this is?" she said. "Did you ask the sorceress?"

She felt him sigh. "I asked her a few questions and was able to determine that Gofraid is the king of Dublin right now."

"When did he reign?"

"He ruled from 934 AD to 941 AD, so we're somewhere in that time span, I would guess."

She lifted her head again, looking at him with shock. "The Dark Ages?"

"More like the Middle Ages."

The shock didn't leave her expression. "Then we're really here. We actually went back in time somehow."

"After what I've seen today, I would agree with that statement."

"Are you scared?"

He shrugged. "I think I'm curious more than anything. But that big snake with teeth… that thing scared me."

"Me too."

Hearing that somehow brought it all home for Destry. Whatever had happened to them was as real as it got. Somehow, someway, a door in time had opened up, and they stepped through it. It was fantastic to the point of being insane, but there was no other explanation.

Frightened and exhausted herself, Destry closed her eyes and fell back against him.

Conor knew she was upset. He pulled her close, his lips against her forehead, kissing her gently to bring her some comfort. To his surprise, she lifted her mouth to his, and he latched on to her hungrily. As her arms went around his neck, he rolled her onto her back and kissed her deeply.

Destry responded to him passionately. With every second that passed, his kiss became more heated, and he licked at her lips before tasting her sweetness when she opened her mouth and invited him in. Her fingers were in his hair, which was still spiked stiff, matching him suckle for suckle as he moved his right hand down her torso and found a full breast. She had such a delicious little body that he just couldn't help himself.

Rather than flinch from his touch, she lifted up her shirt

and unhooked her bra at the front. Conor's hand came into contact with the heated flesh of her naked breast, and he groaned softly in excitement, feeling the nipple harden in his palm. He was trying to stay quiet; God help him, he was *desperately* trying. There was a four-year-old and an eight-year-old just a few feet away, and he didn't want to wake them. But he couldn't stop himself from exploring Destry, something that was becoming less like exploration and more like reacquainting. Even as he fondled her soft breasts, it was as if he already knew their texture and softness. He already knew her body.

He had to taste her.

He moved his hot mouth to a nipple, and Destry had to slap her hand over her mouth to keep from making noise. As Conor furiously suckled, Slane suddenly moved in his sleep, rolling into his brother and sending them both sliding off the bedding. The boys ended up in a little heap on the floor, still halfway on the blanket, and Conor and Destry froze, watching to see if they'd wake up. But both boys were sleeping so heavily that they weren't even aware of the fact that they had rolled right off the bed.

Conor grinned at Destry, who waggled her eyebrows. Then she latched on to Conor's mouth and kissed him hotly.

Their passion took flight, and clothes began coming off in the darkness. Conor left her breasts and yanked off her jeans, planting himself between her legs as he worked his mouth across her flat belly. The smell of her, the taste of her, was feeding his frenzy, and he moved his right hand from her breasts to the junction between her legs. So far, she wasn't flinching from his touch—in fact, she seemed to be encouraging him. He could feel her squirming beneath him, and it excited him like nothing he had ever known. When he reached her inner thigh and he realized that her pubic area was completely waxed, he groaned with excitement.

"Shh," Destry whispered, her hand over his mouth.

Conor kissed her fingers, one by one, before descending on the pink folds between her legs. Destry's knees came up at the delicious sensation, and a moan escaped her lips.

"Shh." Conor grinned as he put a hand over her mouth.

She rewarded him by sucking on his fingers, stroking his index finger with her tongue as he performed oral sex on her. Driven beyond endurance by her heated tongue and sexy body, Conor sat back on his heels and lifted Destry onto his waiting erection. He didn't want to grind her tender back into the rough mattress, so he sat on his heels while she straddled his lap. As the boys around them slept like the dead, Destry wrapped her arms around his neck, straddled his thighs, and gave herself over to him completely.

The scent of their lovemaking stirred strong, buried memories. She began to recall innumerable nights like this, wrapped around the man she loved, feeling his power deep within her. She began to recall the depth of her feelings for the man, the love and adoration she felt that was more powerful than anything that had ever existed. She found his mouth, feeling his goatee scratch her tender lips but loving the sensation. She kissed him deeply as he thrust into her, knowing that, at last, she was finally where she belonged.

"Oh, Conor," she breathed into his mouth. "I love you so much."

His arms tightened around her. "I've never loved anyone else but you, sweetheart," he murmured against her lips. "You are my heart and soul. I will always love you, in this life or the next."

They made love deep into the night.

℃ℬ

THE NEXT DAY, Conor awoke at daybreak because he heard Padraigan moving around in the great room.

He blinked, struggling to orient himself because he didn't recognize where he was at first. He didn't recognize the mud walls or sloping roof. But he quickly realized that Destry was in his arms, sleeping the sleep of the dead pressed up against his warm body, and the events from the previous day and night flooded his mind. He remembered Dowth, the flight to Padraigan's cottage, the snake with teeth… everything.

Most of all, he remembered the feel of Destry, and his limbs grew warm at the thought. He'd never known anything so passionate, satisfying, or erotic. It was as if he was finally and completely whole. As long as she was with him, as long as he had her love, he could move mountains.

Another thing he quickly realized was that they were both quite naked. He felt rather bold and caddish having made love to her in the presence of sleeping children, but there wasn't much he could do about that in hindsight, so he carefully disengaged himself from her with the intention of looking for his pants. But she groaned when he moved, and he put a hand over her mouth, silencing her when she opened her eyes.

"Shh," he whispered, kissing her nose. "The boys are still asleep."

She was still half-asleep herself. "Where are you going?"

He kissed her again and slowly moved to sit up. "I need to find my clothes," he whispered, spying his jeans next to the bed. "I'm without a stitch on. And so are you. If the boys wake up and find us like this, we'll have a lot of explaining to do."

Destry blinked, rubbing her eyes as she looked around. The boys were still dead asleep, but she realized that Conor was correct—she was stark naked. She sat up, her arms covering her substantial breasts.

"Oh, brother," she said. "Where are my clothes?"

Conor was fighting off a grin as she tried to cover herself up. But her double-D cup breasts could hardly be contained by her slender arms, and he lost himself for a moment, burying his face in the delightful cleavage. She gasped, giggled, then groaned softly as he moved her right arm aside and suckled gently on a peaked nipple.

"Conor, don't," she gasped, her face in the top of his head.

He lifted his head, kissing her lips. "I'm sorry," he whispered. "I got carried away. You seem to have that effect on me."

She grinned at him, quickly feeling hot and horny as he played with her nipple. It wasn't so much a want for him but a need; she needed the man more than she could comprehend. Her body was crying out for him, having been denied for the months and years and centuries of their separation, and last night had evidenced that.

Now that she had reacquainted herself with him, fragments of memories about the man and her love for him returning, she had to make up for lost time. She slanted her lips over his, plunging her tongue into his mouth, and Conor fell back on the bed, taking her down with him. This time, however, she climbed on top of him, straddling his belly as she ferociously kissed him.

Conor could feel her naked body against him, her wet heat rubbing against his belly, and it was all he could take. He was intoxicated with her. He cupped her buttocks, and when he thrust a finger into her, she groaned into his mouth and pushed her pelvis against his finger, simulating intercourse. Conor groaned softly in return, as wildly aroused as he had ever been in his life, then lifted her up and planted her onto his fully engorged erection. He could feel her warm tightness as she slid down over him, accepting his sensual intrusion into her body.

Destry drew away from his mouth as she sat up, taking his hands and placing them on her breasts as she began to ride him. Knees on the ground, she rolled her hips forward and plunged as he fondled her breasts, her head back and her long hair tickling the tops of his thighs. Twice, she started to groan, and twice, Conor put his hand up to gently cover her mouth, reminding her that they didn't want to attract any attention. What they were doing was between the two of them—her supple and shapely body welcoming his power deep inside her as it had so many times before, in so many forms. At the moment, there was only the two of them, re-experiencing something they had both sorely missed. It was a rebirth.

Destry plunged down on him, again and again, hearing him hiss with the pleasure of it. Conor watched her as she made love to him, marveling at her beauty and perfection, before sitting up and pulling her against him, suckling her nipples as she continued to ride him. Destry was so highly aroused that in little time, she was climaxing, wave after wave of pleasure rushing over her as Conor repeatedly thrust himself deep.

He felt her orgasm throbbing around him, and he answered by releasing himself deep into her body, taking so much pleasure with it that he bit his lip. He could taste the blood. But he still continued to move, feeling her multiple orgasms that ended up reducing her to a quivering shell in his arms. Her entire body was throbbing against him, and he moved his mouth slowly over her neck and shoulder as the tremors eventually died away.

Destry remained straddled on his lap, weak and limp, as he held her close. He could feel her heart thumping against him. Her hair was in her face, all over his shoulder, and as he loosened his grip, she lolled back. Her head rolled back as well, and Conor grinned as she remained lifeless and boneless in his arms. He leaned forward, kissing her neck, the swell of her breasts, and eventually a soft nipple. When he suckled her tenderly, her head came up.

"No," she whispered, pulling his head back. "Not again. We really should get dressed before these kids wake up and catch us."

He grinned up into her half-lidded face. "I'd rather do this."

She grinned in return, a delightfully sleepy gesture. "Me too," she whispered, "but we're going to have to wait for more privacy. We've already risked being caught twice, and I really feel dirty having done this in front of these kids, but…"

They had let their lust get the better of them, and they both knew it, but there was something so overwhelming about feelings they were awakening that it seemed to supersede all else.

Conor sighed in agreement, in disappointment, realizing their bodies were still fused and lifting Destry up by the waist to withdraw from her. But the moment he did so, another orgasm washed over her, and she threw her head forward, biting off her cries on his shoulder as a powerful climax surged through her body. It was unexpected and deliriously sweet. Her teeth pushed into his pale flesh, leaving a mark.

Conor couldn't control himself, and he lowered her back down onto his semi-erection, grinding his pelvis against her as he greedily soaked up the last few tremors of her orgasm.

Breathlessly, Destry tried to stop him, but she couldn't quite get the words out of her mouth in time before he withdrew from her again and caused yet another orgasm. Her face ended up in his shoulder again as she struggled not to scream, but when Conor went to put her on his erection again, she prevented him. They could go on all day if they didn't stop, because the experience was like nothing either one of them had ever known, something magical and emotional that went beyond a physical need.

It was magic.

"Are you okay?" Conor finally whispered.

Destry nodded weakly. "Uh-huh."

"Can we get dressed now?"

She lifted her head wearily, smiling. "What's stopping you?

"*You* are."

"Complaining?"

"God no." He rubbed his nose tenderly against hers. His eyes locked with hers, and, for a moment, they just stared at each other. "Any regrets?"

She shook her head. "No," she whispered. "Absolutely not."

"You're sure?"

"Yes."

"Good." He pulled back to look at her, his dark blue eyes intense with emotion. "Because I love you. I'll love you until I die."

She smiled, moving a soft hand to his rough cheek. "I love you too."

He stared at her, a smile eventually coming to his lips. "I know it doesn't make any sense, but nothing has ever felt so right. The moment I saw you, I knew I loved you. I've always loved you."

She leaned forward, kissing him sweetly. "It's so strange," she said as she pulled away. "Pieces of memories are coming back to me, but I really can't figure out if it's because I'm imagining them or because they're truly memories from some past life. But the memory of you… it came back so strongly last night. The moment you touched me, I remembered you. I remembered everything, and now I can't seem to let you go."

He nodded. "I know what you mean," he whispered. "The second I touched you, everything came flooding back. Your taste, your scent, your curves… everything."

She smiled at him, her hand on his cheek, rubbing his stubble as she gazed at his face. He was such a handsome man.

But before she could say anything more, Padraigan suddenly entered the small doorway, her arms full of clothing. Unimpressed by Conor and Destry's naked state and the fact that Destry was still straddling Conor's lap, the little sorceress went to the bed and dumped the pile.

"Your clothing, great lord." She turned to the pair. "I managed to salvage some of it when Geric confiscated the Cashel. I have these possessions and more. After you dress, I shall show you."

Destry was wrapped up in Conor's enormous arms, so she wasn't entirely exposed, and Conor was sideways, so he wasn't providing a completely naughty display, but they were both very uncomfortable with an audience to their nakedness. More than that, it was readily apparent what they had been doing. If Padraigan had been in the next room or even the next county, she would have easily heard them.

But the sorceress seemed unconcerned. She rummaged through the pile and pulled out some kind of white robe. She turned and held it out to Destry.

"My lady?" she said. "May I assist you?"

Destry didn't have a clue what the woman was saying. She looked to Conor for help, and he took pity on her. Destry had no recollection or knowledge of a former language. It had made the situation particularly disorienting, but, so far, she hadn't complained about the communication barrier.

"She wants to know if she can help you dress," he told her.

Destry lifted an eyebrow. "I don't think so," she said. "Thank her, but tell her that I'll dress alone."

Conor relayed the words, and Padraigan laid the robe back on the bed and quit the room. When she was gone, Destry jumped up and went for her bra and panties, which were in a silky pile next to the bed.

Conor watched with great appreciation and admiration as she slipped on her lacy panties followed by the lacy white bra. She had a fabulous body, the most beautiful he had ever seen. His hungry gaze moved up her silky thighs, lingered on the lacy panties, before moving up her torso to her full breasts. He was thinking very dirty thoughts again as she bent over and picked up her jeans.

He stopped her. "Wait," he said quietly. "If we're going to be stuck in this time, the last thing we want to do is stand out. We need to blend in, and that's not going to happen if you wear those jeans."

She looked at the jeans in her hand, nodding when she realized he made some sense. Her gaze moved to the flowing white robe that Padraigan had laid upon the bed. Jeans still in hand, she moved over to the garment and observed it with some doubt.

"All right." She sighed heavily as she folded the jeans up and set them aside. She picked up the white robe, realizing it was like a giant, flowing muumuu. It was very soft, and she rubbed it against her cheek, looking at Conor with a grin. "It's soft. I think I can wear this."

He smiled in return, his gaze once again trailing down the curve of her back and coming to rest on her delicious buttocks. He just couldn't help himself. He stroked her rounded butt cheek, squeezing it, before bending over to nibble at it.

Destry giggled and pulled away from him. "Come on," she said. "If you keep doing that, we'll never get dressed."

He waggled his eyebrows in resignation and stood up. Destry burst into snorts of laughter when she saw that he was semi-aroused again.

He pursed his lips with mock fury as she laughed. "It's not funny," he told her.

She continued to giggle softly as she pulled the dress over her head, immediately loving the feel and fit of it. It clung to her beautifully, as if made for her. As Destry smoothed at the garment, she realized that it *had* been made for her. Running her hands up and down the arms, noting the texture of the fabric, she glanced over to see Conor examining the leather pants that Padraigan had left on the end of the bed. He had pulled his boxer-briefs on, so he wasn't completely nude as he stood inspecting the stitching on the inseam of the pants.

Curious, Destry went to see what had him so fascinated. "What's wrong?" she asked.

He shook his head, riveted to the stitching. "Nothing," he said. "I was just looking at the craftsmanship on these breeches. The leather is sewn together with very fine strips of leather. It's really remarkable."

Destry tried hard to see what he was looking at, but, as she wasn't a scientist like he was, it really didn't mean all that much to her. So she bent over the end of the bed where Padraigan had laid the pile of clothing and began pulling out various garments. There was a long, dark green article that looked like a robe, a faded yellow one with beautiful beadwork around the neckline, and several others. She ran her hands over the material, seeing that it wasn't like any material she had ever seen in her life. The green garment was made from wool, very fine, but the weave was uneven. The yellow garment was silk, she was sure, but it was also uneven, and the color wasn't uniform. Everything was fastened with tiny hand stitches, and the hems of the garments weren't sewn at all, but all things considered, they seem to be very well made.

As Conor pulled on the leather pants, Destry took the long green robe and put it on over the feather-soft dress she already had on. She was delighted to see that the long sleeves on the green garment had slits in them, allowing the eggshell-colored dress underneath to show through. The robe also had a belt with fine tassels on the end, and she tied it around her waist, emphasizing her slender torso and large breasts.

By the time Conor looked up from lacing the front of his leather pants up, the sight of her in the flowing robes made his heart leap in all directions.

"My God," he breathed. "You're a lovely creature."

She was fussing with the tassels, looking up with a grin when he spoke. "Thanks," she said. "I really have no idea if these are even supposed to go together, but they seem to. Am I wearing it right?"

He looked her over with his critical Celtic eye, having her spin in a circle for him. He nodded with satisfaction.

"There has never been another woman on this earth as beautiful as you," he said decisively. "You're spectacular."

Her grin broadened. "You're sweet; thank you," she said, but her grin faded. "I'd love to shower and shave right now, but I'm guessing that's not going to be possible."

He shrugged, tugging at the leather breeches before he reached down into the pile on the bed and began hunting for a shirt of some kind.

"Probably not," he replied. He found a woolen shirt, or what he thought was a woolen shirt, big enough to fit his frame and pulled it over his head. "There's a whole host of things we need and don't have. I need to talk to Padraigan to see where we can at least get soap and basic hygiene needs. What we can't buy, I can make."

Her eyebrows lifted. "What can you make?"

He shrugged again, straightening out the tunic. Destry moved forward to help him straighten out the back of it, smoothing the tunic against his very broad back.

"A toothbrush, for example," he said. "They were made out of water reeds or green branches, something that frayed easily. We can make toothpaste out of soda and mint, all mashed together. Soap can be made from any number of oils that occur naturally and lye, or lotions from almond oil or beeswax. I promise that you'll not do without, sweetheart. We'll keep your skin soft and your smile bright."

Her smile was back. "You can make all of that? Where did you learn to do it?"

He returned her smile. "Back in the early days when I was still going to college, I worked several Medieval fairs all around Ireland. Since I'm such a big lad, I was always some kind of warrior, but during those years I learned a lot about ancient processes with food and other things. I learned how to make soap, candles, certain medicines, things like that. It's come in very handy to pass down to my students. I'm a walking dictionary for all things ancient."

She sighed. "If I have to be stranded in the past with someone, thank God it's you," she said, watching him wink at her. "I have to tell you that I'm still feeling a little disoriented. What's our plan of attack for this morning?"

Conor eyed the boots that Padraigan had dropped at the foot of the bed, massive things made from cow hide. He picked one up and began to inspect it.

"I'm not sure," he told her. "I need to talk to the sorceress and try to figure some things out. Meanwhile, you can get the boys up and ready for breakfast."

He was nodding toward the boys. Destry turned to see that they were just starting to stir. Little mouths were yawning. She shook her head, grinning.

"Now they wake up," she commented softly. "We made so much noise last night and this morning that it would have awoken the dead, but those three slept right through it."

Conor fought off a grin. "Thank God they didn't wake up," he muttered. "We didn't need an audience for what we were doing, but I'm not sure I would have been able to stop had they woken up, so I'll thank God for small mercies. The lads can sleep through anything."

Destry was grinning because he was, and went to pull on her shoes, fancy modern sneakers with straps and rhinestones.

"I never grew up with brothers, so I can't attest to boys' ability to sleep through anything, but I know my sister and I were very light sleepers," she told him as she slipped on a shoe. "We heard every little sound in the house."

Conor pulled on both boots, inspecting them on his feet and realizing they were a perfect fit. "I'll be damned," he muttered, running his hand over the sole of the shoe. "These fit as if…"

He trailed off, and she sat down next to him on the foot of the bed, looking at the boots. "As if they were made for you?"

Her voice was soft, and he looked at her, feeling the weight of their situation settle, while he had been fairly detached from it since they woke up. For some reason, the boots seemed to bring it home. If he thought hard about them, he thought he might remember them somehow, like a distant dream just lingering below the surface.

Gazing into her bright blue eyes, he nodded with some reluctance. "Yes," he murmured. "This just keeps getting weirder and weirder. These shoes fit perfectly."

"And you're surprised?"

"It's not that." He sighed. "I guess… I guess I'm just not as resigned to all of this as much as I thought."

"Why?"

He shrugged. "It's all so overwhelming," he said. "Just when I think I've accepted it, something happens and I realize I really haven't."

"Like Dark Ages boots that were made for you?"

"Yes."

She gave him a sweet smile and laid her head against his shoulder. "Don't go to pieces on me now," she said softly. "I can't guarantee how I'm going to hold up if you don't stay strong."

He shifted, wrapping his arms around her and pulling her close. He kissed the tip of her nose, her tender mouth. She was soft and delicious, and he was in the process of kissing her more deeply when Slane suddenly groaned, a grumpy little sound, and sat bolt upright. He rubbed his eyes, frowning when he saw

Destry and Conor in a tight embrace. As they watched, he stood up, eyes still half-closed and a frown on his face, and wedged himself in between them.

Destry giggled while Conor was forced to let her go as the four-year-old plastered himself against her. She wrapped her arms around the little boy as he snuggled against her and promptly fell back asleep.

Conor shook his head and stood up, feeling the fit of the boots and clothing, acquainting himself with something that felt oddly familiar.

As if they belonged to him.

Padraigan entered the room again, this time with a bucket of water, which she handed to Conor. He took it, having no idea what to do with it, but set it on the broad windowsill as Padraigan moved to Mattock and Devlin, who were still sleeping on the floor. She shook Mattock by the shoulder before doing the same to Devlin. The boys groaned and stirred, rubbing their eyes and sitting up from a deep sleep.

Mattock blinked when he saw his father standing there in familiar clothing. His young face lit up with delight as Devlin, catching sight of the same vision, jumped up and ran to Conor, throwing his arms around the man's waist.

"Dada," the boy said, nearly weeping. "You're really here. I thought I'd dreamed you."

Mattock joined his brother, his face shining up at Conor adoringly. "Dada, will you ride with us today?" he asked.

Conor had one hand on Devlin and the other on Mattock, smiling at boys that he was increasingly convinced he'd fathered.

Like last night, the memories were coming back to him in pieces, but he knew for certain that they were recollections and not his imagination. The feelings associated with them, the emotion, were far too strong to be anything else.

"Ride with you?" he repeated, turning to look at Padraigan. "What does he mean?"

Padraigan smiled as she crouched on the floor, rolling up the bedding. "You would take your boys riding with you every morning, great lord," she explained. "You would go about your duties, checking posts and meeting with your generals, and bring the boys. You said it was important for them to understand their duties to the land as well as to the people."

By this time, Destry had stood up from the bed, the four-year-old still clinging to her. His little head was on her shoulder, his arms around her neck. Hugging the boy, Destry made her way over to Conor and the other two.

"What are they saying?" she asked.

Conor looked at her with the boy wrapped all around her and grinned, putting his hand on Slane's back.

"He looks like a parasite." He snorted.

Destry grinned. "He has no intention of letting me go."

Conor's eyes glimmered at her. "Neither do I." He winked at her before glancing back at Devlin and Mattock. "In answer to your question, the boys wanted to know if I was going to take them riding. Padraigan said that it was something I would do with them every morning because I told them it was important for them to understand their duties to the land as well as to the people."

Destry's expression turned warm. "That sounds like something you would say. Call it a hunch, Conor, but I would guess that you were a pretty amazing king."

His appreciative smile grew, but he was prevented from answering her as the boys began to clamor around him, grabbing his hands and pulling him from the small chamber. Destry followed with Slane still clinging to her, pausing in the open doorway, as Padraigan followed them out into the yard.

"You cannot ride, great lord," she told him. "You would risk being seen."

Conor turned to look at her, catching a glimpse of the burned body of the dragonlike creature near the crude stable. In the light of the new morning, he stared at it, being reminded yet again that he had awoken to a different place and time.

He drew in a long breath, resigning himself, forcing himself to focus on the situation at hand. He had no choice. The reality was all around him.

"So what do you suggest?" he asked. "I can't hide out here the rest of my life."

Padraigan was resolute. "I shall go into town and bring back your trusted men," she told him. "They will counsel you on what has happened in Ciannachta since you have been away. Then you will know what you must do."

He nodded simply because he couldn't think of anything else to do. They just couldn't hide in the woods for the rest of their lives. If he had a kingdom to rule, and people waiting for his triumphant return, then they'd better get about it.

"All right." He waved her on. "I'll wait here."

Padraigan smiled. "Your men will be very glad to know you have returned. We have waited so long for this day."

"How long?"

She didn't hesitate. "Three hundred and sixty sunrises, great lord," she told him. "We have waited a long time."

Conor smiled because she was. Swiftly, she turned for the barn, instructing the boys on their chores while she was gone. Mattock and Devlin made unhappy faces but begrudgingly did as they were told, going to feed the chickens and milk the fat cow.

Conor stood out in the yard, watching the boys go about their duties. He could see Destry inside the doorway of the little cottage, brushing her hair with her fingers, as Slane, now out of her arms, followed her around by holding on to her skirt. Conor had to grin at the little boy who was attached to his mother like glue.

And then it struck him—*his family.*

If he'd had any shadow of a doubt before, seeing Destry with Slane, seeing the older boys going about their chores, and listening to a white witch speak of things so natural cemented into his heart and soul that this was where he belonged. As he'd told Destry, he'd always felt out of place, a man who didn't belong in the modern world he was born into. Here he was now, and all things were as they should be. He had Destry. He had his boys. He had everything.

He was back where he belonged.

He turned around, holding out a hand to Destry. With Slane still clinging on to her skirts, she made her way to Conor, taking his hand. He held it tightly, kissing it as he composed his thoughts.

"What is it?" Destry asked. He seemed distant and pensive. "What's on your mind?"

Conor grunted as he looked around. Then he sniffed the air. "Smell that?"

Destry sniffed too. She shook her head. "I smell trees."

"Exactly," he said. "No smog, no smells of the modern world. I suppose I had my doubts about this entire situation even until a few minutes ago, but walking out here, smelling the smells and hearing the birds and wind through the trees… I'm not feeling any more doubts. As much as I knew you belonged to me the moment I met you, right now, I feel like this belongs to me, too. I belong here. Whatever has happened to us, maybe it wasn't a mistake. Like Padraigan said, maybe it really *was* magic. It was something that was meant to happen."

Destry was listening to him seriously. "I guess all things happen for a reason," she said with surprising acceptance; like him, she was coming to understand the reality of their situation. She looked down at Slane sucking his thumb and holding her skirts, and smiled. "I told you last night that I know my children. These boys are mine, and you are their father. I don't know how this happened, but I'm not going to question it. After what we've been through the past day or so, I'm willing to take a few things on faith. So now what?"

He sighed, putting his arm around her, grinning when Slane pushed his way in between them and clung to Destry's leg. "Now, we have a whole new world out there," he said softly. "Just think about it—I'm supposed to be the king. You're my queen. I've got an evil brother who's stolen my throne. I want the damn thing back."

Destry smiled at his animated speech. "I'll help you."

He looked at her, bending down to kiss the tip of her nose. "I think you already have," he said. "I wouldn't be here it if wasn't for you. You brought me back, Destry. You gave me my destiny."

She hugged him, trying not to squish the child between them. "Padraigan said that time and space couldn't keep us apart," she said quietly. "Whatever I did, I was meant to do it. *We* were meant to do it. But I think I'm a little afraid."

"Afraid of what?"

"Afraid for you," she said, gazing up at him. "Your brother

went through a lot of trouble to separate us. He's not going to be happy to see you. These guys have swords and stuff. They're going to try to kill you."

He grinned. "I told you that I can fight with swords, feet, fists, and anything else they throw at us," he said. "You don't need to be afraid, but you need to be smart. Listen to what I tell you and what the white witch tells you. I didn't find you after a thousand years only to see you taken away from me again."

Destry lifted her eyebrows in agreement. "Same goes for me," she murmured. "You have no idea what it would do to me if you were killed. God, it sounds so scary even to say that. We're facing a whole new world out there."

He kissed her forehead. "New and deadly and beautiful," he said. "We have the opportunity to shape the world, I think, or at least our little corner of it. Are you ready for it?"

Destry looked out over the green, green foliage, enormous trees reaching for the untamed sky, and the beams of light piercing their way through the canopy. There was such raw beauty to it, and when she gazed up at Conor, all she could see was her past, her present, and her future.

"I'm ready," she said, laying her head on his chest as Slane begged to be picked up. "It sounds corny, but as long as we're together, I'm ready for anything."

"Me too," he whispered. "I love you, sweetheart. Until the end of time, I will love only you."

She smiled at him, a genuine and heartfelt gesture that sent his heart fluttering. "I love you too," she whispered.

He kissed her and picked up Slane, who wanted to go with his mother and not his father. Conor handed the boy over to Destry just as Mattock and Devlin raced over to him, explaining that they had seen something magical and wonderful near the barn. Conor thought they mentioned a faerie of some kind, but he couldn't be sure. The modern man, now ancient ruler, was ready for anything as he went to see what had his boys so excited.

This was his world, and he intended to master it as he'd done once before. This time, there would be no failure. He was back.

The high king had returned.

# CHAPTER TEN

T HE BUSTLING COASTAL city of Ciannachta was a sight to behold, but for Padraigan, it was a sight she'd seen many times.

And she was wary every time.

Ciannachta was a large community clustered around the south side of the mouth of the River Boyne as it met the sea, a fishing village mostly, but one with a good deal of commerce because of the location across the sea from the Welsh coastline. It was also a village that had been repeatedly attacked and burned by the Northmen and then rebuilt by the stubborn Irish, who refused to allow their village to die. It was a cycle of birth and death and rebirth that kept Ciannachta alive.

Padraigan hadn't been in Ciannachta in months, mostly because she was afraid of being recognized. Everyone had known and revered the white witch, at least until Geric took control. These days, she didn't want to attract the attention of villagers, well-meaning though they might be.

High atop the mound near the riverbank sat Cashel Cian, the crown jewel of the village, a fortress that was a great and powerful achievement. The cashel itself, the wooden and stone keep with the heavily thatched roof, was on the top of the mound, while the grounds for the army were down below. A wall, built from wood and stone, surrounded not only the cashel, but the entire village. In the distance, farms spread out against the rich green countryside. Everything smelled a bit salty and earthy, like the sea grass that grew in droves along the shore.

Padraigan had missed that smell. Inland, where she'd been hiding, the scents of the sea didn't permeate.

Her objective this morning was to find three of Conor's most loyal men, men who had left the army when Geric took control. They knew what Geric had done to his brother and would not, could not, serve such a man. They had been the men in command of the king's army, and once they left, the army fractured. Men loyal to Conor had departed, but those who needed the food and shelter remained.

At least, that was what Padraigan had heard. She had heard that no one in the army loved Geric and the men he'd brought in to command his men and keep order were mercenaries, Northmen from the group of raiders he'd become friends with.

An Irish army being commanded by Northmen was never a good thing, and that was why Padraigan knew that the army, or what was left of it, would rise up if they knew their high king had returned.

But first, she had to find the high warrior.

Bradaigh mac Neil was his name.

Bradaigh came from a long line of warriors, back a thousand years to the time when the Romans had conquered Britannia and a few of them came to Hibernia, or Ireland, and nosed around. There had been no invasion. They never even tried. But Bradaigh's ancestors were there to greet them and chase them off. All Bradaigh knew was war, and rumor had it that after Conor's disappearance, Bradaigh had gone north to serve other lords, but then Padraigan heard that he'd remained on the outskirts of Ciannachta with his mother's family, living on their farm.

She intended to find out.

Her first destination was the avenue of the smithies, where the blacksmiths worked with common fires and the acrid smoke of burning steel rose up in the sky. Two of Conor's men had become tradesmen there, two of his commanders, who remained in the city. Padraigan had seen them there, once, when she came to town to procure ingredients she could not gather in the wild. Specifically, she was looking for Auley Bannan and Brone O'Donnagh. She knew they would recognize her on sight, so perhaps that was why she'd avoided them over the past year, fearful news of her presence might reach the cashel. She had children to protect.

But now, exposure was necessary.

The smell of hot steel assaulted her nostrils as she entered the avenue. There were dozens of smithies working from their stalls, some using the common fire for their work but others having their own bellows and forges. The ground was muddy and slick from the rains that had come over the past several days, littered with slag from the fires, but the avenue was busy. Cloaked, and with her usual walking stick that she didn't need except for protection, Padraigan tried to blend in with the crowd.

It was mostly men, however, which made her stand out. A petite woman in a pale cloak wasn't exactly masculine. The sooner she found Auley and Brone, the better. If they were even still here.

She wasn't one given to fear, but at the moment, she could feel the familiar palpations in her chest. Fear that the men had somehow moved on. If Conor had any hope of regaining what was his, he needed his loyal men. Even a man as great as Conor couldn't do it alone.

Then she heard it.

Shouting caught her attention off to her right. She was between stalls, so she moved out into the avenue, peering down toward the area where she heard the shouting—in time to see a big, burly man with black hair and a busy black beard as he regaled some men with a story. The shouting was coming from him because he clearly couldn't tell the story in a quiet manner. But Padraigan knew that shouting because she'd heard it innumerable times before at Cashel Cian, when that very man bellowed orders to the army of the high king.

Auley Bannan had been found.

Padraigan couldn't help the surge of hope. More than that, it was a surge of delight. She had known Auley for many years, and, at one time, he'd even spoken of a desire to marry her— but that had been before Conor's disappearance and her dedication to duty. She'd fled with Conor's children, and any talk of marriage ended. She'd often regretted that, but never more than she did at this very moment as she beheld her tall, strong Auley.

Gathering her courage, she moved in his direction.

Auley was a great storyteller. He always had been. He had an audience of a few men standing around, watching him stoke the fire in his own forge but making no effort to do any actual work. Auley was more devoted to his stories than to his craft at the moment.

Padraigan moved to the area behind his stall, watching from

a distance as Auley shouted and laughed.

And on it went.

Auley had never been short-winded. He was vivacious and bright, well-seasoned and interested in the people around him. That had served him well when he'd commanded Ciannachta's powerful army because, above all else, he could communicate with the men. He understood them, and they worshipped him.

When Geric took command, he'd worked hard to woo Auley, who had known Geric since he was a child and had hated him for as long. Geric had pleaded and threatened, but in the end, Auley refused to serve him. Only Geric's respect for the man had allowed him to leave Cashel Cian unharmed. Whether or not Geric knew Auley had set up a trade on the avenue of the smithies was anyone's guess, but Padraigan suspected that he knew. As long as Auley didn't take up arms against him, Geric would leave him alone.

But that was about to change.

Hopefully.

Auley's storytelling went on for quite some time as Padraigan hung back and watched. It seemed that the men of the avenue of the smithies didn't grow tired of telling stories and gossiping like fishwives. Padraigan could hear them speaking of some merchant's daughter and a pirate who had taken her to Anglesey. They joked about the two-headed grandchildren the merchant would have.

And on it went.

Eventually, the conversation stopped and the men actually went back to work, including Auley. He had two young apprentices with him. One of the boys had nearly seen her, but she'd ducked away before eye contact could be made. Now that Auley was back in his stall, however, it was time to make her presence known. She couldn't wait much longer.

There were great piles of peat behind the stalls that the smithies were using to fire up their forges, and Padraigan hung back by the pile, beneath the shade of a yew tree that wasn't particularly healthy because of the acrid smoke it was swamped in from day to day. She could hear Auley telling one of the boys to gather more peat, but when the boy evidently had his hands full with something else, Auley suddenly appeared to collect the peat. He was short-tempered, clearly unhappy at having to do such a menial task, and Padraigan stepped out from behind the yew tree, in full view.

At first, Auley didn't see her. He hadn't looked up from his pile of peat. But he caught sight of her cloak, something white in the corner of his eye, and glanced up with disinterest. At least, at first there was no interest. But the moment he realized who it was, his eyes widened.

"Padraigan?" he whispered as if afraid to even say her name. But his mouth popped open as reality dawned. "*Padraigan!*"

She smiled timidly, holding up a hand to quiet him. "It is I," she said softly. "It has been a long time, Auley."

He dropped the peat in his big hands, too startled to hold on to it as he faced her. "A very long time," he said incredulously. "But… you're *here*. You're truly here!"

Padraigan nodded as she moved within arm's length. "I am."

"Where have you been?" he demanded, then quickly looked around to make sure no one had heard him. Given Padraigan the White was a marked woman, he didn't want any witnesses to their conversation. "I have been looking for you for an entire year. Where did you go?"

"To safety," she said. "I must speak with you, Auley. Something wondrous has happened."

"What is it?"

Padraigan looked around, and because she was doing it, Auley did it too. He knew she was nervous. Hell, he was nervous for her. Thanks to Geric and his wizard, there was a price on her head.

Quickly, Auley grasped her by the wrist and pulled her over against the back wall of his stall. "*What* are you doing here?" he whispered. "If you were in hiding, you must go back where it is safe. I will come to you when I can."

Padraigan couldn't help but notice that he hadn't let go of her hand. Long-forgotten feelings threatened to stir again at the mere sight of him.

"I will return, but you must come with me," she murmured. "Auley, Conor has returned."

He stared at her in shock. "Conor… he's come back?"

Padraigan nodded quickly. "Aye," she said. "He has returned with Etain, but it has taken me all this time to bring them back. Olc's curse was complete. They do not remember me or anything about their lives here. Etain cannot even understand my words. She speaks a language I have never heard before. But Conor… he remembers, Auley. It is coming back to him. He is coming to understand who he is and what he must do, and you must come to him. He needs you."

Auley was clearly astonished. "By God's holy order," he muttered. "He actually returned."

"He did."

"I will be honest when I say I did not believe he would."

Padraigan couldn't argue with that. "Olc may be powerful, but my magic has been known to move mountains," she said, looking around again to make sure no one was around. It had become a habit with her whenever she was in town because Geric had soldiers everywhere. "You must come right away. Where is Bradaigh?"

Auley was struggling to overcome his surprise. "He fled," he said. "You know he fled when Geric took command of the kingdom. Bradaigh had to flee or risk death. Geric knew that Bradaigh would not swear fealty to him."

"Where did he go?"

Auley pondered that question for a moment. "I am not entirely sure," he said. "I heard he'd gone to serve the high kings of Uliad, to the west."

"But you do not know for sure?"

He shook his head. "I did not want to contact him and risk Geric discovering his whereabouts," he said. "Wherever Bradaigh is, he is safe and away from Geric and his Northman dogs."

Padraigan understood. "But Conor has returned, and he needs his high warrior," she said. "Can you not locate him?"

Auley hesitated. "If Conor has indeed returned, then that would be reason enough to locate him," he said. "But I must be very careful in doing so."

"How will you go about it?"

Auley thought hard on the question. It was one he'd pondered once, briefly, back in the days when Conor first disappeared and everything was in chaos—but as he'd told Padraigan, he let Bradaigh go for fear that any contact might bring Geric to the high warrior. Geric had soldiers everywhere, but worse than that, Olc of the Eye had spies all over the land. He had flocks of ravens that spied for him and men in the shadows who watched for enemies.

Finding Bradaigh would be dangerous indeed.

"Before he fled, I remember him speaking of a young woman he was fond of," Auley said. "Do you remember her? Cara was her name. Her father was a weaver."

Padraigan's brow furrowed. "I think I remember hearing a rumor," she said. "I did not know the lass."

Auley nodded at the memory of the young woman with long, pale hair and a pretty smile who had Bradaigh, the consummate warrior, fairly smitten. "He wanted to marry her," he said. "Can you imagine? Coming from the *laoch ard* who lived and breathed war, he actually found a woman he wanted to marry. But that all ended when Geric came to power."

*Laoch ard.* The high warrior. Big, handsome Bradaigh with the dark hair, pale skin, and dark eyes. Conor was proud of the man whose battle tactics could put other men to shame, a man who had been both friend and advisor to the king. He had been more of a brother to Conor than his own ever had.

"What about the lass, Auley?" Padraigan asked. "Do you think she might know where he is?"

Auley shrugged. "'Tis worth a try," he said. "And Brone… he must know that our king has returned as well."

Padraigan nodded eagerly at the mention of Conor's third great warrior, a man loyal to the bone. "Find Brone and tell him," she said. "Bring him when you come."

"Where shall we go?"

Padraigan pointed east. "Along the main road to Navan," she said. "Do you know where the graves of our ancestors are located? The big hills along the road?"

Auley nodded. "I do."

"I will meet you there at sunrise tomorrow."

The light of hope began to glimmer in Auley's eyes. "We will be there," he said. "Brone is working for a merchant in

Gardner's Hill, but I will fetch him. We will come."

"What is Brone doing with a merchant?"

"He protects the man's goods."

"And Bradaigh?"

"I will go now and find the lass. Mayhap she knows where he has gone."

That was all Padraigan could do. The wheels were in motion, and she was beginning to feel some hope. She could see it in Auley's face that he, too, was optimistic.

Her timid smile turned genuine. "The high king has returned, Auley," she whispered, squeezing his hand. "This time of darkness with Geric will come to an end. Our great lord will see to that."

Auley nodded, grinning because she was. "It was agreeable to see you again, Padraigan."

"And you, Auley."

"Be cautious as you leave the city. Geric's men are still about."

She nodded, feeling more than the light of hope in his expression. There was renewed interest there as well, joy at her appearance as old memories stirred.

But Padraigan couldn't give in to them. She was on a mission that was not yet complete, as restoring the kingdom of Ciannachta meant more to her at the moment than her own romantic feelings.

But it had done her heart good to see Auley.

"I will see you at dawn," she said, finally letting his hand go. "Take care that you are not followed, by land or by air. Olc's ravens are everywhere."

Auley's smile faded. "They do not bother me nowadays," he said. "I am confident they will not follow me."

"Be sure of it."

He simply nodded, watching her as she scampered away, losing herself in the mews that existed against the backs of the stalls that lined the avenue of the smithies. It was a dirty lane, full of dogs and debris, but it was the best place for Padraigan to be. Auley knew how much it would mean to Geric to get his hands on Conor's white witch.

But now, there was hope for the future.

Auley had a woman to see.

# CHAPTER ELEVEN

"THERE WERE A lot of high kings," Conor said. "Every county had a high king. Clans had high kings. But Ireland overall had high kings that were recognized as *the* kings of Ireland."

He was sharpening a blade as he spoke on a bright afternoon, with light filtering in through the canopy above and birds singing overhead. Destry had never seen so many birds shitting all over the ground—and on her, if she wasn't careful.

Over in the crude stables, the boys were mucking out the dung and putting it into a big pile. A cow and calf milled around the small corral where Mattock's pony had once lived.

"So this Gofraid guy is the king of Dublin right now," she said. "But he's not *the* king of Ireland?"

"No," Conor said, pausing. "The one thing you need to know about Irish history is that it's very complicated. Incredibly complicated. Certain kings descend from certain groups, so the fact that I'm supposed to be the high king of Ciannachta just means I'm another high king in a land that's full of them."

"But I'll bet you make your mark."

He smiled modestly as she grinned at him. "You're sweet,"

he said, looking back to the blade he'd been sharpening. Then he paused again and looked around. "Is it just me, or do you also feel a sense of... I don't know... peace around here? There's something strangely normal about all of this to me."

Destry was watching the boys clean out the stable. "There's definitely a sense of peace when weird lizard creatures aren't attacking," she said. "Has Mattock said anything to you about his pony?"

Conor looked over at the boys, who were now encouraging Slane to shovel the cow dung. "No," he said. "But you can tell that he's sad. He's over there picking up shit from his dead pony. That has to hurt."

"He needs a new pony."

Conor nodded. "I'll have to ask Padraigan where we can get him one," he said. "I must admit that I'm eager to go into the village. I really want to see an authentic Medieval village for myself. You know—do a deep dive."

Destry snorted. "That's the professor in you."

"You're darn right," he agreed firmly. "It's a hell of an opportunity."

"To do what?" Destry said as the mood abruptly turned serious. "Did you ever think about that?"

"About what?"

She sighed and looked at the clothing she was wearing, running a hand over the skirt. "It's not like you can take this experience back to your students," she said. "Maybe you clear up some myths or misconceptions, but what do you do with the knowledge? Nothing. We're stuck here, so there's nothing you can do with it."

He looked at her, sensing sorrow and maybe even despair. Something about the way she'd said it gave him a clue that she wasn't viewing all of this as clinically as he was. Maybe she wasn't accepting the situation as much as he was willing to. This was his element, or at least he knew a good deal about it, but she knew absolutely nothing. She may as well be on the moon for all she knew about ancient Ireland.

He had to keep that in mind.

"That's true," he said steadily. "But until we can figure out a way home, maybe we do something important while we're here. You said I would make my mark. Maybe you will, too."

Her brow furrowed. "How?"

He reached out to take her hand, something that came so completely naturally to him. As if he'd done it a million times before in a thousand different lives. Everything about her blended into him, becoming as crucial to his survival as breathing.

"You're a trained nurse," he said. "Can you imagine what you could do for these people with your knowledge of healthcare? Think about it, Des. Healthcare in this era was nonexistent."

Destry could feel him caressing her hand even as she watched the boys in the distance as they carried loads of dung out to the pile.

"You would know more about that than I would," she said. "But I'm sure they had a lot of holistic methods. Those can be very good."

He lifted his eyebrows. "And very bad," he said. "No one washed their hands, hygiene was very spotty, and take something as normal as childbirth—a pregnant woman faced the same odds as a man heading into battle. In fact, women were often given a hero's funeral if they died in childbirth. The risk was the same."

Destry could understand that. She knew something of the history of medicine and healthcare as part of her degree, so she knew he was right. "Then maybe the biggest mark I can make is with hand washing and general hygiene," she said. "But it's not like it'll be for the entire world. Just these people."

"These people who will go on to share the knowledge," Conor said, blowing at his blade. "Ciannachta is a port city, with ships sailing to parts of the known world. Information can spread, so don't sell yourself short."

Destry pondered what very well might be her future in this strange and foreign land. But that brought up a point. "And there's something else," she said. "I don't know this language at all. You're going to have to teach me enough to get by."

"I can do that," he said. "What language did you take in school?"

"Four years of French."

"Were you any good?"

"Top of my class."

"Can you speak it conversationally?"

She shook her head. "Not really," she said. "There's no chance to do that where I live in California, but I can speak some Spanish. In my line of work, being multilingual is a plus when dealing with patients and their families."

"Then you can pick up on Gaelic," he said confidently. "I'll start with the basics."

"Now?"

"Can you think of a better time?"

She couldn't. He put his blade and stone aside, reaching out to take her hand and leading her out into the dirt area beneath the canopy of trees. The corral and barn were to their right, the cottage behind them, and he came to a halt. Releasing her hand, he went off to find a couple of sticks, then returned to her and handed her one of them. Then he smoothed out a big patch of dirt and began to write with his stick.

"We'll start with some basic words," he said. "For example, the things around us—the cottage, the barn, the trees. That kind of thing."

He started to write in the dirt. The boys, who had been watching as soon as he brought Destry into the dirt clearing, gradually set aside their rakes and shovels and gravitated in their direction. Soon, they were standing on either side of Destry, watching Conor write in the dirt. The older boys had some education, but not the manner in which Conor was teaching. They didn't recognize the letters he was forming. Conor finished with the last word and turned around to see that he had a full class watching him.

He grinned. "Look," he said, pointing to the boys. "You have three more teachers. We'll all help you. *An cuidich thu i?*"

*Will you help her?*

The boys looked at Destry, and Slane slipped his hand into hers. She smiled at them, squeezing the little hand in her palm. They weren't quite sure what Conor meant, but they nodded anyway.

Conor pointed to the first word he'd written.

*Bothan.*

"That means cottage," he said. "*Bothan.*"

He pointed to the cottage, and the boys nodded, pointing as well.

"*Bothan,*" Destry said. "Cottage."

"Exactly," he said. "But it conjugates differently. Just like the English language has different words for a dwelling, like home and house and cottage, so does Gaelic. If you want to tell the boys to go to the cottage, say *rach don taigh*. It essentially means go the house."

Destry nodded. "*Rach don taigh*," she repeated. "I'll remember."

He believed her. Something in those bright blue eyes spoke of great intelligence and brilliance. He'd seen it from the start with her. Not only was she beautiful and sensual, but she also had a brain. She was magnificent.

*His queen.*

The more he looked at her, the more he knew that.

She was his everything.

When the boys realized what he was doing, they jumped in to help. It wasn't in the writing of the words or even the discussion on how verbs were conjugated or proper grammar. It was much more functional and simpler. They began to point at things and tell her what they were.

Rock.

*Creag!*

Tree.

*Craobh!*

And on it went, with Conor explaining the nuances of the words and spelling them in the dirt. Even Slane, the littlest, got into the act, dragging Destry all over the yard and pointing out bugs and leaves.

That went on for about an hour until Conor distracted everyone by taking them back over to the corral, where the little calf was being frisky. He had to take back the lessons or they'd never get anywhere. As the boys climbed into the corral to play with the calf, laughing happily as the little animal butted them, Conor handed Destry a stick and pointed to the dirt.

"Write what I tell you to write," he commanded softly.

She looked at him curiously. "Like what?"

"Write 'rock' in Gaelic."

She grinned and promptly scratched out *creag*, remembering how he'd spelled it. He flashed his big teeth.

"Very good," he said. "How do you say 'go to the house'?"

Destry replied without hesitation, "*Rach don taigh.*"

Laughing, he pulled her into his arms and hugged her tightly. "How do you say 'I love you'?" he whispered.

She paused, pulling back to look at him. "I don't know," she murmured. "You never told me how."

He kissed her before answering. "*Tha gràdh agam ort.*"

She repeated it softly. "*Tha gràdh agam ort.*"

He nodded. "Very good," he said. "You are an excellent student."

She smiled, gazing into his handsome face. "I think it's more that you're an excellent teacher," she said. "It feels like you've done this before."

He started to laugh at her obvious referral to his profession, but then Slane let out a shriek as Mattock teased him about something. In fact, both older boys were teasing him about something, and the adults turned to see what the commotion was about. Mattock had a rock or a stick or something that Slane wanted as he and Devlin passed it back and forth between them.

Conor released Destry and headed in their direction. "Enough," he said evenly, snapping his fingers and causing an instant cessation of the tussle. Glancing at the sky, he could see that it was at least midday, if not a little later. "I'm hungry. Let's find something to eat."

Immediately, the boys began to scramble. "I know, I know!" Devlin said, trying to sprint ahead of his brother back toward the cottage. "I know where the food is!"

The boys were already rushing toward the cottage, except for Slane, who was holding Destry's hand and sucking his thumb. Conor held out a hand to Destry, who took it, and he led her and Slane back to the cottage, where Mattock and Devlin were already pulling things out of the hearth and out of what was the crude kitchen area. Here they were, back in that little cottage, feeling more comfortable with it, and everything, as the day went on.

At least, that was Conor's hope. He was trying to orient Destry, hoping it would ease her sense of despair and confusion, and so far it seemed to be working. She seemed to be relaxing.

He just needed to find some sense of normalcy, whatever that happened to be.

Food was normal enough, and one thing Conor noticed was that there were lots of eggs. It seemed to be a staple, and he'd seen the coop near the cottage, filled with little black and white birds. He'd had eggs the night before and also that morning for breakfast, and now the older boys were producing more boiled eggs along with that thick-crusted bread and hunks of tart, heavy white cheese. They'd eaten the remains of the chicken stew for breakfast, so it was just the eggs, bread, cheese, and purple berries that were like blackberries, only smaller and lighter in color. Conor made sure Destry had plenty as the boys put it all onto the table.

"You know," Destry said as Slane climbed into her lap, settling down with his thumb still in his mouth, "I have been feeling kind of useless, but I think I know how I can help."

Conor was peeling one of the hard-boiled eggs. "What do you mean, you've been feeling useless?" he said. "You're not useless."

"Yes, I am," she said quietly, picking up a piece of the bread because that was all she could manage with one hand with Slane occupying the other. "I mean, you speak the language. You can fight. You understand this world. Honestly, I'm just dead weight right now."

"You're *not* dead weight," he insisted, eyeing her. "You're a trained nurse. We just talked about how that skill set is going to be hugely helpful. You know things about medicine that I couldn't possibly know. I think you can really help people, more than I ever could."

She shrugged as she took a bite of bread. "Maybe," she said. "But we'd have to get into a medical situation for me to prove it, and I'm not sure I really want to tempt fate like that. Aside from my medical background, I was thinking that I could do some of the cooking. I'm a pretty good cook."

"Then it only underscores that you're the woman of my dreams," he said, half joking. "Because I like to eat. I don't think you know that about me yet."

She laughed softly, watching him shove whole boiled eggs into his mouth. "Actually, I've sensed that," she teased. "But cooking is something I can do. I took some cooking courses because my former fiancé wanted me to learn so I could cook for him. I could make a hell of a good soup if I can get my hands on chicken bones and carrots and celery."

He nodded as he chewed. "Make stock?"

"Exactly."

He swallowed the bite in his mouth. "This period in time didn't have a lot of the food that we consider commonplace," he said. "No tomatoes or potatoes. No zucchini."

"That's okay because I don't really need those things,"

Destry said. "But I do need herbs and salt and pepper. I need onions and garlic, any vegetables we can find, and I can make my own noodles."

He was quite interested at that point. "What do you need for noodles?"

"Flour, eggs, salt."

"That's it?"

"That's it."

He grinned. "Then let's get you what you need," he said. "I can kill a chicken for the meat and bones, and onions and garlic were known and used at this time. They were fairly common, so there are probably some around here. Maybe the boys know where to get flour and vegetables, or at least grain we can make into flour. Have you ever done that?"

Destry shook her head. "No, but I'd be willing to try."

That was what Conor wanted to see—the desire to integrate and at least try to accept and even participate in the world around them.

At that point, he began to speak to Mattock and Devlin as Destry held Slane, who was asleep in her arms by now. She couldn't understand what was being said, but the older boys were nodding to whatever it was. When the three of them got up from the crude table and began to poke around in the baskets around the hearth, Destry carefully stood up, carried Slane into the other room, laid the child down on the bed gently, and pulled a rough coverlet over him. Silent as a ninja, she backed out of the room, but there was no door, so she shushed Conor and the older boys as they rifled through the baskets.

"If you're trying to tell us to shut up, say *sàmhach*," Conor told her. "I have a feeling that with three lads, you'll need to know that word."

Destry chuckled. "Probably," she said, looking at what they'd pulled out of the dusty baskets. "I see onions, I think."

Conor picked one up and handed it to her. "Turnips," he said. "There are also leafy green vegetables. I think it's spinach."

Destry picked up the big bunch of dark green leaves. "Did they have spinach in the Middle Ages?"

He shrugged. "They did, but I don't know if they had it in Ireland," he said. "But it's some kind of edible leaf. There's also a basket of grain and a bigger basket of oats."

Destry put the leaves down and looked at the grain, scooping it up and letting it run through her fingers. "Barley," she said. "I can try to make barley flour. It's actually good to bake with."

"That must be what Padraigan makes the bread from."

Destry brushed her hands off. "Probably," she said. "Are there carrots in there?"

There were. Carrots, very small onions, and turnips that were wilted. They came across dirty, strangely shaped radishes and a sack of dried green peas. There were also two chicken carcasses, wrapped up in cloth and stored under a table, and an earthenware dish covered with a cloth that Conor discovered to be bread dough, left to ferment. As it turned out, there was quite a bit of food in that crude little cottage.

"She must have a garden, don't you think?" Destry said once they'd inventoried everything. "She seemed so paranoid about being seen that I can't imagine she would go into town and shop for this stuff on a regular basis."

Conor turned to the boys and asked them about a garden, to which they nodded their heads and indicated that it was somewhere outside.

"She has a garden," Conor said to Destry. "Do you want to check it out?"

She shook her head. "There's plenty of stuff to use here," she said. "Do you think she'll mind?"

"I doubt it," he said. "She'll probably appreciate it."

Destry started to roll her sleeves up. "Then let's get started," she said. "I need to find whatever she uses to make flour with. Some kind of stone or mortar and pestle, I would think. Or even just a couple of rocks. Anything hard."

Conor began to look around him for something like that. "I'll see if I can find it," he said. "But remember that this won't be like cooking on your stove at home. This is like cooking over a campfire. It's pretty rustic if you're not used to it."

Destry shrugged. "If this is where we're going to live out the rest of our lives, then I need to get used to it," she said. "If I try to integrate a little, it'll be easier. Maybe I won't feel so disoriented. I really need to be doing something productive."

He was glad to hear that she was being logical about it. "Then do what makes you happy, sweetheart," he said, a glimmer of warmth in his eye. "I'll be here every step of the way."

She gave him a half grin. "To help me grind flour?"

His eyes narrowed, but it was with humor. "Are you telling me that you want me to do woman's work?"

"I want you to put those enormous muscles to work, big boy."

He chuckled, pulling her against him and kissing her on the top of the head as she went to work. In fact, she seemed rather eager about it now that she was focused on something industrious, and he let her do her thing.

The first order of business was to find a pot for her stock, and Destry spied a big iron cauldron tucked in the corner of the hearth. It was old and dusty, but after thoroughly wiping it out, Conor hung the thing on the arm over the fire for her because it was quite heavy.

"I need clean water, and lots of it," Destry told him. "I also need any herbs there might be around here—thyme would be great. Rosemary and dill, too. Anything at all. Do you think the boys would know if any of that is around here?"

Conor brushed his hands off and stood up from the hearth. "I'll find out," he said, grabbing Mattock by the shoulder and steering him toward the door. "We'll go hunt down some herbs and anything else you can use. Will you be okay while we wander around?"

"Of course."

Mattock opened the door into the yard beyond, and Conor grasped Devlin, leading the boy outside after his brother. That left Destry alone with sleeping Slane.

She had to get organized.

 C𝕭

Padraigan could smell something cooking.

Approaching the settlement from the west, she could smell it through the trees.

It had taken some fancy footwork for her to return home.

As always, the white witch was terrified that she would be followed from the village. That had been her fear on the first day of Conor's banishment, and it continued to now. Even though the Ciannachta army had dwindled because of a dislike for their new king, there were still those who served Geric and would know her on sight. The flock of ravens was always a particular threat. The last thing she wanted was to be followed, and any time she went into the village, she always went to great lengths to ensure her safety and the safety of the boys she protected upon her return home.

But there seemed to be more of a sense of apprehension since Conor had returned. Up until that point in time, there had been caution and there had been anxiety, but there had also been hope. Hope that the king would return and restore the land and its people. That hope was fulfilled yesterday, but now, the white witch found herself with a new set of worries.

The fear that the king would be discovered before he could regain his throne.

From the village by the sea, there was a road that went straight west, and it was that road that Padraigan usually took to and from the town. Her little settlement was about five miles from the village, south of the road and buried in an area that most people stayed away from. There were ancient mounds in the area, and the superstitious townsfolk were afraid to venture too far into the verdant and mysterious land, which was exactly why she had chosen it.

Shortly after Conor and Destry had been banished, Geric sent out patrols to hunt for the king's white witch and his three sons, who were of great concern to him. As long as the boys lived, there was always a chance of rebellion, so Padraigan had learned to hide them well and cover her tracks whenever she was traveling.

She had no reason to believe that she could let up her guard, even a year later.

Therefore, it took quite some time to travel back to her abode because of all the safety measures she had to take. Out of necessity, she had to take the road west, but there were smaller paths that branched off from the road, livestock trails, and she used those to travel. She went south and then west and then south again, and then north for a short way, and then she would pause and wait to see if anybody had been following her. Usually, she would wait at least an hour, and when no one appeared, she would continue west hurriedly.

Today she had followed her usual path—west and then south, and then west again and then south again. She had crossed over streams and through meadows and into thickets that were so dense that it was nearly impossible to break through them. Her little settlement was planted strategically in the midst of several ancient structures, and over the course of the year she had used spells to shield the dwellings from prying eyes.

That did not work, however, with all creatures. That had been demonstrated by the demon that visited them last night. That wasn't the first time one of those demons had come, but thankfully, they weren't too frequent, as those creatures had been greatly dwindling in number over the years. They were hunted and skinned. Soon, they would be no more, but it couldn't be soon enough for Padraigan.

Now that the afternoon was beginning to wane, Padraigan knew that she was close to the cottage. Even though she knew by the landmarks around her, she would have known that there was a home nearby simply from the scent in the air. Somebody was cooking, and she suspected that it was her queen. She had known Etain since they were children, and she knew that the woman was quite conscientious. She wasn't afraid to get her hands dirty. In fact, when she was queen, Etain had taken an active role in managing her husband's kitchens. Padraigan knew that the queen liked to feed her family well, and even if Destry did not remember her life as a queen, there was something deep inside that did. There was something deep down that was awakening in her.

The smell in the air was evidence of that.

But so was something else.

As Padraigan drew near, she began to hear voices in the bramble.

At first, she was leery and came to a halt. But listening for a couple of moments told her that she recognized at least some of the voices. Then a deeper voice chimed in, and she recognized that one as well. Cautiously, she stepped through the brush and into a clearing that was full of flora and fauna.

It was also full of people.

Mattock's head popped up as she came through. He was bent over something, as was Devlin, with Conor standing behind them. Three pairs of eyes were suddenly looking at her, and she smiled.

"I see that you are all quite busy," she said. "Are you hunting for something?"

"Herbs," Conor said, scratching his cheek where an insect was crawling. "Destry is making a meal, and she asked for herbs. I thought the boys would know where to find them."

Padraigan's smile broadened. "I thought I smelled something," she said. "But our great queen does not need to lower herself to the cooking duties. I will happily continue the task."

Conor shook his head. "She needs to feel useful," he said, glancing up at the sky. "We've only been here a short time, and she's still not sure of everything. Feeling useful keeps her mind off our situation."

Padraigan understood. "And she does not know our tongue," she said. "That must be very difficult."

"It is, but we were teaching her some words this morning,"

Conor said. "She is very intelligent. She'll learn."

"Then let me remind her, great king," Padraigan said. "Everything she was is buried deep inside her. It is still there, but it must be coaxed forth. When she sleeps tonight, I will sing to her. She will remember that which has been forgotten."

Conor's brow furrowed. "Sing to her?" he repeated, but then it occurred to him what she meant. "You mean magic? You'll cast some kind of spell?"

Padraigan nodded. "The song of poets," she said. "It will help her remember."

Conor wasn't sure what to say to that. He was trying very hard to accept what had happened to him, but when it came to her sorcery, he was still hesitant—even after he saw her transform his sons back into their original state. He accepted what had happened in a scientific sort of way, whatever the explanation could be, but believing it was something pulled out of thin air was altogether different. This king, the one who had been through so much, thought differently from the old Conor.

Padraigan sensed that.

"Let us finish gathering what our great queen needs," she said, shifting the subject of her sorcery. "What may I help with?"

Conor shrugged, watching the boys pick green plants and leaves out of the earth. "We're looking for the herbs and anything else she can cook with," he said. "Garlic, onions… anything like that."

Padraigan began to plow back into the bramble, pushing it away enough to expose a little patch of earth and what looked like thick grass growing out of it.

"This is where I find much of our food to sustain us," she said, ripping out the thick grass, which turned out to be wild chives. "Your sons know this, and that is why they have brought you here. I keep a garden of vegetables close by, but for the wild things, we know where to come."

She was tearing out quite a bit of the wild onions and handing them over to Mattock, who was collecting everything by using the front of his tunic as a basket. "These are leeks," she said. "There is more over here."

She seemed to know everything, so Conor followed along as she ripped things out of the earth and put it in Mattock's tunic-basket. There was feathery dill, spikey rosemary, chives, leeks, and other things to use in a stewpot. She directed the boys to gather certain things, and when Mattock's tunic was full, she instructed them to hurry back to the cottage so their mother could use the ingredients. She and Conor followed behind at a leisurely pace.

"I wanted to send them ahead, great lord, because I must speak with you," she said quietly. "I saw Auley. He is coming to see you at dawn on the morrow."

Conor looked at her. "Auley?"

Padraigan nodded. "Auley Bannan," she said, realizing he had no clue who she was talking about. "He was the man who commanded your army. No man shouts as loud as Auley. He was much revered by your men. Do you not remember the name?"

Conor was trying hard to. "Maybe it will come to me," he said. "Were we friends?"

"The closest," Padraigan said. "There are two more men he is going to seek. One is a warrior who would carry out your orders without question, a man who is more muscle than brains, but he would walk through fire for you. His name is Brone."

That name didn't sound familiar to Conor either, but he nodded as if it did. "Brone," he repeated. "I won't forget that. You said there were three?"

Padraigan nodded. "The third is your high warrior. His name is Bradaigh mac Neil, and he is the finest warrior Eire has ever seen. He was like a brother to you. I am confident he shall be again. But these men are the most powerful in the kingdom, next to you, and Geric knows this. When you were banished, the three of them chose to flee rather than serve him. They will serve only you. I am certain you can imagine how furious this makes your brother."

Conor lifted his eyebrows. "I am coming to suspect there is a great deal about me that infuriates him," he said. "The deeper we get into this… this situation, the more I'm coming to realize how serious this all is."

"It is, great lord," Padraigan said firmly. "It is serious, and it is dangerous. That is why we must be so careful with things even as usual as cooking smells."

"What do you mean?"

Padraigan sniffed the air. "I could smell whatever my lady is cooking even from far away," she said. "I do not roast meat openly. Other than smoke from the cooking fire, I try not to prepare anything that can give us away."

Conor inhaled. "I only smell smoke from the fire."

"I smell boiling chicken carcasses."

He looked at her curiously. "You do?"

She nodded. "And now she intends to add herbs to that? It will smell also."

Conor appeared regretful. "I didn't think of that," he said. "Should we throw it all out and bury it?"

Padraigan shook her head. "Nay," she said. "To dispose of it would be to waste it—but we must be more careful in the future."

Conor understood. Such was the way of his new world.

The cottage was coming into view now. They could hear the boys' voices because the door was open, and they were clearly excited about their bountiful harvest. As Conor and Padraigan approached, they could see Destry standing just inside the door, taking plants and leaves and things out of Mattock's tunic. She was laying everything on the crude table as Padraigan caught Devlin's attention and instructed the boy to feed the animals for the night. As the middle son ran off, Mattock finished cleaning out his tunic-basket and shook it out of any dirt and debris, before going to stand next to Destry as she examined everything on the table.

"This is lovely," she said, though he only understood her smile. Picking up the chives, she inhaled deeply. "God, what a gorgeous smell. These are spectacular."

By this time, Conor had entered the cottage, as had Padraigan. He put his hand on Mattock's shoulder.

"The boys knew just where to go," he said. "Padraigan called those onions leeks, but I think they're just chives. I think 'leek' is a catch-all term for anything onion."

"They smell wonderful," Destry said. "But what's this?"

She was holding up what looked like a spring onion, and Conor took a sniff. "That's wild garlic," he said. "Smell it."

She did, thrilled with the onions and garlic that had been brought back. She picked through the herbs, rinsing them and roughly cutting them before tossing them into the pot along with the garlic and onions. As Padraigan moved around in another chamber, Destry was in her element boiling the chicken carcasses with the wild herbs. It would make a rich and satisfying broth.

As the sun began to set and the boys went about their chores, including Slane when he woke up from his nap, Conor pulled up a stool next to Destry and watched her as she stirred the boiling stockpot and tended the fire. There was warmth in his expression while he observed as she, in her own words, made herself feel useful.

Possibly feeling as if she'd done this before, once.

Like for him, ancient memories were finally beginning to stir.

"You look very comfortable doing this," he said softly.

She looked up from putting another piece of wood on the fire. "Do I?" she said, grinning. "I've never cooked over an open flame. Not even a barbeque."

"Why not? I hear they barbeque a lot in California."

She laughed. "They do, but barbeque is a man's domain," she said. "My father never let me when I lived at home, and I just never did it when I lived on my own. This is all new to me."

"You're doing a good job."

She shrugged as she looked back at the bubbling pot. "I hope the stock is good," she said. "I still need to find something to grind the barley into flour. Maybe Padraigan has something I can use."

He sat forward on the stool, his elbows resting on his knees. "Speaking of Padraigan, she told me a couple of things," he said. "The first is that she evidently found one the men who used to serve me, and he's supposed to be here in the morning. And the second is that she doesn't cook using anything smelly, like onions and garlic and stuff."

"She doesn't?" Destry said, confused. "But that food was in the baskets."

"I know," he said. "But maybe she just eats it raw. I really don't know. She doesn't cook it because the smells carry, and she doesn't want the wrong people to find her hideaway."

It was obvious that none of that had occurred to Destry. "Oh, crap," she said, concerned. "I didn't even think of that. Should I dump this out?"

He shook his head. "Finish it," he said. "She thinks that we're safe for now, but whatever you make should last us for a few days. No more cooking with smelly things."

Destry looked around at the crude kitchen and everything in it. "But she made that chicken and barley stew we ate," she said. "How did she cook the chicken?"

"She probably boiled it rather than roasted it," he said. "In any case, we need to be careful. Smells carry."

Destry nodded. "I will," she said. "I'll just boil everything from now on, I suppose. But what about stuff like baking bread? That smells for miles."

"We'll have to ask Padraigan what she does."

The last thing Destry wanted was for them to be discovered. Based on what she'd been told, that would be catastrophic, so discovering that even cooking was dangerous for them dampened her enthusiasm to feel useful.

"I'll be careful," she said. "But let me get the rest of this out of the way so we have something to eat tonight. Will you ask her about flour or something to grind up the barley with?"

He nodded and rose from the stool. "Sure," he said. "But one more thing."

"What?"

"Padraigan says that she's going to sing to you tonight after you go to sleep and teach you Gaelic."

Destry snorted. "Seriously?" she said. "So I'll dream about it and wake up speaking it?"

"Something like that."

Destry didn't seem to give too much credence to that. "If true, that would be awesome," she said. "I'd like to speak to the boys. And I'd like to understand what's being said. But teaching me in my sleep? I don't know about that."

He rested his big fists on his hips. "Why not?" he said. "You saw her make the boys out of dwarves. I wouldn't discount anything she says too much."

The smile faded from Destry's face. "Do you really think she can do it?"

"I suppose we'll find out," he said. "If we're going to live the rest of our lives here, then you'd better know the language."

He turned to find Padraigan, but Destry stopped him. "Conor," she said. "Do you really think we're going to live the rest of our lives here?"

He paused. "I don't know, sweetheart," he said. "For now, we're here. There seems to be a reason why we're here. I know it's difficult to comprehend that we've really gone back in time, but for now, that's where we seem to be."

Destry took a long, deep breath and stood up, wooden spoon in hand. "I've been thinking," she said. "Maybe there's a medical explanation for all of this."

"Like what?"

"Like we're both suffering from some kind of hallucination."

"Just the two of us?"

Destry shrugged. "Maybe being in that mound and then something violent happening has somehow put us both into some state of unconsciousness where we're imagining all of this. Like a shared dream."

He lifted an eyebrow. "Have you ever heard of anything like that? Ever?"

She shook her head. "No," she admitted. "But people who take hallucinogens tend to feed off one another and create a kind of shared hallucination. The power of suggestion is strong."

He didn't want to completely discount her, but he couldn't agree with her. "I think that might be a little far-fetched."

"No more than going back in time," she pointed out. "No more than the woman in the other room making little boys out of dwarves. This is all far-fetched, Conor. All of it."

She was getting worked up, and he went to her, putting his hands on her shoulders to ease her. "I'm sorry," he said. "I wasn't trying to call you crazy. But I'm not sure a shared hallucination is really possible."

"Why not?"

He moved his hands down her arms until they came to her fingers. He held them up, kissing them. Even the one still holding the spoon.

"Because this is real," he said softly, taking the spoon from her hand and setting it on the table. "Your flesh is real. I didn't imagine or dream or hallucinate making love to you, Des. You are the most real thing I've ever touched. What has happened to us is real, and we just have to make sure we survive it."

Those were the magic words, as far as she was concerned. *We have to make sure we survive it.*

Destry sighed heavily. "Yesterday when Padraigan was so eager to get us away from the mound, I thought she was crazy," she said. "But everything that she's told you… I was afraid yesterday. Today, I'm trying not to think about it, but when you tell me that smells carry and I have to be careful with what I cook, and that there are men out there looking for us… God, Conor, I am fucking terrified. I hate using that word, but I really am. I just want to go home, but we have no home to go to. Right now, this *is* home, and evidently, everyone around here wants us dead."

She was starting to get agitated again, and he pulled her over to one of the rustic chairs and sat down with her on his lap.

"Listen to me," he said quietly, his head against hers. "It's natural to be afraid. After everything that's happened to us in such a short span of time, it's a miracle that both of us aren't shut up in a closet somewhere, losing our minds. We both acknowledge that this whole situation is terrifying and disorienting, but panicking about it will not solve the problem. I know you get that. Right?"

Destry was verging on tears by this point, but she nodded. "I do."

"Logic and reason are the only thing that's going to help. Right?"

She nodded again, reluctantly. "Right."

He kissed her cheek. "You're strong," he said. "You're strong and resilient. Instead of looking at this as being a terrifying situation, look at it the way I'm trying to look at it."

"How's that?"

He squeezed her gently. "That we're here for a reason," he said. "You read books about this kind of thing. Fantasy books. You see fantasy movies about time travel. But it really happened to us, which means the universe or God or whatever you believe in has singled us out for something really important. You and me, two people who didn't even know each other last week. We're *meant* to be here, Des. We just have to find out what the reason is, because whatever it is, it's damn important. Would you agree with that?"

Destry took a deep breath. "I would," she said. "That all makes a lot of sense."

"Good," he said. "So just keep that in mind whenever you're feeling scared. Something put us here, and I don't think we're meant to die. Why put us here just to get us killed?"

She looked at him then. "That's true," she said. "But according to Padraigan, there are people out to kill us."

He snorted softly. "If we can't outlast or outsmart guys from the Middle Ages, then we're not worth much," he said. "We're smart, educated, and strong. And I know something else."

"What?"

"That I can't do this without you," he said, pulling her close. "I need your strength and your level head. I need the feeling I get when you look at me with a twinkle in your eye. Maybe I haven't known you all that long, but my soul has. And the memories are coming back."

She broke down in a grin, wrapping her arms around him and hugging him tightly. He gave her a big squeeze, burying his face in the crook of her neck, taking a few moments simply to savor her. It was becoming more natural with each passing moment, the two of them together, in each other's arms.

What Conor said was absolutely correct—memories were coming back. Their spirits knew one another, more and more by the minute.

Destry finally pulled away from him and stood up. She squared her shoulders and grabbed her wooden spoon again.

"That's the second time you've given me a pep talk like that, and there won't be a third," she said. "I'll be okay. Let me finish what I'm cooking, and tomorrow, your men are coming here. That's the next step in all of this."

"It is," he said. "We'll find out what's really going on and what I need to do in order to get my kingdom back."

Destry smiled again. "Kingdom," she murmured. "Doesn't it feel weird saying that? Weird but also… right."

He nodded as he stood up. "It feels normal," he said. "I feel like I belong, Des. You will, too. I know you will."

Destry put her hand to his cheek, watching him kiss it. "I'm sure of it," she said. "But I know something else."

"What?"

"I couldn't do this without you, either."

He broke down in a grin, pulling her against him and kissing her tenderly. They were interrupted when the cottage door opened and the boys returned. With their chores finished, they were looking for food and possibly entertainment from their father, and begged for stories before the evening meal was served. Conor complied, but not before he asked Padraigan for something to grind the grain with, and she produced a stone bowl and a long stone, items that were well used. Once it was all explained to her, she understood clearly what Destry wanted to do.

As Conor told the boys stories of ancient warriors, Destry and Padraigan made flour and then mixed it with eggs and milk, making dumplings, which were boiled in the stock that Destry had made. Destry felt oddly comfortable with Padraigan working at her side, as if they'd done it before, perhaps countless times. There was a level of friendship there that was difficult to describe, but Destry could feel it. Even if she couldn't communicate with the small woman, it was as if she didn't really have to. She knew her.

*Once, we were as sisters,* Padraigan had said.

Somehow, Destry wasn't feeling so lost and disoriented

after all.

Later that night, after an excellent meal of dumplings, bread, and more boiled eggs, Destry drifted off to sleep with Slane sleeping beside her and the other boys at her feet. Conor, however, deliberately remained awake because he wanted to see how Padraigan was going to sing the song of poets and teach Destry their language as she slept.

He had to admit, he was a little skeptical.

As he stood in the doorway and watched, Padraigan lay down next to Destry as she snored softly, and then began humming a tune that Conor had never heard before. Soon, she was whispering lyrics along with the tune, only Conor realized that she was murmuring incantations—odd, echoing incantations that seemed to come from the very walls, as if the cottage itself was singing. He even put his hand on the wall and, sure enough, could feel the vibration.

It was the strangest thing he'd ever witnessed.

The casting went on well into the night. Conor ended up sitting at the table, listening to the song, but the wait proved to be too much, and he laid his head on the table and promptly fell asleep.

When morning came, he awoke next to Destry with no memory of how he'd gotten there. Padraigan was gone and the sun was peeking in. As he yawned and tried to remember how he'd gotten there, Destry rolled over, stretched, and promptly smacked him on the head. Distressed, she quickly sat up and put a gentle hand where she'd hit him.

"*Tá brón orm,*" she said. *I'm sorry.*

It didn't even occur to her she'd said it in Gaelic, but Conor was blown away.

More mystery from a land that seemed to be full of it.

# CHAPTER TWELVE

T HE STREET OF the weavers was perhaps the busiest street in all of Ciannachta.

It was a street that contained more then weavers. There were barrel makers, a few merchants who sold dry goods, and even a wheelwright. Because there were weavers on the avenue, there tended to be livestock also. Some of the weavers would insist on inspecting the coats of the sheep whose masters were trying to sell them. Sometimes there were even goats, for they had fine hair that could translate into fine thread.

The weavers on this avenue could make anything from thread to fabric. They each specialized in something different. Given that the village was at the mouth of the river where it joined the Irish Sea, there were always vessels bringing commodities as well as taking them back across the sea.

The weavers, as well as the rest of the village businesses, had suffered much under the rule of Geric, but they were trying to come back.

They were working hard at it.

Auley found his way onto the street shortly after the noon hour. He hadn't been on the street in several months, at least since Cashel Cian fell. Truth be told, he didn't much venture away from his own stall, fearful he might attract too much attention from the wrong people. Geric left him alone so long as he wasn't being obvious or causing trouble. But that didn't mean that Auley was ignorant from what was happening with the new king.

Far from it.

He kept abreast of the movements of the army as well as any political dealings going on, at least the ones that were apparent. What had been widely apparent since Geric took control was the number of Northmen that had invaded their village. It was well known that most of Conor's army had departed when Geric came to power, and in order to fill those gaps, Geric had struck some sort of deal with men who had historically been their mortal enemies.

They started appearing shortly after the new king assumed the throne, and even now, Auley could see them in the avenues. Sometimes they did business with the merchants, but mostly they simply took what they wanted, and no one fought back. They knew if they did, they would lose their business and perhaps even their life.

Auley had to deal with those men in his own business, though they seemed to stay away from him because he was a very big man who could easily handle a sword. He didn't have to deal with them the way some of the merchants did, and that included the weavers. He'd heard tales that the Northmen would simply take as they pleased, leaving the weavers without anything to sell. There used to be more merchants on this avenue, but with the advent of the Northmen, several of them had simply gone elsewhere.

On this afternoon, he didn't see any Northmen on the avenue of the weavers, which was a good thing. He was looking for a girl named Cara, so he began making inquiries. He was trying to be very casual about it because he didn't want to arouse suspicion. If Cara was here, he didn't want to chase her away. He was looking for a man, and he hoped she held the key.

On his third inquiry, to a very old man who was weaving an exquisite piece of fabric, he was told that Cara was the daughter of Cavan the Tongue, a man who had a stall at the very end of the avenue. Auley thanked the old man and moved toward the indicated stall, though he was curious to know why a man would be called "the Tongue." Perhaps it implied the gift of speech. In any case, Auley was cautious as he approached the stall, which seemed to be one of the larger ones on the avenue.

It was a long stall with stone walls and a low ceiling. Auley hit his head as he entered, noting a very long, somewhat dark structure. Rubbing his forehead, he saw a customer or two, and an older woman trying to sell them some thread. He didn't see anyone else, so he politely stood back by the door and waited.

The older woman saw him and greeted him, but she was busy with the customers who eventually bought a bundle of blue-dyed thread. She took their coin, gave them the thread, and then encouraged them to return soon as they headed out of the door.

Once they were gone, she turned to Auley with an oddly hungry expression on her face. "What's wantin', young lord?" she asked. "Something for your wife? What does she need?"

Auley shook his head. "I am looking for a woman," he said. "I am told she is here."

Her eyebrows lifted in delight. "If you are looking for a woman, *I* am here."

"Is your name Cara?"

The woman's face fell. "Nay," she said. "What do you want with Cara?"

"I come with a message."

"Give it to me and I will tell her."

Auley shook his head. "I must give it to her directly," he said. "Is she here?"

The woman frowned. "Who are you?"

Auley could hear the suspicion. "I mean her no harm, I swear it," he said. "But I have come with a message for her. Will you at least tell me if she is here?"

She looked him up and down. "Who are you?" she demanded. "What do you want?"

He remained calm. "My name is Auley," he said. "I am a smithy, and I have a stall over on the avenue of the smithies. I am a man of means and of good reputation, but I must speak to Cara. Is she here?"

The woman eyed him, backing away. "I'll not give you any information," she said. "Go away now. I will not speak to you."

With that, she rushed off, heading toward the rear of the long stall that was crowded with bales of wool, yarn, and other textiles. She lost herself somewhere in the back, because he could hear her grunting fearfully.

Auley watched her go, wondering why the woman was so suspicious. That seemed odd.

Feeling disappointed that he'd come to a dead end, he left the stall, but not the area. He wasn't going to give up so easily.

There was a mews behind the stalls, a small and dirty alley-way that contained rubbish and carts and other things stored by the merchants. Auley ducked back to the mews, staying low, hiding behind the edge of a cart that was a few stalls down from the one he'd just visited. He thought that he might catch the older woman coming out of the rear, and perhaps she would lead him to Cara. She hadn't given him a straight answer about Cara, whether she was at the stall or whether she even knew her, but her skittish response to his query told him all he needed to know.

She knew Cara.

Auley waited.

Some merchants lived where they worked, meaning some stalls had living quarters attached to them, but that didn't seem to be the case with this stall. As he'd hoped, he caught the older woman bolting from the rear of the stall, rushing away from him and onto one of the main roads that carved through the town of Ciannachta.

He followed.

It was busy on this day before market day, so Auley was able to pursue her without much trouble. There were people, trees, wagons, and muddy roads, and he slipped by all of it, following the woman who was heading to the northern part of the village, to an area of larger homes that sat along the River Boyne.

There were fewer people on this end of town, causing Auley to become more creative in the way he concealed himself. The woman hadn't been watching her back, which worked to his advantage, and he followed her right up to a home that was built of stone and heavy timber, with an enormous front door. She banged on the door a few times, calling to whoever was inside.

Auley crept closer.

Finally, the door opened and the woman asked for Cara. Auley could hear her. She made no attempt to enter, but he crept up behind her about the time a lovely woman with pale hair came to the door and addressed the older woman pleasantly.

Auley made his move.

"Are you Cara?" he asked, coming up behind the older woman and pushing her aside. "My name is Auley. I've been sent with a message for you."

The older woman shrieked, and Cara, puzzled by the question and the entire situation, started to panic because the old woman was. She screamed and stumbled back as Auley came through the door, but he hadn't taken two steps when something was flying at his head. Had he been any slower, it would have decapitated him. He fell to the ground as a heavy sword embedded itself in the door behind him, then he rolled to his knees and leapt to his feet. He grabbed for the nearest weapon, which happened to be a chair, and swung it at the man behind the sword with all his might. The man took the brunt of it, but he didn't fall. He didn't even let go of the hilt of the sword stuck in the door. As Auley balled a fist to throw into the man's face, he came to an abrupt halt.

He recognized the face.

His eyes widened.

"Bradaigh?" he gasped. "*Brad?*"

Bradaigh mac Neil looked at Auley with equal surprise. Those dark eyes against that pale face were something Auley had seen many times in his life. The high warrior of Ciannachta was before him, and the sight brought him comfort that he didn't even realize he'd missed.

"Auley?" Bradaigh said incredulously. "Is it you?"

Auley nodded with glee. Suddenly, he and Bradaigh were in an embrace, relieved and joyful at the unexpected reunion. Bradaigh, usually a reserved man, let his guard down for the moment.

He pulled back, looking Auley in the eye. "By all the saints," he muttered. "I can hardly believe it is you."

"It is me."

"And you are well?"

"Very well," Auley said. "And you?"

"Quite well," Bradaigh said. Then he stepped back, looking over Auley's shoulder. "All is well, love. Come to me."

Auley turned around to see Cara coming away from the wall where she'd been cowering fearfully. She took Bradaigh's outstretched hand, and he pulled her against him.

"This is my old and dear friend," he told her. "This is Auley Bannon. You have heard me speak of him."

Cara, bright and young and lovely, but also still a little scared, nodded unsteadily. "I have," she said. "Welcome to our home, Auley. Blessings upon you."

"My lady," Auley said as he dipped his head, but then he looked at Bradaigh curiously. "*Our* home?"

Bradaigh nodded. "We have been married for several months," he said. "We live here with her mother and her father and her aunt, whom you apparently followed here."

Auley grinned. "May your marriage be as strong as your heart, lad," he said softly, looking between them. "I'm sure you're wondering why I'm here. Do you have a moment to speak with me?"

Bradaigh nodded. "For you, anything," he said, letting go of his wife so he could yank the sword out of the door. "Sit with me. Let us speak of old times."

They'd upended the room with their brief fight, so Cara and her aunt were righting chairs and the table. Bradaigh and Auley took a seat as the women rushed off for food and drink.

"You were never the sentimental type, Brad," Auley said as

he settled back in the chair. "You know I've had a smithy stall not far from the street of the weavers, don't you?"

Bradaigh shrugged. "I knew you were there," he said. "I've seen you on occasion, though I did not want to speak to you. Geric has eyes everywhere. Someone would report back to him that we were plotting if they saw us speak."

Auley nodded. "I know," he said quietly. "That is the same reason I never sought you out. I was afraid we'd be seen."

Bradaigh's gaze lingered on him a moment. "But something has changed," he said. "How did you know where to find me?"

"Because you were sweet on Cara before Geric came," he said. "I did not know if you were with her, but I thought she might be a place to start. I knew her father was a weaver, so I followed the trail."

"And it led to me," Bradaigh said. "Why? What's amiss?"

Auley looked around to make sure there was no one around before leaning forward and lowering his voice.

"Conor has returned," he whispered. "Padraigan has come to me. We have been summoned by our king."

Bradaigh's eyes widened. "He came back? From the nether realm?"

Auley nodded. "He is back, along with Etain."

Bradaigh could hardly keep the shock off his face. "By all the saints," he murmured. "I do not understand... How? Olc banished them both, and surely they were gone forever. But they're back?"

"So Padraigan told me."

"Is she sure?"

"I am certain she would not have lied to me."

"And you are convinced this is not a trick?"

"Padraigan would die before seeing us come to harm. You

know that."

Bradaigh nodded quickly. "I do," he said. "'Tis only… I simply cannot believe it. I never thought I would hear that he had returned."

"I told Padraigan that we would come to him tomorrow," Auley said. "I suppose we shall see then if this is real or not. Conor was sent to the nether realm. Hopefully something did not return with his face and voice, claiming to be him."

Bradaigh eyed him warily. "A demon?"

Auley shrugged as if anything was possible, something that unsettled them both. But they knew Padraigan and knew she was trustworthy. She wouldn't have summoned them if the return of the king was not true.

But the whole thing was simply mind-blowing.

"We must find Brone," Auley said. "He will want to join us. The last I heard, he was employed by a merchant in Gardner's Hill. I saw him a few months ago when he came into town with his lord. We spoke a few words of greeting, but nothing more. It simply wasn't safe."

Bradaigh nodded. "We will go now," he said. "It sounds as if there is no time to waste if we are to meet our lord tomorrow morning."

Auley sat there a moment, a pensive expression on his face. "You realize what this means, don't you?" he said. "This is the beginning of our return. Even as I say it, I can hardly believe it. I did not think we would ever see Conor again."

"Nor I."

"And you are prepared to wrest back his throne?"

"I was ready the moment it was taken from him."

That was the high warrior in him. Auley didn't reply as Cara and her aunt returned with drink and food, waiting until the women deposited their load and cleared the chamber before speaking again.

"You must send your wife and her family out of the town," he said in a low voice. "It will not be safe for them here if you are to fight against the usurper."

Bradaigh picked up the pitcher of ale, pouring his friend a cup before he poured one for himself. "I know," he said steadily. "Like you, I never really thought this moment would come, but even so, I planned what I would do if it did."

"What will you do?"

Bradaigh set the pitcher down. "My wife's family has a home in Dundalk," he said. "I will send them there. They will be safe while I do what I must do."

Auley took a drink of his wine. "There is much we need to plan," he said. "I've not paid much attention to Geric and his movements, but I do know that he has a large contingent of Northmen with him. They make up more than half of his army."

Bradaigh snorted softly. "Thieves and murderers," he muttered. "They only swear fealty because he has given them most of what was in the Ciannachta coffers, or so I have heard. He lets them roam the streets of the town and do anything they wish. They steal goods, women, and anything else they want. Ciannachta has become their personal Garden of Eden. But they have one flaw—they have become fat and lazy over the year. There are no battles for them to attend, so they are not prepared for any action against them."

"You know this for certain?"

Bradaigh nodded. "I have been watching," he said. "I still know men at the castle, men still in the army. They tell me what is happening. In fact, right now, Geric has taken most of his men north to loot and pillage because they have nearly picked Ciannachta clean. They've gone to raid, which means there are hardly any men at the castle. If Conor is truly returned, now is the perfect time for him to confiscate Cashel Cian. There would be very little resistance, if any."

Auley hadn't known any of that because, as he'd said, he simply didn't pay attention to the movements of Geric and his Northmen mercenaries.

"And you think the men left behind would show loyalty to Conor?" he asked.

Bradaigh nodded. "Without question," he said. "From what I've seen, the men left behind are of our kind. The Northmen have gone with Geric."

Auley stared at him for a moment, realizing that this was indeed perfect timing. "We must find Brone," he muttered with quiet urgency.

Bradaigh nodded without hesitation. "We must," he said. "Gardener's Hill, you said?"

"I did."

Bradaigh's dark eyes glittered. "This is a moment I did not think we would ever see," he said. "But now that it is here… I have missed the feel of a sword in my hand. I have missed my calling, Auley. Living the life of a weaver… though I love my wife, it was an unhappy thing for me. God sent you here today. He sent you to me. I will once again do what I was born to do."

Auley could see the fire in his eyes. "You are the high warrior, Bradaigh," he said.

"And you are the master commander."

Auley lifted his cup in salute. "Long live the king," he whispered.

Bradaigh lifted his as well.

Within the hour, they were off to Gardner's Hill.

# CHAPTER THIRTEEN

"YOU'RE SURE YOU told him dawn?" Conor asked.

Padraigan nodded patiently. "They will be here, great lord. Have faith."

It was a misty, cold morning. The day had dawned dark, with a heavy fog hanging over the land, as Padraigan and Conor had made their way out toward the mound of Dowth.

Truthfully, it was a strange experience for Conor, who had been here two days ago when his life had suddenly changed. This was where it had all started. Now that he was back, he found himself peering into the passageway where he and Destry huddled before they'd been blown out by forces beyond their control. He'd told Destry that they were essentially stuck in this time period, but stuck with a purpose. The more time passed, the more he was coming to believe that. Somehow, someway, fate had put them here for a reason.

He was sticking to that theory.

"You miss your home."

He heard Padraigan's soft voice behind him as he peered into the mound. He turned to look at her. "I do," he said. "It's the only one I remember."

"You wish to return, great lord?"

He shrugged. "I would like to eventually," he said. "But I will tell you what I told Destry—that I feel as if we've been brought here for a reason. Maybe that wizard you told me about banished me to the nether realm, just like you said. I'm not disputing that. But we were brought *back* for a reason. I'd like to find out what that reason is."

Padraigan took a few steps toward him. Wrapped in a heavy cloak against the mist, she looked tiny and fragile.

"I did indeed bring you back for a reason, great lord," she said. "Olc's magic may be strong, but mine is also strong because of my feelings for you and our great queen. Ciannachta is a city of people who loved and laughed and respected you as their king. You were someone to be admired greatly. When your brother banished you, a veil of darkness was cast over the city. You must bring back the light."

He looked at her seriously. "Is that the only reason?" he said. "Because I need to restore myself to the throne? What is so special about this town that it needs me again?"

Padraigan's gaze lingered on him a moment before she lowered her head, pulling the cloak more tightly around her small body.

"It is not simply to restore you to the throne," she said. "You have been away too long. The memory of your past life has been removed from your mind. But there is a battle playing out at Ciannachta, and if you do not win, this land will be lost. Gods are using men to do battle against one another, and the battle at Ciannachta will only get worse. We are coming to a moment of peace or of fire. There is a fork in the road, and we must choose the right path."

Conor knew all there was to know about the Irish mythological cycle, an incredibly complex web of legends and tales that made up Irish history. Many of the original tales were written centuries ago, something that over the years took shape and form, becoming the basis for analysis and interpretation in the eighteenth and nineteenth centuries by great scholars. But Conor believed that all legends had a basis in reality, and as he listened to Padraigan, he was coming to think that she was speaking about some of these ancient legends. They had to start somewhere.

Maybe that's what she meant.

"What gods?" he asked. "Who is using men to do battle?"

Padraigan was looking off into the mist now. "I did not tell you all of this when you first returned," she said quietly. "You were confused enough without my telling you everything, but the truth is that you are needed, great lord. Your brother's wizard, Olc, is a son of Cichol, a demon of chaos. Your brother listens to Olc because he tells him what he wishes to hear. He makes it so Geric can rule your lands. He puts more greed in your brother's heart because he wants something from him."

By this time, Conor was looking at her as if she'd gone mad. "Wait," he said, thoroughly perplexed. "You said Cichol? You can't possibly mean Cichol Griscenchos?"

"The *Fomoire*."

Conor's jaw dropped. "Fomorian?"

She looked at him, seeing his shock. "You came from the nether realm," she said. "Surely it cannot surprise you that the wicked roam the earth in many shapes and in many centuries. It is always there. The *Formoire* are here in our time, great lord, and they want your kingdom. How do you think you were banished so easily? They used their power to do it."

Conor had to make a conscious effort to shut his mouth. He

was absolutely gobsmacked. Padraigan was speaking of the mythical race of misshapen and evil monsters that were said to have once populated Ireland. Most scholars thought they were simply a mutation of pagan gods, but if he was understanding Padraigan correctly, they weren't legend.

They were real.

He could hardly believe what he was hearing.

"Jesus," he muttered, looking away and trying to wrap his head around what she was telling him. "Formorian? Seriously?"

He was muttering to himself, but Padraigan was listening. "Were there no demons in the nether realm, great lord?"

He sighed, running a hand through his red hair. "Not in mythical form, no," he said. "And I wasn't in the nether region. I was living a thousand years in the future, right here in Ireland. There were no Formorians or gods or witches or demons that I know of."

"They have all been destroyed?"

"They must have been," he said, turning to look at her. "Are you telling me they actually exist?"

Padraigan nodded. "They are in our world," she said. "There is a prophecy, great lord, a prophecy of old. It is said that a great king will rise in the east and begin the banishment of the *Formoire*. We have been waiting for a long time for such a warrior-king, and I believe it to be you. The banishment of the evil that walks our lands must begin somewhere. It must begin with you. That is why I returned you. That is why you are here. The salvation of Eire must start with you."

Conor was having a difficult time keeping the astonishment off his face. "So the destruction of these… these legends begins with me?"

"I believe so."

More insanity for Conor to wrap his head around. He had to think about that seriously for a moment, but it didn't take him very long. Since arriving here two days ago, he'd seen some very strange things—lizard creatures, dwarves becoming children, and so on. Things his scientific mind couldn't explain, which was creating a massive quandary within him. Now, Padraigan was telling him that he was to fulfil a prophecy of sorts. He'd told Destry they'd been brought back for a reason, and the white witch had just handed him that reason on a silver platter.

*The salvation of Eire must start with you.*

Those weren't words he'd ever expected to hear, but on the other hand, his entire life had been about his country and his culture. It was ingrained in him more deeply than anyone he knew. His heart bled green; his soul was entrenched in the earth of his birth country.

And now this.

Somehow, it didn't seem so outlandish. As if everything in his life had pointed to this moment.

"Okay," he said, sighing sharply. "I suppose I have no other choice but to go on a little faith here. If you say this is why I'm here, then I'll take you at your word. But first, I want to know who you are. Clearly, you're a sorceress, so what... *what* are you?"

Padraigan smiled faintly. "I am what you see, great lord."

"Are you mortal?"

She cocked her head. "I am *Tuath de,*" she said. "My soul is immortal, but the flesh upon me bleeds as yours does."

Conor snorted, rolling his eyes as he realized what she meant. "Fuck me," he mumbled to himself, overwhelmed with the irony of it all. "Tuatha de Danann. She's from a race of demigods."

He was chuckling, trying not to lean to the side of madness in all of this. Destry had once suggested that this experience was some kind of mass hallucination, and, at the moment, he was trying not to agree with her. It was *all* madness. But after what he'd seen, he supposed there was truth to it.

All of it.

He was caught up in what was commonly known as an Irish mythological cycle.

And he had a purpose.

"So you're my white witch," he said. "I'm going to have to trust you because I still don't remember anything. You're going to have to tell me everything I need to know for whatever purpose I've been born to accomplish."

"I will do all I can, great lord."

"Good," he said. "Because not remembering anything is going to be a problem. I've got to—"

He was cut off by noise in the brush off to his right. Something was coming through the thick bramble, and he turned to face it, admittedly feeling some nerves. Maybe it was another lizard creature, or maybe it was more naked guys out to attack him. He was dressed in his kingly garb this morning, and that included the gorgeous sword Padraigan had given him, but he really didn't want to use the thing and damage it.

He hoped he didn't have to.

Three men suddenly emerged from the foliage, and Padraigan reached out, touching Conor's arm.

"Those are your loyal men, great lord," she said, a smile on her lips. "Do you not recognize them?"

Conor peered at them closely as they came near. The men, three big men, were looking at him in shock. They came closer, without speaking, before taking a swift knee several feet in front of him, lowering their heads in a sign of respect.

"Great lord," one man said, awe in his voice. "Praise God and the saints that you have truly and finally returned to us."

Conor looked at the three lowered heads before glancing to Padraigan with uncertainty, but she nodded encouragingly. He cleared his throat softly.

"Get up," he said, but realized that didn't sound very kingly. "Rise. Please rise."

They did, looking at him with varying degrees of emotion. Conor swore he saw tears in the eyes of a couple of them. There was a big man with shaggy brown hair, an equally big man with black hair and pale skin, and then a tall, sinewy man with dark blond hair to his shoulders and freckles all over his face. That man was on the verge of weeping.

The emotion in the air was palpable. Something warm and healing and full of hope. Conor had never felt anything like it, but it was there. It was like dust upon the wind, falling upon them, mingling with them, fortifying this moment that was as unexpected as it was joyful.

Conor cleared his throat again.

"You know who I am?" he asked them.

All three of them nodded without hesitation. "Our prayers have been answered, great lord," the man with shaggy brown hair said. "When Padraigan told me yesterday that you had finally returned, I will admit that I had my doubts. But I doubt no more, great lord. Forgive me my momentary weakness."

Conor could see the sincerity in their faces. He wasn't quite sure what they expected from him at that moment, so he did what he thought he should do—he walked up to the man who had just spoken and looked him in the eye.

"I was told by Padraigan what had happened," he said quietly. "I will admit that I remember nothing. Whatever happened to me destroyed my memory of this place and this time. I am told that the three of you are my loyal men, so I will have to ask forgiveness that I don't remember you. But I want to. I hope you will help me do that. What's your name?"

The man with the shaggy brown hair had warmth in his eyes. "Auley, great lord," he said. "I am Auley Bannan. I am the commander of your army."

Conor could see, in that simple sentence, that there was great affection for him. It was all over the man's face, which made Conor feel more confident about this strange situation. Clearly, these men felt something for him, so if he'd truly had any doubt that he was who Padraigan said he was, then that doubt was evaporating.

Something inside him was becoming fulfilled.

The ancient Celtic king was beginning to rise.

"Auley," he repeated. "I will not forget your name."

"Thank you, great lord."

Conor turned to the next man, who seemed to be struggling to hold back his emotion. The man with black hair and black eyes looked as if he would burst forth with tears had he any less self-control.

"I am Bradaigh mac Neil, great lord," he said before Conor could ask. "I am your high warrior. We were like brothers, once."

Conor could see the deep feeling in the man's heart. It was in his eyes, in his manner. "And we will be again," he said. "I am sure of it. You will help me remember our bond."

Bradaigh nodded smartly. He looked as if he wanted to say more, but he refrained, being a man of action more than a man of words. Somehow, Conor sensed that. Looking at him, looking at all of them, gave him a bizarre sense of déjà vu, which meant that somewhere deep inside of him, more memories were beginning to stir. God, he hoped so, because he wanted to remember everything. This life he'd once been part of and would be again. He was going in blind to an incredibly dangerous situation, and he was desperate to know all he could. He had told Destry that he didn't think they'd been put here just to be killed, but the truth was that these were dangerous and deadly times. They could very well be killed.

As he'd once said, he simply wanted to survive it.

The third man was looking at him with obvious glee when he turned to him. This man was tall, lanky, with the biggest hands Conor had ever seen. He wasn't as restrained or reserved as the other two because his entire body was twitching with the happiness he was feeling.

"And you?" Conor asked. "What's your name?"

"Brone, great lord," the man replied. "I am your *laoch meargánta.*"

Conor's brow furrowed. "Reckless warrior?" he repeated. "That sounds rather dangerous. What do you do in battle?"

"He is the first man into a fight," Bradaigh said, eyeing Brone with both approval and disapproval, a strange combination. "Auley gives the orders, and Brone carries them out. Men follow him without question. Reckless warrior is simply what we've taken to calling him over the years, but his formal title is first warrior. The first man into the fight and the last one to leave it. You will never meet a braver man."

Conor understood. His gaze lingered on Brone, and simply from the man's giddy expression, he could easily see why he was called reckless. He just had that look about him. But he'd managed to survive all these years, so there had to be some restraint in him, somewhere.

Conor found himself looking at all three of them, reconciling himself to the men who had helped him command. And who had fled rather than serve his brother.

"Padraigan has told me everything," he said. "I know about Geric and I know what he's done. I know what his wizard did to me and my wife, but Padraigan has brought us back. The problem is that we don't remember anything. Up until last night, my wife didn't even speak the language. We've been in another place and another time, where we had lives and friends and families. We knew nothing of this world we now find ourselves in, so I will rely on you men to help us. There's a kingdom that needs me, so I'll need all the help I can get."

The three men all nodded, but Auley spoke. "Understood, great lord," he said. "Just know that we are very glad to see you. Truthfully, we weren't sure we ever would when we heard you'd been banished. Men that Olc of the Eye banishes don't return, so whatever magic Padraigan cast upon you is very strong. Very strong indeed."

Conor glanced at the little sorceress, who smiled timidly. But his attention returned to his men. "I'm back in body and spirit, but not in mind," he said. "I need you to tell me everything you know about Geric and the men who support him. I'm hearing he has Viking mercenaries helping him."

The word "Viking" didn't mean anything to them, as that wasn't a word widely used until later centuries, and Conor could see their confusion. He quickly corrected himself.

"I mean Northmen," he said. "Mercenaries from the land of the Danes. If we are to regain the kingdom, then I need to know what you know."

Now, the men understood. There wasn't any hesitation in telling Conor what he needed to know. Even if it involved a personal opinion or two with regard to Geric.

"Your brother was an old evil from the days of his childhood, great lord," Bradaigh said grimly. "He always envied you. Before you married your wife, he tried to steal her from you, but your love for her was too strong. Many of us… we thought you should have killed him long ago. He has only, and always, been a threat to you. But you would not do it, stating that you only had one brother and that to kill him would be to lower yourself to being a murderer. But still, Geric plotted and planned against you until that dark and terrible night over a year ago."

Conor was listening intently. "The night he had me banished?"

Bradaigh nodded. "It was a peaceful night, like any other," he said, thinking back to that troubling moment. "I remember it well. We'd heard of a buildup of raiders to the north, but that wasn't unusual. We've had Northmen on these shores since the days of my ancestors. We were keeping watch on them, but as we watched the group to the north, a group landed to the south. They moved up at dawn, and that was when hellfire began to rain upon us. There was a battle."

"Where was my army?" Conor asked.

Bradaigh shifted uncomfortably. "Sleeping," he said. "We sent out regular scouts to watch the land, but the scouts were killed before they could report the movements of the men from the south. They caught our army off guard, and Geric had spies inside the castle. They bolted the hall doors, where the army was sleeping, while those same spies opened the gates. After that… after that, the Northmen ran free. I came to you, along with Brone, and we attempted to help you escape, but we were not successful. We were all captured except for your wife and sons. They managed to break free through the drainage ditches beneath the cashel. They ran for freedom."

Conor knew the basics of what had transpired from Padraigan, but hearing the details was something different. It was so strange, like hearing a movie or a book plot, only this was for real. This really happened in a minor kingdom in Ireland at the beginning of the Middle Ages, one event in a history full of such events spread all over the world. Men seeking to conquer, other men seeking to hold what they had. He was a professor of history, and he knew these stories. He'd studied them and he'd taught them. He'd always felt such a kinship with tales from ancient Ireland, so much so that he'd actually changed his surname to reflect his passion and affinity. Now, he knew why.

Because the same thing had happened to him.

It was a stunning realization.

"I'm told that my wife took my sons to Padraigan, who cast a spell upon them so they would not be discovered," he said, watching the men around him nod. "And my wife? She returned to the castle?"

Bradaigh continued, "She returned to plead for your release. Your brother had always had a passion for her, and she tried to use that against him. She hated your brother, but she was willing to do whatever was necessary in order to gain your release. You are not going to like what I am about to tell you, great lord, but you must understand why she did it. It was because she loved you. Geric promised her that if she gave herself over to him for one night that he would free you."

Conor knew exactly what he meant and felt bile rise in his throat. "And she agreed?"

Bradaigh nodded with reluctance. "She did," he said. "But your brother went back on his word. She was forced to watch as Olc banished you to the nether realm. When your wife refused to become Geric's queen, he moved to kill her, but Olc convinced him to banish her as well. Both of you, lost in the nether realm with no memory of each other. That would be a fate worse than death for two lovers."

Conor closed his eyes tightly for a moment, digesting what Destry had gone through for him. That wonderful, sensitive, beautiful woman had risked everything for him. It was because of him she'd been sent to the nether region. It was because of him she'd slept with a man she hated, trying to secure her husband's release. He was positive she didn't remember that and he wasn't sure he should tell her, but it only made him love her more.

And hate a man to his very bones that he'd never even met. *Geric.*

"The spell wasn't strong enough to keep us apart," he finally said. "She found me and I found her. We didn't know one another, but the feelings were there almost instantly. There are some things magic can't destroy, and love is one of them, so we've returned and I've got a kingdom to take back. I need your help. Will you do it?"

The three men nodded without hesitation. "We will, great lord," Auley said. "That is why we've come. We must retake the cashel right away because Geric has taken his mercenaries and gone north. There are barely any men left protecting the fortress. It would be a simple thing to do it now."

"But what about the men left behind?" Conor said. "We'll still have to fight them, and we don't have an army. It will take more than four of us to do that."

Auley and even Bradaigh were shaking their heads. "You do not understand," Auley said. "The men left behind are men who were loyal to you, who serve Geric because they have nowhere else to go. Most of the army left when you were banished, but a few remained. Show yourself to them and they will be loyal to you once again."

Conor didn't want to doubt these men, but it seemed like a stretch. "That's putting a lot of faith in men who have been serving another king," he said. "Maybe they like him."

More heads were wagging. "No one has any love for your brother, great lord," Auley said firmly. "The villagers, the army you left behind… no one. They pray for your return, but we must move now while Geric is gone. Surprise is on our side."

Conor could see the logic, but he still had questions. "And once we take the castle with the small contingent left behind, what happens when Geric returns?" he said. "Clearly, he has an army with him. Highly trained Northmen, it sounds like. These men are trained and bred for war. He'll come back and overrun us if we can't build up our army to sufficiently hold them off."

"As I said, many men fled the city when Geric took your throne," Bradaigh said. "All we need do is spread the word throughout the countryside that you have returned. You had thousands of men loyal to you, good lord. If they know you have returned, they will come back. They will fight to the death for you."

"Then why didn't they do it before, when Geric took my throne?"

"Because most were trapped in the hall," Auley said. "Geric and his mercenaries had time to secure the cashel before they opened the doors, and at that point, the men inside were prisoners. They had no weapons, nothing to fight with. They resisted for a time but too many were killed, so they stopped. In fact, you told them to so no more would be slaughtered, but I'm sure you do not remember that. The men were given the choice of joining Geric's mercenary army or being banished, and most chose to leave. They are scattered."

"And you think we can gather them before Geric finds out I've returned?"

"I believe we can, great lord."

Conor thought seriously on that, looking to Padraigan, who didn't look so pale or so frail at the moment. She had some color to her cheeks, maybe from the hope in her heart. It had been a year of fear for her, fear and waiting, and this was the moment she had waited for. All of this had been her doing, so she agreed with the men she'd brought to Conor. They needed their king to lead them.

Conor knew that. He could see it in their faces. They were all looking to him for leadership and strength. He realized that all of those ancient warfare classes he had taken, and given, were about to be put to practical application.

He was ready.

"Okay," he finally said. "Come back with me to the cottage and we can plan out how we're going to do this. For what it's worth, I'm sorry you three have been caught up in this. As I said, I don't remember any of it, but it sounds like maybe that's a blessing. Especially the part about Destry—I mean, my wife, and what she had to do in order to free me. And then the bastard betrayed her. She doesn't remember any of that either, so please don't bring it up. Some things are better left unsaid."

The three warriors nodded solemnly. Padraigan had already begun walking, heading in the direction of the cottage, and Conor began to follow as his men gathered around him.

*His men.*

That was the weirdest thing in the world to him, but on the other hand, not entirely weird. He immediately felt comfortable with them, as if he'd known them all his life.

And he had.

The return of the high king was imminent.

# CHAPTER FOURTEEN

THAT CRUDE LITTLE cottage in the middle of nowhere was becoming a hive of activity.

Three days after Destry and Conor were blown through the passageway at Dowth, men began to gather. Word had been spread through the small farms and villages to the west of Ciannachta that the king had returned, and men were being summoned to the burial lands of the ancient ones. The area was taboo, but they came anyway.

They began to trickle in, little by little.

The men were so glad to see Conor when they arrived that some actually wept. It was both a powerful and strange experience. They began to set up an encampment to the south of the cottage because so many of them were coming in from the countryside that they needed some place to live while the battle was being planned. Since time was of the essence, they had to move quickly, so the men who had joined them were immediately put to work on making spears and clubs and other weapons using material from the land around them.

The meadow to the south turned into a bustling settlement.

Because of that, Conor had cautioned Destry from straying

from the cottage, but he gave no such warning to the boys, who wandered into the encampment and were treated like little kings by the men. Conor's three warriors seemed nice enough, however, and they were quite respectful of her. They only came into the cottage when invited, and only when Conor was there. They didn't say much to her, but that wasn't strange considering she was their queen and any conversation with her was improper unless Conor was involved.

Destry didn't really mind. She remained in and around the cottage, keeping up with her cooking duties and trying to assimilate into the world her life had become.

After Padraigan had sung the song of poets to her, it took Destry about two days before she realized that she was speaking Gaelic. She could still speak English just fine, but she understood, and could respond to, Gaelic. The boys would chatter at her and she would understand all of it, which was something of a miracle in her mind. Whatever Padraigan did to her had worked, something that fascinated her to no end.

That was just one example in a long line of things that were rare and unusual in this strange new world. After the shock of landing in the middle of this new life wore off, the reality of what they found themselves in began to settle deep. No phones, streaming services, or food delivery. No shower—no bathroom as Destry knew them. A bath was a luxury, and Padraigan didn't have a dedicated washroom. The toilet was a hole in the ground next to the creek behind the cottage. One squatted over it, did one's business, and wiped with whatever one could find— leaves, grass, or whatever.

Since hygiene was important to Destry, something she refused to compromise on more than she had to, she had Conor help her make the toilet area more acceptable. They gathered big, soft leaves to use as toilet paper. He helped her rig up a wall of leafy branches around the hole in the ground for more privacy. He even took one of the stools from the cottage, sawed a big hole in the middle of it, and put it over the hole in the ground so she had something to sit on when she did her business. Destry insisted they keep a big bucket of water next to the stool so that when they were finished, they could clean up with it and also use a little to wash the waste down into the creek, which was fairly deep and flowed quickly. That was the best they could do for a toilet at the moment, but she wanted to get her hands on some vinegar to clean the toilet and try to keep the smell down.

That wasn't a priority, however, and it became even less of one as men from Conor's army began arriving. Conor was tied up with them most of the time in planning the coming invasion of Cashel Cian, leaving Destry and the boys mostly on their own. Even Padraigan was wrapped up with the building army, so Destry and the boys took charge of their living quarters. That meant changes were in the air, because Destry was determined to "modernize" their abode.

After the toilet was built, she set about either rigging a shower or somehow creating a bathtub. The simplest thing seemed to be rigging a shower, and she did so with the help of Mattock and Devlin. There were several buckets around because of the livestock, so she had the boys grab one. The next thing they needed was a rope, but they couldn't find one until Devlin suggested they use old vines. That turned into a big project, as they took old, wild flowering vines that were past their prime, braiding them to form a long rope, which was secured to the bucket.

Then came the tree.

Out back, by the toilet next to the stream, were several trees, and Destry put the boys on collecting more leafy branches to build a stall under a larger branch of one of the trees. There were three sides to the makeshift stall, with the fourth side facing the stream, and Mattock and Devlin took delight in poking a big hole in the bottom of the bucket and then using the wooden piece they'd popped out to act like the stopper. After being looped over the branch, the bucket simply needed to be filled with water—then one would pull the plug, and it became a showerhead of sorts. Although it would be high maintenance, it was better than nothing. Destry couldn't wait to try it.

Conor came home that evening after having been with the men all day long, and she proudly showed him what she'd rigged up. The older boys were quite proud of it also. He grinned at her ingenuity, thinking it looked like it might come down on top of her, but he didn't say so. He congratulated her for trying.

Then came the obvious question of soap and shampoo, at least from Destry. Conor was able to secure soap from Padraigan, who had purchased it in the village months ago to use on the boys. The little woman kept a clean house, and clean children, and the hard, lumpy soap was part of that. Once Destry realized she had a bar of soap that smelled of peppermint and rosemary, she was absolutely determined to try out her new shower.

Conor had to help her, of course, and it turned into a not-so-simple production. Buckets of hot water had to be lugged outside and put into the bucket over the tree trunk. Conor had also secured a coverlet around the stall for more privacy as Destry stood underneath the bucket, stark naked, and pulled the plug, letting the hot water beat down over her. It was marvelous. But Conor had to fill the bucket seven times because the soap, while fresh and efficient, was made from tallow, which was difficult to wash out of her hair. She had to rinse it several times before it all came out. After that, Conor wrapped her up in a blanket and carried her back to the cottage so her feet wouldn't get dirty.

The shower had been great, and she felt much better, but it had been a hell of a lot of work. Much to her disappointment, Destry didn't see herself doing it again anytime soon. Conor promised her that he'd try to find an acceptable bathtub.

As the sixth day after their arrival dawned and Conor went off to find his men again, Destry braided her hair and donned a soft white shift with a pale green robe that went on top of it. It was cinched at the waist, giving her a glorious figure.

After the shower adventure the night before and everything she'd experienced over the past several days, she was coming to see just how rustic of a situation they were in. No cream, mascara, or lotion for her skin. Conor had fashioned toothbrushes with soft green reeds that grew on the banks of the creek, and they brushed their teeth with a mixture Conor had made up of salt, mashed wild mint, and a little bit of wine. It wasn't great, but it was better than nothing.

Medieval living had been quite interesting.

Destry couldn't say that she hated it, but she longed for a deep-soak tub and her favorite bath products. Some lip balm would be nice, too, because her lips were constantly dry. Makeup would also be a godsend, but there simply wasn't anything—and, Conor told her, she didn't need it anyway. She was a natural beauty.

She'd had a headache the other night and no aspirin, although Conor told her that willow bark powder would serve a similar purpose. All things she was unfamiliar with, but he wasn't. The problem was that ever since the three warriors appeared, he'd been off with them daily, and she'd been left with the boys. She hadn't seen much of him.

But she knew something big was building.

She tried to be patient.

The weapons that the men were building were piling up. In fact, on this misty morning, there was more activity than usual. She wandered outside, still close to the cottage, peering to the south and seeing the encampment, which had grown overnight. She couldn't really tell, but she knew there had to be hundreds of men there at the very least. Hundreds of men who had returned to help Conor regain the kingdom that had been wrested from him.

And then Conor stepped into her line of sight. She could tell by that bright red hair. He was also at least a head taller than any other man around him, his warriors included.

She watched him as he spoke to his men and inspected the spears they'd fashioned. It made Destry smile; technically, she'd only known him a few days. About a week, by her calculations. But already, they'd lived a lifetime together, and evidently, a lifetime before that. She'd heard of soul mates, of course, but she'd never imagined that she actually had one. That lost wedding seemed like a lifetime ago.

Everything seemed like a lifetime ago.

It was heading toward noon, and she knew the boys would be hungry. It seemed that they were always hungry. She'd made pea soup the night before, with carrots and onions and the dried peas she'd found in a sack, so now she headed back into the cottage to warm that up for the boys, who were still out in the barn doing their chores. They had Slane with them, teaching the four-year-old that hard work was good, but every once in a while she could hear him squeal as something didn't go his way. The child was a squealer, something that probably wouldn't work well for him in a land of strong and determined men, including his father. He was definitely a mama's boy, and although Conor hadn't said anything about that, at some point, he probably would.

Even little boys had to grow up sometime.

By the time noon rolled around, Destry had the pea soup heated up, with bread and boiled eggs on the table. She also took some of the precious beef fat that Padraigan had pur-chased from the butcher in Ciannachta some time ago, fat used in food preparation, and melted it down. There was an entire sack of turnips, and she cut a few of them thinly before frying them in the beef fat like potato chips. Sprinkled liberally with salt, they weren't bad at all.

Those went on the table about the time the boys came in, and although they were initially puzzled by the crispy bits of turnip, they soon decided they were quite tasty. Between the pea soup, the eggs, and the turnip chips, they had a significant meal.

Conor appeared in the doorway when the boys were about half finished, inhaling deeply the scent of the meal.

Destry grinned.

"I thought you'd come running when you smelled food," she said. "Sit down and eat. There's plenty."

Conor didn't have to be told twice. He moved to the table, lifting Slane off a stool so he could sit down. He lifted up one of the still-warm chips.

"What are these?" he asked, taking a bite. "Are these the turnips?"

Destry nodded as she fried more. "Definitely," she said. "They're much better when they're cooked or fried. I wish I had some parmesan cheese. That would make them really delicious."

"They're already delicious," Conor said, taking a handful. "Very clever of you. You're getting the hang of this."

Destry's smile faded as she fished out some brown chips. "I'm trying," she said. "I still wish I had a bathtub."

"I'll find you one, I promise."

"I know you will," she said, glancing at him affectionately. "I wasn't trying to harp on it. But speaking of bathtubs, how's it going out there? Looks like we had more arrivals overnight."

Arrivals had nothing to do with bathtubs, but the way she said it made it a funny transition.

"We did," he said. "We've got about six hundred men out there, and that's not even half of them, I'm told. But there's no more time to wait, so we're moving into Ciannachta tonight."

Destry stopped and looked at him. "What are you going to do?"

Conor had an egg stolen out of his hand by Devlin, and he scowled at the giggling boy before answering. "Move into the city under the cover of darkness and take the castle," he said. "Auley and Bradaigh know it inside and out, so I'm just along for the ride."

"Are you going to be fighting?"

"If there's resistance, I will."

Destry's gaze lingered on him for a moment before returning to her turnips. She fell silent after that, removing all of the chips from the beef fat and moving the iron pot off the fire so the fat could cool. She brought the chips over to the table in a bowl, setting them down so the boys could pounce on them.

She sat down opposite Conor, but when she reached for an egg, his big hand closed over hers.

"What's the matter?" he asked softly.

She looked at him. "What makes you think anything is the matter?"

"Because you've suddenly gone silent," he said. "What's wrong?"

She shook her head. "Nothing," she said, holding up a chip. "I was just busy cooking these things and didn't want to burn them, so I was focused. Do you think they'd be better with some salt and rosemary sprinkled on them?"

"I think it would be better if you were honest with me."

Destry almost denied it again but thought better of it. She lowered her gaze as she spoke.

"I guess I'm just processing what you're going to do tonight," she said. "This all seems to be happening so fast. A week ago, you were standing on top of Dowth, teaching your class. Tonight, you're leading a castle siege. Honestly? It's terrifying. I'm terrified for you."

He lifted her hand and kissed her fingers. "I get it," he said. "But I find it pretty exciting. Don't be angry with me about that, but I feel like this is what I was born to do. I really do."

"But it's so dangerous."

He toyed with her fingers. "Do you remember the first time you came to my office on the college grounds?"

"I do."

"Do you remember all of the weapons and stuff I had on the walls?"

"Of course."

"You asked me if I'd ever used them."

"I remember."

He kissed her hand again. "I'm better trained in those weapons than almost any man out in that encampment," he said. "I've dedicated my life to the study of ancient Ireland and all that entails. I never imagined in my entire life that I'd actually have a chance to participate in that history, but that's exactly what I'm going to do. It's an incredible honor. I know this is scary for you, but you're going to have to trust that I'll be okay. I told you that I don't think we've been brought here just so I can be killed. We have a greater purpose, and I'm going to find out what that purpose is. Okay?"

She finally looked at him, taking a long, deep breath. "Okay," she said, resigned. "But I'm still scared."

"I completely get it."

"What do you want me to do tonight?" she said. "Am I coming with you?"

He shook his head. "No," he said. "You're going to stay here with the boys. I'm taking Padraigan with me because I may need her, so you'll be alone. Bolt the door and stay inside. Don't go outside for any reason. I'll leave you with knives and clubs in case you need them, but I want you to remain here, nice and safe. Okay?"

She nodded. "Okay."

He smiled encouragingly at her and returned to his meal, telling the boys that they'd better not eat the rest of the eggs. He gently teased them, they responded, and, for a moment, Destry just sat there and watched it all, thinking that it seemed completely normal and domestic. She felt as if she'd been in this situation before, countless times, listening to the conversation between the boys and their father.

Her boys.

Her husband.

A husband who was going to war and might not return.

"I have to ask this," she said after a moment. "I'm not trying to be a buzzkill or whine about it, but I have to ask you something."

He looked at her. "Ask what?"

"What happens if you don't come back?"

"I will."

"But for the sake of argument, what if you don't?" she said. "What do I do?"

The warm expression on his face faded. "It won't happen, but if it does, you stay with Padraigan," he said. "Don't leave her side, ever. And you raise our sons to be strong, fearless men. They've got a hell of a mother, Des. I know you'd make me proud, so I'm not concerned about it. I know you'll always do what's best in the end."

Destry nodded as if his answer satisfied her. But then she burst into quiet tears and fled the cottage. With a heavy sigh, Conor followed.

He found her out back, on the banks of the creek, wiping at her cheeks as she watched the water flow. He came up behind her and wrapped his arms around her, holding her tightly as she wept. He buried his face in the side of her head.

"I know this is a lot," he whispered. "Believe me, I know. I get that this whole thing is frightening. But this is why we've come here, so I can't avoid it. Padraigan told me that a battle of good against evil is happening now with Ciannachta, that the same wizard who banished us to the nether realm is from a race of evil supernatural beings. Padraigan is from a legendary group of demigods. That's why she can work magic. Crazy as it sounds, she says there's some kind of prophecy about a great king rising to help free Ireland from oppressors, and she thinks

I'm that king. *That's* why we're here. And I believe with all my heart that this is what I'm meant to do."

Destry was still sniffling, her arms wrapped around his arms as he held her. "So we're in a land of witches and wizards and demigods?" she said. "That's just insane, Conor."

"We've both seen a grain of truth."

She couldn't deny it. She continued to sniffle as he held her, and both of them watched the creek flow gently by. Conor hugged her tightly, kissing the side of her head to give her some comfort.

"What to hear something funny?" he asked, trying to change the subject a little.

"What?"

"I found out today that I'm known to the people in the kingdom as *Conchúr Dearg*."

"What does that mean?

"Conor the Red," he said. "But the word *dearg*—it's the same pronunciation as Derga, the name I took for myself. Weird coincidence, right?"

Destry chuckled. "I'm coming to think there are no coincidences in our world, Conor," she said. "Everything we discover like that are just pieces of a larger puzzle, falling into place."

"That's exactly what I was thinking."

"You know what else I was thinking?"

"What?"

"That I'm going to miss you when you leave."

Conor's response was to turn her around and kiss her deeply. He didn't want to talk anymore, because they'd talked the subject into the ground as far as he was concerned. Now, he just wanted to touch her.

Destry gave herself over to him as she always did when he

held her, because the pheromones between them were over-whelming—and if there was one thing she had learned about Conor, it was that he liked to touch her.

He also liked to have sex. A lot. Not that she minded, because she loved it as much as he did, but they had done the deed every night and every morning since their arrival, in spite of Destry saying that she felt dirty doing it in front of the boys. They hadn't yet woken up to their parents' activities, thankfully, but it was only a matter of time.

One of the things Destry had done in the small room they'd all been sleeping in was move their bed—the one she and Conor slept in—and hang a coverlet up to shield it from where the boys slept. A futile gesture, given the size of the room, but an important one to Destry.

But out here in the yard, with no witnesses, they could do as they pleased.

Lips still fused to hers, he pulled her around the tree that held the makeshift shower, using the crude stall enclosure as protection from any prying eyes. Conor managed to disengage himself from her lips and turn her around, bending her over and putting her hands against the tree. Once she was bent over in front of him, it was a matter of tossing her skirts up, pulling down her panties, and driving into her from behind.

Destry moaned from the pleasure of it, moving her hips back to meet every thrust. Conor definitely had what was called BDE—big dick energy. The man was hugely hung, and Destry was convinced she could never sleep with another man ever again after she'd had Conor. Not that she ever intended to, but it was more the realization that she'd finally found what she'd been looking for. Not simply the physical size of the man, but everything about him. His mind, his humor, his gentleness, but also the way he touched her. He was a sweet, thoughtful lover. He was the complete package, something she'd been searching for her entire life. Everything about him was so familiar.

She knew she could never be without him.

He was her alpha and omega, her first and her last.

He was everything.

Conor hadn't been going for very long before he climaxed. Destry felt him throbbing within her, and was so highly aroused that his spasms threw her over the brink. She cried out, gripping the tree so tightly that she tore bark off. He leaned over her, his hands on her torso, her breasts, between her legs, everywhere he could touch her, and she let him. He remained embedded in her, simply for the comfort and pleasure of it, but his roaming hands managed to work her into another orgasm, which only made him hard again when he felt her pulsing around him.

Soon, he was making love to her again, moving in and out of her slowly, his fingers playing with her nipples as she bit into her arm to keep from crying out. Another orgasm from Conor, smaller than the one so recent, but pleasurable nonetheless, and another one from Destry, and he finally pulled her up so that she was clutched against his chest. Because he was so tall, he was no longer embedded in her, and his semi-flaccid cock was against the small of her back.

While Destry reveled in the powerful love and physical attraction between them, Conor was having a completely different experience. She couldn't see the tears in his eyes as he held her, thinking of what Bradaigh and Auley had told him. Goddamn the fact that it had suddenly popped into his head, but it had.

He was thinking about how Destry had been forced to sleep

with Geric, a man who was supposed to be his brother but a man he didn't remember. That faceless bastard had forced Destry to do unspeakable things with a body that belonged only to him. He didn't blame her; never would he blame her. But the sacrifice she had made for him threatened to tear him apart. There was a very small part of him terrified he might get himself into that situation again, and he knew that Destry would do what she needed to do in order to free him.

That—and only that thought about the entire upcoming situation—scared him to death.

"Conor?" Destry said softly.

His head had been buried in the top of her head. "What?" he asked, muffled.

"What's wrong?"

He opened his eyes and lifted his head from her hair. "What do you mean?"

"Because you're breathing unsteadily," Destry said. "What's wrong?"

Conor didn't know what to tell her, but he suddenly realized he'd been on the verge of sobbing. As he released her, he quickly wiped at his wet eyes. "Nothing," he said. "Just living in the moment. This is everything, Des."

Destry pushed her skirt down, adjusting the shift that he'd hiked up so he could get at her breasts. "I know," she said, turning to face him. "It really is. I never knew there was passion like this."

"Love like this."

She smiled. "That's what I meant," she said. "I've known you about a week, and I love you as if I've been doing it my entire life."

"You have."

She laughed. "I just wish I remembered all of it."

He glanced at her as he cinched up his breeches, a knowing gleam in his eye. "Even if your mind doesn't remember, your heart does," he said. "So does mine. That's all that matters."

Destry gently pushed his hands away and finished tying off the breeches for him. She smoothed down his tunic and finished dressing him as he stood there and let her. He loved it when she fussed over him.

When she was satisfied, she looked him over. "You're pretty damn handsome," she said. "I thought so the moment I first met you, but you seem to get better with age."

He grinned. "I've got a smoking hot girlfriend, so I have to look good."

Her smile faded. "Only your girlfriend?"

"Only?"

"Everyone says I'm your wife. You don't feel like I'm your wife?"

He quickly pulled her into a tight embrace. "I didn't mean anything by the comment," he said. "You're my wife, my girlfriend, my mistress, my heart, and my soul. You're everything. There hasn't been a title for what you are to me, Des."

"Queen," she whispered.

He laughed, hugging her. "That you are, sweetheart," he said. "You are my queen in every sense of the word. I'll never call you anything else but queen, ever again. I promise."

She looked up at him, smiling. "That's better," she said. Then she pulled away and took his hand. "Let's find the boys. You need to spend some time with them before you go."

He squeezed her hand as they began heading back toward the cottage. "Definitely," he said. "In fact, I've been thinking about them."

"The boys?"

"My family in general," he said. "You know that I changed my surname to Da Derga, but that was before I knew what my real legacy was."

Destry glanced at him. "You mean Conor the Red?"

He nodded. "Right," he said. "Most kings were given a nickname of sorts, to differentiate them from others with the same name. The European kings did the same thing—Charles the Bold, Charles the Fat, and so on. But for the Irish, the surname was really the big deal. That really differentiated your branch of the family from someone else's."

"So you don't like Da Derga anymore?"

"You really want to go by Destry Da Derga for the rest of your life?"

She started laughing. "I don't care," she said. "I'll go by whatever you decide. Maybe the Red's Wife?"

He chuckled. "Doesn't have a good ring to it," he said. "I was going to say that I've learned a lot over the past few days, hanging out with the soldiers. Not only did I learn I'd once been called Conor the Red, but because I came back from the nether realm, they're starting to call me *an rohan*—it's a name that basically means spirit or spiritual."

"Rohan," Destry repeated. "Isn't that from the Lord of the Rings? Like, the riders of Rohan?"

He nodded. "It is," he said. "But Tolkien was a philologist."

"What in the hell is that?"

"A language expert," Conor said. "He invented the Elvish language in the book and called it *Quenya*, but more to the point, he used parts of other languages for Middle Earth. Rohan was one—the word appears in other languages and has a few different meanings. For Gaelic, the proper name Rohan, for example, if we were to name a child that, means spirit or spiritual. That's what the men have taken to calling me."

"It's a nice name."

"I want to take it for my surname," Conor said. "Da Derga was for the man who didn't know he had a role in the Irish mythological cycle. But now that I know, Rohan is more fitting. For our children, Mac Rohan, meaning son of Rohan, will define our family for centuries to come. Maybe that name is my legacy in the end."

Destry smiled. "I like it," she said. "Destry Rohan sounds better than Destry Da Derga."

"I think so, too."

They came around the side of the cottage in time to see the boys in the corral with the little calf again. They'd finished their chores and were goofing off, but once they saw Conor and Destry, they ran toward them, with Slane bringing up the rear.

"Dada!" Devlin yelled as they came close. "If Mattock is to get another pony, may I have a pony too?"

Conor lifted his eyebrows thoughtfully, glancing at Destry, who was fighting off a smile as she picked up Slane. Boys and their toys, from century to century, didn't change much.

"Who said Mattock was getting a pony?" Conor asked.

Devlin pointed at Mattock, whose face fell with disappointment. "I'm not getting a pony, Dada?" he asked sadly. "Deneb is gone. He was my only friend. I thought… I had hoped…"

Conor stopped the boy by putting a hand on his shoulder. "Of course you will get a pony," he said, looking at Devlin. "And you. You will be men soon, and all men should have a horse. Right?"

Mattock and Devlin nodded eagerly. Conor smiled at the

boys who looked so much like him and Destry, something that still surprised him. He should have been used to it, but he just wasn't. It only served to underscore that this entire situation they found themselves in was real.

Very real.

That brought about another thought.

"Then we'll talk about ponies when I return," he said. "But for now, I have a very important job for you both. Are you listening?"

Again, the boys nodded, and he continued.

"I am going to Ciannachta with the army tonight," he said. "I am not sure how long I'll be gone, but when I am away, you will be in charge of your mother's safety. That means you remain in the cottage. That means you don't let anyone in, and you don't go out except to feed the animals. But you go right back in and lock the door. If you have to, you bring the cow and calf inside the cottage to keep them safe, because another one of those *fiacla nathair* may come back, and I won't be here to fight it off. Do you understand me so far?"

The boys had grown serious because he had. "We will protect mother and Slane," Mattock said. "They will be safe."

"Good," Conor said. "But now that I think of it, I think you need to bring everything inside the cottage to keep it safe—the chickens, the cows, everything. There's the small room that Padraigan sleeps in, and they can all go in there. I know it's going to smell, but I just don't think it'll be safe leaving them out at night if I'm not around, so I think you need to go about preparing that room for them. Put hay in there. Make a place for the chickens to go, and then put them in there. Move firewood and grass and everything you need for the animals inside so you don't have to go out while I'm gone."

Destry, with Slane on her hip, had been listening. "How long do you think you'll be gone?"

Conor shrugged. "No more than a couple of days, I think," he said. "This is temporary, but I think it's necessary just to be safe."

Destry felt better knowing that he didn't plan to be away very long. Somehow, what he was doing didn't seem so dangerous if it was just a day or two, and that brought her a false illusion of comfort. She was looking for details like that to cling to.

"But what about going to the bathroom?" she asked. "If we have to urinate, we have to come out to the outhouse."

"That should be okay during the daytime," he said. "But travel in twos—one watching out for the other. Mattock, I will leave swords and clubs, so you will be armed. You can come out here during the day to relieve yourselves, but at night, you're going to have to use a pot. Nobody goes outside at night, at least until I get back."

Everyone nodded solemnly because Conor's tone suggested this was a command and not simply a plea for cooperation. When he looked at everyone to make sure they understood, he pointed toward the corral.

"Go," he said. "And hurry, because the army is leaving soon. I want you to be done before I go."

Mattock and Devlin took off at a run while Slane, now sleepy, laid his head on Destry's shoulder. Conor turned to the pair, smiling at Slane and putting a gentle hand on the boy's head.

"Put him down for a nap," he said. "I need you with me. We have to make this place rock solid before I leave."

Destry looked at him curiously. "What do you want me to

do?"

"Gather water, mostly," he said. "If you are going to be bottled up in that cottage, you're going to need water. You'll need firewood. And I want to take a look at the door to make sure the bolt is solid. I'd like to secure the windows better than they are, too."

Destry turned for the cottage, carrying Slane, as Conor headed off to gather whatever he needed to gather. By the time she'd put Slane down for a nap, Conor had returned with a few men, and they were going over the three windows in the cottage—one in each of the rooms—and the front door.

Padraigan, who had been with the men, returned also and explained that the cottage had already been built when she took up residence. Whoever had lived there had basically left everything behind, which explained why there was furniture and beds and even dried food. The cottage windows had shutters that were shut at night, but Conor wanted them, and the door, reinforced. As Destry went to find enough buckets and things to collect water, Conor and his men went to work on the doors and windows.

The hammering and work went on most of the afternoon. Everyone had their tasks, and they completed them to the best of their ability. Mattock and Devlin moved the cow and calf into the small chamber that Padraigan had been using, making sure to secure the animals and give them lots of grass and water. The chickens went into the same room, wandering around and staying clear of the cow and her calf. It was hilarious watching the boys, determined to please their father, chase the chickens all over the place before finally catching them.

The afternoon flew by.

As sunset approached, Conor and the men had succeeded

in reinforcing the door and the shutters. They were quite sturdy now, and as the sun began to go down, the encampment began to buzz with activity. They were getting ready to head out, and Conor was expected to join them, so he herded everyone into the cottage and stood at the door as if to block them from trying to get out again.

He pulled Destry to him. "I'm told the castle is about ten miles to the east," he said. "It'll take us a few hours to get there, is my guess, but we need to move slowly and carefully. Bradaigh and Auley have already spoken about how they plan to take the castle."

"How?" Destry asked.

A twinkle came to his eye. "You don't remember this, but when you were fleeing the castle after Geric invaded, you took the boys and fled through the drainage system," he said. "That's how Bradaigh and Auley plan to get in—the same way you got out."

Destry was trying very hard to be calm and confident about the whole thing. "Then no big fights right off the bat?" she said. "Like, no storming the citadel or anything?"

Conor shook his head. "No," he said. "We'll send men in through the drainage pipes, and they'll get to the gate and open it for the rest of us. There's supposed to be very few men guarding it, which is why we needed to move so quickly. My guess is that we'll take it with very little bloodshed if that's the case. So let's hope it's still the case."

"Let's hope."

The noise from the encampment was growing as men pre-pared to move out. They could both hear it. Conor looked at Destry as if he wanted to say something meaningful and poignant, but she could see he was having a difficult time.

Maybe it was because he thought *she* was having such a hard time, so she knew she had to be tough. She didn't want him to worry about her when he needed to focus on himself and whatever he needed to do ahead.

Smiling, she stood on her tiptoes and kissed him. "Go on," she said. "We'll be fine. But if you get back here in a couple of days and I'm climbing the walls because of too much cow shit and restless kids, you'll just have to deal with it."

He started laughing. "I will apologize to you when I see you for keeping you cooped up with that mob."

"You'd better," she said, grinning. "Now, go. I'll be fine. But you take care of yourself, Conor the Red. You have a family who loves you and needs you back."

He smiled, leaning forward to kiss her again. "A wife I love madly," he murmured. "I'll be back."

"I know."

With that, he headed off toward the encampment. Destry smiled bravely, watching him go, even waving to him when he turned around to look at her. But once he was through the foliage and into the encampment, he disappeared, and she closed the door, bolting it.

Then, and only then, did she shed tears for his safety.

*Come back to me, my love.*

She had no idea what she would do if he didn't.

# CHAPTER FIFTEEN

*Somewhere north, near Belfast*

"YOU MUST RISE, great lord. Awaken."

The tent made of animal skins and roughly woven woolen fabric smelled like animals had roosted. It smelled rank, of blood and sweat and the disgusting mess that men made when they cared nothing for what people thought of them. A horrible smell that went beyond what men normally emitted, but something tinged with death.

*Evil.*

Geric the Usurper stirred upon his bed.

He hated the name, but that was the name not only his mercenaries had given him, but also the people of Ciannachta. He shouted at his people, repeatedly, demanding they call him Geric the Brave, but no one would. Even the mercenaries laughed at him when he told them to simply call him the king. They would speak among themselves in their own language, laughing at Geric but trying to pretend they weren't. He had hired them and was still paying them, so as long as the money held out, they'd continue to show him the respect he'd paid for.

But even that was questionable.

"Great lord? Rise. We must speak."

Geric heard that voice again, and he groaned, opening an eye to see Olc standing a few feet away, lighting an oil lamp. His *draoi*. Wizard. The old man with the impossibly black hair for his age and a face that looked like the sole of an old shoe. He had black eyebrows that grew upward, making him look as if a strong wind was blowing him right in the face. Wearing robes that were probably older than Geric was, he stood in the weak light of the lamp.

"What is it?" Geric groaned. "What's so important that you felt compelled to awaken me?"

Olc shuffled over to a stool near Geric's bed. He pulled it up to the side of the bed and lowered his boney body upon it.

"Are you alert enough so that we might have a conversation?" he asked.

Geric opened both eyes and looked at him. "Do I not look awake?"

"You do," Olc said. "I simply want to be certain. It would seem we have some concerning news."

"What news?"

"Your brother has returned."

Geric stopped rubbing his face and yawning. Suddenly, he was quite alert, and he looked at Olc suspiciously. "What's this you say?" he said. "That is impossible. Who told you such lies?"

"My ravens."

"Your ravens are mad," Geric muttered, now sitting up and swinging his legs over the side of the bed. "And they are birds. Men do not speak to birds."

"I do," Olc said, cocking one of those wild eyebrows. "You do not call the ravens mad when they tell you something you wish to hear. Now you do not wish to hear that your brother has returned, but he has. My ravens have seen him."

"Impossible."

"He has reclaimed his army, and they took control of Cashel Cian two nights ago."

Geric looked at him as if he'd lost his mind. "Are you serious about this?"

"I am."

"But his return is impossible! You assured me!"

Olc watched his young king work himself up into a state, which wasn't unusual with Geric. He was always in one agitated state or another.

"It is the doing of the white witch," Olc said. "Her powers are formidable. I warned you of this. I told you that I could send them to the nether realm, but it was possible they could be brought back. I told you that repeatedly. It seems that they have, indeed, returned."

Geric was starting to realize that this wasn't some fever dream. Olc was completely serious. Disbelief turned to shock.

"Then Conor is truly returned?" Geric said with awe. "He's come back from the nether realm?"

"He has come back, and his queen with him."

Geric's jaw dropped. "*She* is returned also?"

"They must have found one another."

Geric stood up from the bed. He was so astonished that he wasn't watching where he was going and tripped over a shoe on the ground. He kicked it, stubbed his toe, and cursed. Then he whirled to Olc angrily.

"He has my castle now?" he nearly shouted. "By all the saints… I should have killed him when I had the chance. I should have killed him and made her watch it all. Then I would have kept her chained to my bed and fucked her every night until she bore my sons, time and time again, so I could breed my brother right out of her. And the sons... my dear little nephews... I should have killed them, too. I told you that!"

Olc was used to Geric's mostly irrational ravings. "If you had killed the children, the village would have risen against you," he pointed out. "If you had killed your brother's men, the same would have happened. You know your brother and his family are well-loved. If you had killed them all, everyone in Ciannachta would have risen against you and your mercenaries. Banishing your brother and his wife and allowing the rest to go in peace, so long as they did not resist you, was the best you could do if you wanted to rule unopposed. I know you understand that."

Geric was seething by the time the old wizard was finished. He stormed over to the tent flap and bellowed for the commander of the mercenaries before returning his attention to Olc.

"I understand that I listened to you when I should not have," he growled. "This is *your* fault. My brother has returned, and now he has my castle!"

Olc didn't change expression, but he lifted a hand, and suddenly, Geric was on the ground. He tried to get up, but an unseen hand to his neck seemed to be pinning him to the ground. He fought it for a moment, looking to Olc in outrage.

"Release me!" he said hoarsely. "By what right do you hold me down?"

Olc still hadn't changed expression. "I earned the right when I helped you overthrow your brother and take his throne," he said in an oddly loud voice that seemed to echo off the soft walls of the tent. "You seem to forget that you would not be king had I not helped you. I do not ask for much, great lord, but I ask for your respect. I have done much for you."

Geric's anger cooled, mostly because he knew that he was in a bad position. Olc could snap his neck without lifting a finger if he wished. He'd seen it before.

"I did not mean to be disrespectful," he said calmly. "My brother's reappearance naturally has me unbalanced. You would not hold that against me."

Olc lowered his hand, and suddenly, Geric was no longer restrained. He sat up, slowly, as the old wizard eyed him.

"It is shocking, but not unexpected," Olc said. "The white witch is powerful. Somehow, she was able to break the curse, and now your brother has returned. That means we cannot retake Cian the way we took it before. They will not be lazy a second time. I will admit, however, that *we* were lazy to leave so few guards at the fortress. I am told your brother took it with no trouble at all. Worse still, those we left behind used to serve your brother. They welcomed him back without resistance."

"You mean we have lost the army we left behind."

"That is exactly what I mean."

Geric sighed heavily. "Then what do we do?" he said. "Conor is not stupid. He will be on his guard, and he will expect me to take his throne again. What shall we do?"

Olc stood up. "I have been thinking on just that issue," he said. "You see, we need Cian. The castle must be held against the white witch and her magic. She stands for the freedom and kindness of men. Her and her kind have long been my enemy. If you wish for conquest and riches, and the continued alliance with the Northmen, then we must have Cashel Cian. We must get it back. But we must be clever about it."

"I am listening."

"Great lord." A tall, rugged-looking man with a crown of

wild, dark hair suddenly stood in the doorway. He spoke with a heavy accent. "I am told you have summoned me. What do you require?"

Geric, still on the ground, looked at the man. "Come in, Ranak," he said. "I have just been told that my brother has returned and retaken Cashel Cian. Olc is about to tell us how to reclaim it. I want you to listen, since this will be your task."

Ranak Hammer Jaw, the leader of the mercenaries, looked at Olc in astonishment. "The Red has returned?" he said. "But he was banished. I saw you do it myself."

Olc nodded patiently. "As I pointed out to your king, the white witch has somehow brought him back," he said. "My spies tell me that the wife has returned also."

Ranak sighed sharply as he looked at Geric. "I told you we should have killed them."

Geric held up a hand. "We have been through that already," he said. "Now, listen to Olc. He has been thinking on the problem. Let us hear what he has to say."

Ranak wasn't receptive. "What is there to say?" he demanded. "Conor's army is no match for mine. We will destroy them!"

Geric wagged a finger at him. "If you do not stop shouting, you will end up on the ground like me," he said. "Shut your lips and listen. Olc will speak."

Ranak may be reckless and murderous, but he wasn't a fool. He knew what the wizard was capable of. Keeping his mouth shut was difficult for him, but he did. He faced the old man, arms folded defensively across his chest and an unhappy expression on his face.

Olc knew Ranak well. He knew the man only spoke with his sword. There was no such thing as a negotiation or strategy. He eyed the big, smelly Northman.

"If you do not wish to be destroyed when the white witch waves her hand in your direction, then we must show cunning in this situation," he said. "My spies tell me that Conor holds Cashel Cian, but they also tell me that the wife and sons have come to live at the castle as well. They are back at Cian like they were before, as if nothing is amiss. It is well known that Conor loves his family and understandably wants them with him. Be clear—that is his weakness, and that is where we shall force him to surrender Cian without bloodshed."

Ranak snorted. "Ridiculous," he said. "I will not hide in the shadows looking for a chance to kill one of his children. I am a warrior; I do not kill children."

"I did not say kill," Olc said. "And I did not say children. Ask yourselves this—what was the one thing Conor loved more than his castle, his kingdom, his anything? What does he value above all else?"

Geric didn't hesitate. "His wife," he said. "I had a taste of the woman, and I understand why. She is a woman beyond compare."

"Then it is his wife we shall target," Olc said. "Not the castle, not even Conor. That is where we made the mistake before—we gave her a choice in the matter. She could stay with you to save her husband or she could go with him, and she chose to go with him. This time, there will be no choice. Queen Etain shall be our key to Cashel Cian."

Geric shook his head. "It will not work," he said. "She will be well guarded. How are we to get to her?"

Olc could see that both Geric and Ranak were doubtful. "We will think of a way," he said. "You could go to battle against Conor, but he will be ready for you. Do you think he will not fight back with everything he has? Cashel Cian is a powerful fortress. Some say unbreakable. He will lock the gates and stay there while we lay siege. This will cost time and money, and meanwhile, Ciannachta will be destroyed. There will be nothing left. You will be a king of ashes. I am telling you that there is a smarter way if you wish to keep your kingdom intact."

Geric looked at Ranak, who simply rolled his eyes and looked away. The Northman hated doing anything other than a full-on attack. It was in his blood. But it wasn't in Geric's blood—he was willing to listen if it meant keeping the city of Ciannachta intact.

He returned his attention to Olc. "My Northman friend loves death and destruction," he said. "He does not like sneaking around."

"Do you want your cashel returned to you in one piece?"

"I want it back the way I left it."

"Then listen well," Olc said. "We use stealth. We infiltrate the city and we watch the castle. Eventually, Conor will open the gates. His scouts will tell him that your army has disbanded, because we are going to split. Some will go to the sea, some to the land. We will regroup at Ciannachta and stay to the shadows, watching for the opportunity to capture Queen Etain. Once we do, we send a missive to Conor—his kingdom for his wife. You know what his decision will be, so he will take his wife and leave, and we reclaim Ciannachta. Why would you do it any other way?"

Geric had to admit that the thought of sneaking into Ciannachta and abducting his brother's wife seemed less dangerous—and maybe even more interesting—than rushing in and laying siege. He could see what the old wizard was driving at.

"We use the element of surprise, do we?" he said.

Olc nodded. "That is the most brutal way of all," he said. "When they least expect it."

"And then what happens to my brother after that? I do not want him running free. He will raise another army to defeat me."

Olc conceded the point. "Then we do what we should have done before," he said. "We kill them all, and your throne will be secure. Your subjects will hate you, but what's a kingdom without a little hate?"

Geric liked that plan. He liked the idea of slinking around, waiting for the right moment to pounce. He liked the idea of seeing defeat in his brother's eyes when he realized he had to surrender his kingdom for the safety of his wife.

And then they'd be done with it once and for all.

With a nod, he agreed to the plan, and Ranak quit the tent in disgust. He didn't like the old wizard, and, truth be told, he didn't like Geric, either. The man was weak-willed and foolish. The only reason Ranak and his men served Geric was because he had mostly drained the treasury to pay them. They were all quite rich because of Geric. But when the money ran out, so would they.

But that brought about a problem.

The return of Geric's brother now put an obstacle between them and the last of the funds in Ciannachta's treasury. They were counting on that money. And that stupid wizard wanted to reclaim the castle in stealth. That wasn't something Ranak wanted to do. Perhaps they'd agree to separate as the wizard suggested, and perhaps they'd even all go to Ciannachta the way they were supposed to—some by land, some by sea. Given his ships were moored near Belfast because he'd sent them along the coast to assist in the current raiding, all he had to do was send them back south. He'd give the command, and his men would attack from both the sea and land, and Conor the Red would be disposed of once and for all.

The old wizard wanted to play games. Ranak was going to make the final move.

When all was said and done, he'd leave Geric with a throne but a raided and burned kingdom. That, for Ranak, was the final victory. In the end, he didn't care about a stupid Irish king. He only cared about his purse.

Geric thought he was doing the betraying when it came to his brother—but Ranak was about to turn the tables.

The victory would be sweet indeed.

# CHAPTER SIXTEEN

*Six weeks later*

MATTOCK WAS HAVING a difficult time staying on his new pony.

It was a clear day at Cashel Cian, with gulls crying overhead and a steady sea breeze. The smell of salt was heavy in the air. Conor, Destry, Bradaigh, and Auley were in the enormous bailey of the cashel, watching Mattock and Devlin ride the new ponies that Auley had brought for them. Mattock's was white and black, while Devlin's was as red as his father's hair. That pony's name was Ghrian, which basically meant *sunny*, while Mattock's horse was named Fionn, pronounced Finn, after a great mythical warrior.

Fionn was giving his new owner quite a time.

"Thank God for Auley and Bradaigh," Conor muttered to Destry, watching the warriors as they gave the boys helpful advice. "I have no idea how to teach them about riding a horse."

Destry snorted. "I know, you sorry cowboy."

"I'd get them both killed."

"Let the Irish knights do what they do best, eh?"

Conor couldn't disagree. He stood back and pretended he

knew everything that Bradaigh and Auley were teaching his boys. He pretended he knew everything about everything, and in a sense, he really did. There was no one in the world in this period in history who was as highly educated as Conor was, so he really *did* know everything about everything.

Except riding horses. That was where he was admittedly faulty.

"When I took the boys into the city yesterday, we visited the avenue of the smithies where Auley used to work," he said. "The commerce seems to be picking up, which is a good sign."

"Anything interesting happening on the smithy street?" Destry asked.

"Mattock saw a saddle there he was in love with."

"A saddle with a blacksmith?"

"Right."

"Doesn't the tanner make saddles?"

"Usually, but the smithy was putting iron stirrups on it. It was a gorgeous leather good."

"And Mattock begged for it?"

"He promised he would work in the stables the rest of his life if I would buy it for him."

Destry chuckled. "And you're thinking about it?"

Conor shrugged. "Maybe," he said. "He's convinced he can ride better with it."

"What did you tell him?"

"That I would think about it."

Destry continued chuckling. Conor was a sucker for his boys, so she suspected that if he hadn't bought the saddle already, he would soon. Also, his scientist's brain had been going crazy with all of the Medieval processes and methods the city presented to him. Everything he'd ever learned in an academic setting, now with a practical application. He was seeing it as it happened.

A college professor's dream.

But it was more than that.

Six weeks after their arrival through the portal at Dowth, Conor could hardly remember the life "before." The life where he taught students and studied ancient history, where he'd changed his surname to Da Derga, much to the chagrin of his father. The life Destry wasn't a part of. He'd never felt particularly lonely, but he had felt solitary. Like something was missing.

Now, he knew what it was.

The woman laughing at his soft side had come to mean more to him than anything in the universe. She was sexy as hell, beautiful, brilliant, and determined. She was also funny, and had him laughing constantly. She lit him up in so many ways that it was difficult to put his finger on one thing in particular that made him love her. It was everything. Everything about her was endearing to him, and he was her slave. No doubt about it. She snapped her fingers, and he jumped as high as she wanted him to.

The past six weeks had been an indoctrination to the life he'd always wanted.

Deep down, he'd been meant for nothing else.

The siege of Cashel Cian those weeks ago had been an astonishingly easy thing. On that night of nights, Conor and his six hundred men had quietly entered the village while Auley and Bradaigh took ten young men, skinny and wiry, and ordered them into the drainage pipes beneath the cashel. They'd come out the other side, into the bailey and stable area, and gone right to the gates without any resistance at all.

By the time those guarding the castle realized what had happened, Conor and his men were inside, and they gathered everyone in the bailey. Conor thought he'd have to convince them to join him or die, but once they saw Conor, there were tears and cheers. Their high king had returned, and Conor had an instant army of over a thousand men, including the ones he'd brought with him.

It had been as simple as that.

Once they were inside and in command, word began to spread that the high king had returned, and the villagers turned out in droves to see him. Conor had stood at the gatehouse, watching the crowds below, the crying and joyful shouting, realizing what his return meant to these people. Padraigan had talked about a darkness settling over the land under Geric's rule, and how the people were suffering, but now he was seeing the proof of it.

His people were thrilled to have him back.

He was thrilled to *be* back.

His first order of business after he secured the castle had been to return for Destry and the boys, and he did so within two days. He brought her, the children, the calf and cow, and the chickens and transported them all to Cashel Cian. Destry's first view of a Medieval city, the sights and smells, had been a bit overwhelming, and once they reached the castle, a lady by the name of Fallon had greeted her with tears.

As it turned out, Fallon used to be Etain's lady-in-waiting. The boys knew her and were excited to see her, but Destry didn't know the woman from Adam. Still, she was very kind and sweet, and given that the boys knew her and loved her, Destry accepted her.

Sort of. She'd never had a lady-in-waiting before, and Fallon's role was as an advisor and confidante, and even a servant. Destry didn't have to lift a finger when Fallon was around, which was both odd and slightly cool.

Life, from that point, grew more fascinating.

So much had happened over the past six weeks, not the least of which were public programs that Destry had started. In the wake of Geric's rule and the fact that he stole so much from his own villagers, or allowed his mercenaries to, some people were literally starving. Very quickly, Destry realized that, and she set up a rudimentary soup kitchen.

That took care of the starving, but both she and Conor knew they had to get the stalled economic engine of the village moving so people could feed themselves. Conor discovered there wasn't much left in the cashel's treasury, so he was careful with what they had. He fronted farmers money for seed, and he also loaned money to bakers and merchants for things like grain and stock, and whatever else they needed to start doing business again.

Slowly, the wheels of the engine began to turn.

Word of Conor's return had spread to the outskirts, and those who had fled when Geric took the throne now began to come back. There was an entire street that had silversmiths and metalworkers, separate from the smithies, and that had dwindled to two or three people struggling to do business. The Northmen had stolen anything of value from these men, so it was difficult to do business with precious metals when one didn't have anything to sell. Conor helped them by giving them money to purchase what they needed. It wasn't much, but it was enough to get started.

Three weeks after Conor's return, business as usual was beginning to happen. Six weeks later, things were ramping up nicely, and they were already starting to repay the loans.

Conor couldn't have been more pleased.

Prosperity, and peace, were slowly returning to Ciannachta.

And that meant two new ponies for Mattock and Devlin. Slane had no interest in horses, but he did have a fascination with carts and wagons, so much so that Conor made a little wagon for him to play with.

It also meant Destry was settling into her new life, or at least becoming accustomed to it, but she wasn't nearly as comfortable with it as Conor was. In fact, for her it had been a curious and sometimes difficult six weeks.

Conor had promised her once that he'd make sure she had acceptable toiletries because of the things he'd learned to make, and he'd kept that promise for the most part. He worked very hard at making sure she had everything she could possibly want for her lips and skin. He found an apothecary in town, a man who had ingredients from all over the known world—and a man that Destry became quite familiar with. He had balms to soothe the lips and skin made from beeswax and butter, along with other oils he wouldn't divulge because they were some proprietary secret. Conor thought he used almond oil or even animal fat in some of his pomades—but whatever he used, Destry had balm for her lips and oil for her skin that soaked in and made it quite soft. It wasn't lotion, but it worked the same way. Better, in some cases.

Face cream or moisturizer was pretty much the same thing. Whatever she put on her body, she put on her face, and her skin was always dewy and soft because of it. Auley, being a smithy, fashioned a razor for her so she could shave her legs and armpits, but she'd cut herself a couple of times before she got the hang of a straight razor. Soap came from the same apothecary, castile-type soap that came from Spain and was made with olive oil. It was great on her hair and, with an ale rinse, had transformed it into something soft and wonderful. Auley had even made her a curling iron, something she could put in the fire and heat up, so although she didn't have all of the modern conveniences and hair products, she had enough that worked for her.

Slowly but surely, life for Destry was balancing out.

Except for one thing.

She was pregnant.

Honestly, she wasn't surprised. She and Conor had sex all the time—and in any place of convenience—and the fact that her birth control pills hadn't come with her when she was thrust into Medieval Ireland really should have made her more careful. But she'd met a man she was deeply in love with, and it was clear she'd had his children before, even if she didn't remember, so making love to Conor without protection was the most natural thing in the world. She'd done it freely and happily and lustily.

And his seed had taken root, as they say.

But he didn't know yet. In fact, Destry was only coming to figure it out herself because she hadn't had a period since arriving in Ireland. Her breasts were swelling and tender, and her belly below her navel seemed to be firm to the touch. She wasn't showing at all, but the symptoms were there.

As a nurse, she was clinical about it, but as a pregnant woman soon to give birth in Medieval times, she was scared to death. She knew what could go wrong. But, as Conor told her the night he laid siege to Cashel Cian, he didn't think they'd been brought back to Ciannachta only to die. She hoped that also pertained to giving birth.

At some point, she was going to have to tell him.

Maybe a day like this was perfect for it. Things were calm, and there were no real worries at the moment. No business to conduct. Conor was out in the middle of the boys as they rode their ponies in a circle, standing next to Bradaigh as he told Devlin to keep his heels down in the stirrups. Destry was still standing outside of the circling ponies, watching the men as they involved themselves with two boys on two ponies. Mattock was much better at riding than Devlin was, but Devlin was trying his hardest to keep up.

Destry smiled as she watched Devlin, the middle boy who was so eager to please. She had a bit of a soft spot for the boy who sometimes referred to himself in the third person as "your Devlin." As she watched him try very hard to get his pony to turn around, Conor broke away from Bradaigh and headed back in her direction.

"Something has occurred to me," he said as he approached. "I think I'm going to have a carriage built for you. You need to have something comfortable to travel in."

Destry looked at him in surprise. "Travel where?" she said. "Are we going somewhere?"

Conor shook his head. "Not now," he said. "But there may be times when we do. Do you really want to ride a horse everywhere? You're a queen, Des. A queen should have queenly transportation."

She grinned. "I haven't really thought about it," she said. "I like riding horses, but if we go someplace far, I don't know if I could sit in the saddle for twelve hours."

"Exactly," he said. "I'll have a carriage made with a couple of benches that we can put cushions on. Or maybe something that kind of slopes back so you'll be more comfortable when you ride. Maybe the boys can join you in it. It'll probably be safer for them."

*No time like the present,* Destry thought. "When you make that carriage, you'd better have them put a baby bed in it."

He looked at her, brow furrowed. "What for?" he said. "Slane is too big to be in a baby bed. In fact, I want to talk to you about him now that you've brought it up. I think he's a little too attached to you. Not that he shouldn't be, because you are his mother and he is young, but maybe we need to start having him spend more time with his brothers and less with you. Padraigan says he's going to be five years old next month. He's no longer a baby, Des."

Destry looked at him as if he was the densest man on the planet. "That's not what I meant, you big dummy," she said. "I meant we're going to have a baby. You didn't get that clue at all."

Conor's eyes widened. Then his jaw dropped. He started to speak, but he ended up choking, coughing furiously as he went to Destry and pulled her into his arms. She kept laughing as he hugged her and tried to recover.

"Oh my God," he said, sputtering. "Are you serious?"

"I wouldn't joke about something like this."

He pulled back to look at her, absolutely stunned. "I didn't mean that," he said. "I just meant… Hell, I don't know what I meant. It was stupid of me to say it. I just… Are you *sure*?"

She was enjoying his shock. "All of my nurse training leads me to believe I am," she said. "Think about it, Conor—have we ever used birth control? And we screw like rabbits, not to put it too crudely. But we do. All the time. Something was bound to happen."

He just stared at her in wonder. Then, as she watched, his

eyes began to fill with tears. "Oh, fuck," he said, blinking. "A baby. You're *really* going to have a baby."

Destry laughed softly and put her arms around him. "That's a good thing, right?" she said. "Our first baby together. Or, at least, the first one we remember. It'll be fine. I feel good. Everything will be fine, I promise."

He hugged her so tightly that he was squeezing the breath from her. "Sorry," he muttered. "I'm just overwhelmed. I never thought I'd ever have a child with a woman I love so much. I mean, I know the boys are ours, but we don't remember them being born. At least, not the experience of it. But this… you said it. This is the first baby I'll remember. And it's with you. It's the best thing that's ever happened to me."

Destry had her arms around his neck, her hands on the back of his head. "Good," she said. "You're happy. I wasn't sure for a moment if you were or not."

"I am," he said, pulling back to look her in the eye. "So happy. You can't even imagine how happy."

"Me too," she said. "But I will admit I'm a little leery of giving birth in Medieval times. No hospital, no modern medicine. We need to find the best midwife in Ireland."

"We will," he said firmly. "I'll talk to Padraigan. She knows everything about everything. You didn't tell her, did you?"

Destry shook her head. "This was your news and no one else's," she said. "I wasn't going to tell anyone before I told you."

He was starting to beam. "Thank you," he said. Then he kissed her sweetly. "I just want a healthy wife and a healthy baby. I don't care about anything else."

"We'll be fine, both of us."

He kissed her again. Then he started giggling. Coming from

a man his size, it was hilariously misplaced. But then someone called for him, and he was forced to let her go as Auley motioned to him from the gatehouse. He headed off, but not before whispering, "I love you," to her.

Heart full of joy, Destry watched him go.

"You told him, did you?"

Destry turned to see Padraigan standing next to her. She cocked her head curiously. "Told him what?"

"About the child you carry."

Destry sighed and shook her head in resignation. "I should have known that you would already know," she said. "*How* did you know?"

Padraigan smiled. "Because you have a look about you that speaks of new life," she said. "It is the look of love, my lady. You love your husband so much that you are honored to bear his children. It gives you joy."

Destry thought it was a sweet way of putting it. "I suppose it does," she said. "But it's one of the things I don't remember. This will be my first child, at least the one I can recall. My training—before I came here—was in nursing. In healing. Giving birth is a wonderful yet dangerous thing, and I want to make sure the baby and I both survive it."

"Of course you do," Padraigan said. "And you shall. This daughter will survive."

Destry's hand instinctively went to her belly. "How do you know it is a girl?"

"Because she told me."

Destry couldn't help but chuckle. Sometimes Padraigan's mysticism was a little far out, but she hadn't been wrong yet. It was both unsettling and amazing.

"Oh?" Destry said. "What else did she tell you?"

"Her name is Anahera."

Destry's eyebrows lifted. "Anahera?" she said. Then she shrugged. "I like it. Very pretty."

"She is excited to meet you."

Destry smiled, hand on her belly. "I think she calls for a celebration," she said. "Let me head over to the kitchens and see what the cooks have for a party."

"This is cause for a celebration indeed."

As Destry headed off toward the kitchens of Cian, Padraigan watched her go. Then she looked to the sky, seeing a large raven riding the drafts overhead. She watched it for a moment before lifting her hand, just a little. The bird abruptly went sideways, then pushed across the sky and back out to sea, as if a strong breeze had caught it and swept it away.

But Padraigan knew differently, because the peace around them was a false peace.

She knew it wouldn't last.

Something dark was coming.

# CHAPTER SEVENTEEN

"**M**AMA, *NO!*"

Destry was trying to dress Slane for the evening meal. Usually, he remained in his chamber and ate with a nurse, an old woman named Freeda who had once looked after Conor when he was a young boy—or at least a young boy in his previous life—but on this evening with the pregnancy being celebrated, Destry wanted him downstairs in the hall.

That smelly, smoky, dank, and damp hall. The place smelled like shit. Literally, like shit. She had no idea what it had smelled like before Geric took command, but it certainly smelled horrible after he left. Destry had spent six damn weeks trying to get that smell out of there.

Meanwhile, they were supposed to eat in it.

But Slane wasn't cooperating with her. Destry was trying to put a clean pair of hose on the lad, but he wanted nothing to do with it. His skinny legs were kicking as she tried to dress him.

"Slane," she said steadily. "Stop kicking. Let me get these on you."

He whined and rolled onto his stomach. Destry flipped him onto his back again. As this was going on, Mattock came rushing into the chamber.

"Mother!" he said. "Look! This has torn. I cannot eat with a torn tunic!"

Destry had both of Slane's legs, holding them so he couldn't kick her. She looked at the tiny tear in Mattock's tunic, in the seam. Somewhere behind her, Devlin was running around looking for something clean to wear. It was chaos in the chambers of the little princes, a normal moment in time with the family she never knew she had until six weeks ago. Destry had gone from clubs and VIP rooms to a Medieval castle and three boys that demanded all of her time. An instant family that, in fact, wasn't so instant.

Sometimes she looked at moments like these and couldn't believe the change.

But she loved every minute of it.

"Let me get Slane dressed and I'll help you with that," she told Mattock. "It doesn't look that bad."

She returned her attention to Slane as Mattock looked at the tear in distress. "I cannot wear it like this," he said, catching sight of Devlin. His eyes narrowed. "He did it. He tried to grab it, but I got it first. This is *his* fault."

The next thing Destry knew, Mattock threw a punch at Devlin and connected. As the boys went down in a pile, Conor came into the room and saw what was happening.

"Mattock," he snapped. "What are you doing to your brother?"

Startled at the sound of his father's voice, Mattock leapt to his feet. "He tore my tunic," he said, pointing to the small tear. "I was punishing him."

At least it was an honest answer, but Conor lifted his eyebrows in disapproval. "If anyone is going to punish Devlin, it will be me," he said. "Do you understand? It's not your job—I mean, it's not your *right* to punish him. It's my right."

He had to put it in terms that Mattock would understand. The word "job" didn't mean anything to him, but the word "right" where it pertained to permission did.

Mattock understood, all too well. "Aye, Dada."

"I don't want to see you doing this again, and most especially not in front of your mother."

"I won't."

"You had better keep to that vow, because I can take the pony away just as easily as give it," Conor said, looking between both boys now. "Do you understand me, Dev? Treat your brother with respect and things like this won't happen. Same goes for you, Matt—treat your brother with respect. Brothers should always love one another and support one another, not be enemies. They should be the one person you can depend on."

The boys nodded, but without much enthusiasm. Conor could see that Mattock, who always liked to look his best, was genuinely upset about the rip in his clothing. Devlin was a slob, but Mattock wasn't. It was one of the personality differences he'd come to discover over the weeks about his boys. They were so different, yet so alike.

Conor inspected the tear for a moment. "Your mother can fix it, I think," he said. "Des? Did you see this?"

Destry was still wrestling with Slane, but she stopped and tossed the hose onto the bed. "I did," she said, frustrated. "I'll fix the tear if you dress Slane. He's kicked me twice."

Conor picked up the hose, eyeing Slane as the boy lay on the bed and gazed up at him apprehensively.

Happy to be away from the kicking child, Destry went to

Mattock and took a good look at the tear. "That's easy to fix," she told him. "Come into my room. My sewing things are in there."

As Destry and Mattock left the chamber, Padraigan slipped in. Conor was standing over Slane and telling the lad he'd better not kick any more, which seemed to do the trick, because he managed to get the boy dressed and onto his feet. As he ran to find his shoes, Conor watched him go.

"I keep thinking he looks like my father," he muttered. Then he shrugged. "Whatever genes are in my family, they're evidently strong."

Padraigan looked at him curiously. "What do you mean, great lord?"

Conor scratched his forehead, realizing she didn't have a clue what he was talking about. "Heredity," he said. "Some families have the same nose or the same eyes. My family seems to have big heads."

Padraigan smiled. "That is because it is filled with great thoughts."

Conor snorted as he looked at her. "I would like to think that's true," he said. "Who knows? Maybe it is."

Padraigan's smile faded. "In your case, it is, great lord," she said. "In your brother's case, he is only filled with ruthless ambition. It is about your brother that I have come."

Conor grew serious. "What about him?"

Padraigan waited until Slane found his shoes and rushed across the corridor to his parents' chamber where Destry was.

When the boy was gone, she spoke quietly. "I believe your brother is nearby," she said. "I have been seeing much raven sign."

"The birds that spy?"

"Aye," she said. "Now that we are at Cian, there is no way to hide from them, but they come. I saw one earlier today. Your brother surely knows that you have returned by now."

"I've had the castle for six weeks. He's had six weeks to find that out."

"I'm sure he knew the very first day we were here," she said. "He is undoubtedly planning how to reclaim the castle."

Conor frowned. "We send scouts out daily," he said. "No one has reported an army approaching."

Padraigan shook her head. "I do not think he will bring an army to your gates," she said. "I have been having dreams of a great mist. I know there is danger in the mist, but I cannot see it. I believe that is a sign of your brother—you cannot see him, but the danger is there."

Conor took her seriously. She'd been right all along about everything else, so he had no reason to doubt her. "Then what do we do?" he asked.

"Be cautious," she said. "Keep the gates closed. Keep your men armed. Geric knows he cannot bring his army to tear down the walls because you will fight him, and then the prize of Cashel Cian will be destroyed and he will have nothing. It would, perhaps, be wise to reinforce the city walls. They are wooden and they burn. But to build walls of rock—that would greatly protect the city."

Conor lifted an eyebrow. "Of course a rock wall would protect the city," he said. "But building a rock wall twenty feet high will take years. It wouldn't make any sense to do it now."

"Then arm your subjects," Padraigan said. "You have an army inside of Cian, but you have a greater army in the city. Arm every subject so they may fight for you when your brother decides to make his presence known. And I believe he will, great lord. You must be ready."

Conor sighed. Not that he didn't believe her, because he did, but he'd hoped that the peace they'd been experiencing would last a little while longer. He had Destry, his boys, and his castle. He was where he belonged. But the man who was his brother, a man he'd never even met, was still trying to get at him. Ruin him.

*Kill him.*

Padraigan was right. He had to be ready.

"Although I know it was futile, I was really hoping Geric just wouldn't come back at all," he said. "Honestly, I never understood why he left in the first place. He worked hard to take the castle and banish me, so why did he leave it the way he did?"

Padraigan lifted her slender shoulders. "He was always quite arrogant," she said. "Why shouldn't he leave? You were gone, and there was no threat. He took his Northmen to raid other parts of the countryside. The Northmen will only stay by his side if he continues to feed their coffers, and he knows that. Ciannachta is nearly destitute, so now, he is looting and pillaging like a Northman to keep his army happy."

"So he leaves his castle to raid other places," Conor said. "But I came back, and now the castle is mine again. And you really don't think he's going to bring that army back to my doorstep and burn the city down on his way in?"

Padraigan nodded. "He needs Ciannachta," she said. "If he destroys the city and the castle, he will have nothing, and the Northmen will leave. If he cannot provide, they will find someone who will."

That made sense to Conor. Geric's army comprised men who valued gold over loyalty. "I'm sorry, but I'm still kind of new at this," he said. "My education is extensive, but the reality of this world takes a little getting used to. It's been that way since the moment I returned. I feel like I have one foot in and one foot trying to get in, if that makes any sense. I don't feel like I'm completely immersed in this life and the way these people think yet. But I'll get there."

Padraigan smiled. "You are doing very well," she said. "You have already done so much for us, much more than any king could have done. I think that, perhaps, going to the nether region was a blessing, because you've returned with knowledge not of this world."

"What do you mean?"

Padraigan lifted her arms in a wide gesture. "Everything," she said. "You have taught the men fighting methods they did not know. You have taught them things about the Romans and the Greeks, and about someone named Edward the First and his warfare methods. You have helped the bakers bake bread again, and you've helped merchants purchase their wares. I think that this would not have been possible had you not been given such knowledge in the nether realm."

"So you're saying that my banishment was a good thing?"

"Perhaps," Padraigan said. "I have never asked you what the nether realm was like. Will you tell me something about it, perhaps when you are not terribly busy?"

He smiled faintly at her curiosity. "Sometime," he said. "But the nether realm was some kind of time-travel portal. It wasn't like I was floating out in space. I ended up over a thousand years in the future, and the world has changed a lot."

"Is it a good change?"

"Some of it," he said. "Medical advances are amazing. Things you can't even dream of. And things like sanitation and education—all good. But there are still wars. There is still famine. Some things never change. But the burial mound we came through—you said it was built by gods. Why did they build it?"

"To travel to other places, like you did," she said. "They came to us and took mates with them. The ancient mound has a name—it has long been called *Caomhnóir Ama*."

"Guardian of Time," Conor repeated. "And it can only be used on the solstice? When the sun is at the right angle?"

Padraigan nodded. "The light is what begins the machine of time," she said. "The light starts the working, like a spark feeds a piece of kindling."

"Then any bright light would start it?"

"It is possible, but for eons, only the sun's rays have fed it." Padraigan looked at him curiously. "What are you thinking? Are you thinking to try to return to the nether realm using another source of light?"

Conor shook his head. "I'm just trying to understand how it works," he said. "And who built it. You're *Tuath de.* Your people didn't build it?"

"Nay," Padraigan said. "It was here long before my kind came."

"Where did your kind come from?"

"Through the *Caomhnóir Ama.*"

It was becoming a circular conversation, one Conor hadn't intended to get into, but he found the subject absolutely fascinating. It was the scientist in him. He wanted to probe her more, but there wasn't time. Destry had organized a lovely feast in the hall and he didn't want to miss it—but before he went to find his wife and children, whom he could hear across the hall, he turned to Padraigan one last time.

"Maybe I'm not thinking of returning to the nether realm myself," he said, "but I wonder if we couldn't send Geric into it. Do to him what he did to me. Clearly, Olc had to open up the portal to send me and Destry through, so why not do the same thing to Geric? Can't you open it?"

It was an interesting question, one Padraigan thought seriously on. "If that is your wish, I can try," she said. "Olc has a spell to open the portal, for I saw it myself. I will think hard on the words he used."

"Then there's a way."

"There is a way."

A gleam came to Conor's eye. "Good."

With that, he left the room and went across the hall, where Slane was now jumping on the big bed he shared with Destry as she finished mending Mattock's tunic. Padraigan had followed, watching as Conor caught Slane mid-jump, grasped Devlin as the boy harassed his older brother, and hauled both of them out of the room so Destry could finish what she was doing.

As he headed down the stairs, he ran into Auley, who was coming up to see what was keeping him from the hall. But he could see right away what it was, considering Conor had his hands full of children. He grinned, watching Conor retreat down the stairs. When he turned to follow, however, he caught sight of Padraigan standing in the corridor.

He paused. "Are you coming?" he asked her.

Padraigan was going to wait for Destry, but she changed her mind when she saw Auley. Nodding, she permitted him to escort her down the stairs that led into another corridor. The passage, lit by fatted torches that burned dark, heavy smoke onto the stone ceiling, was empty for the most part.

Once they hit the bottom of the steps, Auley turned to her.

"I've not seen you all day," he said quietly. "I looked for you, but I did not see you."

Padraigan's pale cheeks took on a hint of color. "It is taking all of my attention to help our great lord," she said. "I have an important task."

"I know," he said as they started to walk again. "You have had an important task since I have known you."

"It is my duty."

"I know all too well."

Padraigan could hear a rebuke in that. "You have a duty as well," she said. "Our great lord needs you. I will tell you what I just told him—I have had dreams of a great mist that hides danger. I believe it means that Geric is near and the threat is approaching, but we cannot see it yet. He knows of Conor's return, and Geric will bring his Northmen."

Auley looked at her with concern. "A battle?"

Padraigan shook her head. "I do not think so," she said. "He knows that Conor has the love of the people and the love of his men. I also do not think he will destroy that which he desperately wants—Ciannachta."

"Then what will he do?"

"Stealth," Padraigan said. "We must watch every road into the city. We must watch every man who enters, every stranger. We must watch the sea. We must arm ourselves and the king's subjects. We must be ready for Geric, for if he chooses to come quietly, then he shall be met with fire."

Auley nodded. Padraigan was as good as any battle commander and, sometimes, far more trustworthy. The white witch was well respected by the men, and Auley most of all—but for him, it went deeper. He'd loved her since nearly the moment he first met her, and the separation of the past year had been difficult for him.

But the six weeks since they returned to Cian had been like heaven for him. It wasn't that they'd spoken frequently, because they hadn't. It wasn't as if they'd had time together in any way. It was simply being around her, and he swore that he wasn't going to let more time go by without expressing his feelings to her. She already knew how he felt, but he hadn't pressed himself. He never had. But in realizing how much he'd missed her over the past year, he knew he wasn't going to make that mistake again. He'd been looking for the right time to speak to her…

Perhaps if he waited, that time would never come.

"Whatever you command, my lady," he said softly. "I will do anything you command."

Padraigan didn't look at him. "The command against Geric will come from the king."

"I did not mean the command against Geric."

Padraigan fell silent for a few moments. Her instinct was to ignore it, but she simply couldn't. He was speaking of things better left unsaid.

"It has been a long time since you and I have spoken of such things, Auley," she said softly.

He was unapologetic. "You know how I feel," he said. "It has been a long time since we have seen one another, and I cannot keep it to myself."

"So you bring it up now?"

"I have been separated from you for a year," he said. "It was the worst year of my life."

They had reached the door that led to the bailey and the hall beyond. Padraigan came to a halt, gazing up at the man who was a good deal taller than she was. She knew that face, that body. She'd dreamed of it from time to time. She also knew the heart within, and it was a good heart.

One she longed for.

One she could not have.

"I am sorry for you," she said. "I have missed you also. But we have spoken of this, Auley. I cannot… You must have a wife, and it cannot be me."

"Then I shall have no wife."

She sighed sadly. "I have a destiny to preserve this kingdom and this king," she said. "It has been my destiny since I was young. When I am finished here, I shall return to my home in the Otherworld until I am called upon again."

She spoke of the magical land where her people lived. Auley had heard of it before. But if she went there, he'd never get her back.

"I want you to marry me and remain here," he said. "I have told you that before. I cannot go to the Otherworld."

"And I cannot disappoint my people."

"Is that more important than the calling of your heart?"

She lowered her gaze, pondering her answer. Auley thought he might have hurt her feelings, delicate flower that she was.

"I am sorry," he murmured. "I did not mean to sound cruel. But is being immortal and alone greater than being mortal and loving one man until you die?"

She lifted her eyes. "I told you that if I marry you, I surrender my immortality," she said. "I did not tell you so you could use it as a weapon of logic against me. I told you because I wanted you to know that my refusal of marriage had nothing to do with you."

"You told me that you loved me, once. Is love not stronger than your destiny?"

"Love is the strongest thing on earth," Padraigan said. "Look at our great lord and lady. Love brought them through the nether realm together. It is why they are here. Love is stronger than anything."

"Then why can you not surrender to it?"

Impulsively, Padraigan put her hand on Auley's cheek. "Because I do not have the choice to do so," she said. "You must understand that my destiny has been preordained. I cannot walk away from it."

"I'm not asking you to walk away from it. I am asking you to become my wife."

She continued to caress his cheek. "You are asking me to give up all that I am."

His features rippled with sorrow. "Then there is nothing I can say? Still?"

Padraigan shook her head. "Not now," she said. "Let us wait until the crisis with Geric is over. Then… then perhaps we may speak of this again. But until Conor is securely on the throne and Geric is no longer a threat, I'm afraid that is where my focus must be. And yours."

That was somewhat promising. Auley took it that way. With a nod, he began walking again, holding out an elbow to her in a polite gesture. Padraigan knew she shouldn't take it, not when he was feeling so low, and she was feeling torn and cruel, but against her better judgment, she took it anyway. His arm was warm and firm and wonderful.

And it broke her heart.

Auley led her all the way to the hall in sorrowful silence.

# CHAPTER EIGHTEEN

H E HATED THIS city.

Geric had hated it since he'd been a child—a city where people had been kind to one another and the land was peaceful. He remembered his father taking him and Conor into the city to meet the people and learn the way of things, to teach his sons to become close to their subjects.

But Geric had only seen subjects to be dominated.

Seoirse—or George—the Wise had been their father, a good and true king who was connected with his people. He had imparted that particular importance to Conor, but not Geric. Geric had no interest in benevolence or being a good king. He simply wanted to rule because of the riches that would belong to him, riches he could hoard or spend as he pleased.

That was all he'd ever wanted.

And he'd had it for about a year. All of that money his father and brother had controlled had become his, and he'd spent it on Northmen who brought him more wealth with their raids.

What he hadn't realized was that he spent more on their services than they brought him, so it was a one-sided relationship and bad financial planning. Still, he felt powerful with

Northmen at his disposal.

Northmen that were in the city now, shielded.

Geric was playing a waiting game.

Ranak had gone to sea with about half of the Northman army, on longships that had been moored up the coast because while some of the army had been raiding inland, others had been tearing apart seaports.

Olc had come with Geric, and, even now, they were planted in a dirty little tavern on the northern edge of the city, just beyond the city walls. Geric had brought one of Ranak's men with him, a fellow by the name of Skeld, and there were about a hundred Northmen in the city, while the bulk of the army were holed up on the outskirts.

Conor was sending out patrols, and it had taken some doing to evade them, but they hadn't been avoided completely. The patrols were seeing signs of encampments that could, or could not, be Geric and his men.

Geric wasn't sure how much Conor knew. But he was certain his brother knew that Geric wouldn't take the return of the true king lying down. He had to know that Geric was waiting for the right time to move.

And move he would.

He intended to enter the city before sunset and find a corner to hide in. Over the past six weeks, he'd changed his appearance so as not to be readily recognized. It never occurred to him that, because of Olc's curse, Conor wouldn't even recognize him. In Dublin, he'd picked up crushed black walnut hulls that turned his light hair quite dark and streaked, and he grew a beard that came in red with patches of white. He realized the citizens of Ciannachta would know him on sight, unlike his brother, so he did his best to change his appearance.

Geric had been in Ciannachta for about two weeks, watching the patrols, getting a sense of the security his brother had. It hadn't been particularly tight, but over the past couple of days, something seemed to have changed. Gates that were normally open were suddenly closed. The castle itself seemed to be heavily manned on the battlements. This told him that, somehow, Conor must have been alerted to his presence, or was at least anticipating his approach.

Or perhaps it was simply Conor being paranoid.

For good reason.

"We must get into the city before they lock the gates," Geric said to Olc. "We'll go to the side of town where the smithies and metalworkers are. We can find shelter in one of the stalls over there. Several have been abandoned, so it should be a simple thing."

Olc had been sleeping sitting up. The noise and smoke of the tavern hadn't bothered him in the least.

He cracked an eye open as Geric spoke. "Where are your Northman friends?" he muttered.

Geric gestured toward the livery. "With the horses," he said. "You know that they prefer their own company. They do not like to mix with the men of Eire."

"Then they can remain in the livery so they are not discovered," Olc said, yawning. "Perhaps you and I should leave now and go into the city. Tell the Northmen to follow before the city gates close. We should not travel in a big group."

Geric nodded. After a moment, he slipped outside to tell the men with him to enter the city later that day. He also instructed them to summon the men who were outside the city, for now was the time to start moving them in. There were other Northmen in the city, blending in with the subjects, because Olc was correct—they couldn't travel in groups or they would look suspicious.

"If we are to go, let us do it now," Geric said.

With that, he stood up from the chair he'd been more or less living in for the past two weeks. Olc, who had shaved his head and eyebrows in his attempt not to be recognized, stood up beside him and pulled his hood over his head.

Geric tossed a coin to the tavern keep and headed outside, to the road that led into Ciannachta. There had been rains a few days ago, and the road was still muddy, still difficult to travel, but he and Olc trudged down it, heading for the northern city gate, which was currently open.

They hurried to get inside.

The town appeared normal enough but for the fact that there were soldiers out on the streets. Geric hadn't noticed that before, so that was something new. The soldiers seemed to be traveling in groups of four, and Geric kept his head down, pulling Olc along. The sorcerer didn't move very well as it was, and on normal occasions would be riding a pony, but not today. Today, he was walking, using a branch that was taller than he was as a walking stick.

Into the heart of Ciannachta they went.

The sky above was deep blue, with gulls screeching over-head—only to be chased away by a vicious flock of ravens. These were Olc's ravens, his *fitheach* army, and there were at least fifteen or twenty of them. Big, nasty birds the size of small dogs that spied for Olc from the air. They came to him and whispered in his ear of the things they'd seen, and Olc had learned to trust them. But they were somewhat conspicuous, and he ordered them away with a flick of his wrist.

The ravens flew toward the castle.

In order to get to the avenue of the smithies, Geric and Olc had to pass by the gatehouse of Cashel Cian. There were few people about, so they kept their heads down and tried to move quickly, tucking in behind those who were walking in the direction they wanted to go. Neither dared to look up at the castle for fear they would be seen and recognized, so they simply moved quickly until they completely passed the gatehouse and headed toward the town center.

The center of Ciannachta had a large well in the middle and several big stones that had been rolled into place as washing surfaces. Women from the city would come and do their laundry, although some went down to the River Boyne to do the same. It was a central area for gossip and conversation, and there were always a few women there, doing their wash and talking. The most recent talk, of course, had been about the return of Conor and Etain, but as Geric and Olc passed by four or five women near the well, they could only hear talk of children.

They continued on.

Just past the city center, the road forked. The right went toward the weavers and merchants, while the left went toward the smithies and livestock area of town, where farmers would bring in their sheep or goats for market.

Geric was slightly ahead of Olc as they headed down the avenue, straight into the avenue of the smithies, when he dared to look up from his lowered hood to get a feel for their surroundings.

And that was when he came to a dead stop.

Olc plowed into him, but Geric didn't apologize. He was fixated on a woman and her son several yards away as the boy looked at a small saddle in the front of a smithy stall. Olc happened to catch a glimpse of what had Geric noticed.

His heart began to race.

"'Tis *her*," Olc whispered.

Geric could only nod.



"PLEASE, MOTHER," MATTOCK said. "Please… I need to go into the town. May I go? Please?"

Destry was in the kitchens of Cashel Cian, a catacomb of rooms set in the sublevel with stairs that led up to the kitchen yard. She had been working with the cook, frying up turnip chips that her family seemed to love so much and trying to get a feel for what kind of cheese she could sprinkle on them. Parmesan would have been perfect, but in the absence of that, she was trying out a couple of hard white cheeses that were strongly tangy. The problem was that they didn't shred very well, and she was trying to figure out how to do it.

Mattock's begging was getting on her nerves. "For what?" she said impatiently.

He was fidgeting. "It… it is a surprise," he said. "I cannot tell you."

"Then you'll have to ask your father."

"Nay!" Mattock nearly shouted, calming quickly when Destry looked at him strangely. "It is a surprise for Dada. I cannot ask him, or he will know."

She sighed heavily and stood up from where she'd been bent over a table working with the cheese. Brushing off her hands, she eyed him suspiciously. "What *kind* of surprise?"

"If I tell you, you will tell him," Mattock said. "But I need your permission to go into town."

"Alone?"

"Aye."

Destry shook her head. "Look, Matt, I don't know what you're trying to pull, but you look edgy."

Mattock cocked his head. "What do I look like?"

"Nervous," Destry clarified. "You look like you're about to rob a bank."

"What is a bank?"

Destry rolled her eyes. "Never mind," she said. "You can't go into town by yourself, but if you do this quickly, I'll go with you."

Mattock frowned. "I do not need an escort."

"Yes, you do."

"But you'll tell Dada!"

"I promise I won't tell him, but we have to do this quickly," she said. "Where are we going?"

Mattock pointed a finger in a general southerly direction. "That way," he said. "I will tell you when we get there. And you will not tell Dada?"

"I won't, but we need to hurry," she said. "We'll run out there and come right back."

Mattock hugged her. "Thank you, *Mamai*," he said, using a childish, affectionate title for her now that he had his way. "Thank you very much. Will you bring money?"

Destry was removing her apron. "Wait," she said. "*I* have to bring money? Isn't this your surprise?"

"But I have no money."

Destry wasn't going to argue with him. Truth be told, she was glad he had asked her, because she'd been having trouble bonding with the boy. He spent so much time with Conor and the other warriors that she rarely had any time alone with him, so she looked at this as an opportunity. He was a serious lad, mature for his age, so this begging wasn't like him. Thinking that giving permission for this secretive venture might endear her to him just a little, she was more than willing to take him into the village for whatever surprise he had planned for Conor.

After telling the cook that she would return shortly, Destry washed her hands quickly in a basin of cold water before heading up to the chamber she shared with Conor to retrieve her cloak. It was a cream color, something Conor had purchased for her a few weeks back, and it was lamb's wool, so it was very soft. She really loved it. She grabbed her cloak and swung it over the simple yellow dress she was wearing, then stopped to take a few coins out of Conor's purse under the bed. Mattock was waiting for her in the doorway, and together, the two of them headed out of the keep.

There was no sign of Conor as they headed to the gatehouse, but Destry caught sight of Brone, who was on the battlements. He wasn't looking at her, but rather in the direction of the sea, so she was able to slip out with just the gatehouse soldiers noting her departure. They offered to escort her, but she called them off because Mattock started to protest, fearful they'd tell his father. Destry had only been out in the city with Conor, and to her it seemed relatively safe, so she didn't see any problem with just her and Mattock making a quick trip to wherever he wanted to go. Just a Mom and Mattock trip.

Out into the city they went.

Mattock was so excited that he couldn't even walk with her. He was a few paces ahead, grinning at her and hoping his fast pace would encourage her to walk faster, too.

"This must be quite a surprise," she said, noting his quick steps. "Where are we going?"

Mattock reached out to take her hand, the first time he'd

ever done that. "To the avenue of the smithies," he said. "I want to show you something."

"What?"

"The surprise."

"Like I said—it must be quite a surprise."

"It is," Mattock said, pulling her along. "Thank you for not telling Dada."

"You're welcome."

"And thank you for not insisting Dev come along."

"He admires you a great deal, Matt. He likes to be with you."

Mattock slowed his pace. "I know," he said. "But sometimes I want to do things without him."

"And that's fine," Destry said. "But remember, he is your brother and he loves you. Not all brothers behave like your father and his brother. Your Uncle Geric is just a very nasty man."

"I know," he said. "I learned that. When I was a boy, he was very nice to me, and we did many things together, but I found out when I was older that he was wicked."

"He sure is."

"Can I ask you what it felt like to be banished to the nether realm?" he said. "Did it hurt?"

It was the first time he'd asked her a question about the "before time," and Destry took the question seriously. "Truthfully, I don't remember what it felt like to be banished," she said. "But I will tell you that where your father and I lived was a wonderful place with wonderful things."

"Like what?"

Destry thought on that, trying to explain it in terms he could understand. "Well, like travel, for instance," she said.

"You know how a ship on the ocean takes people from one port to another?"

"Aye."

"Where we lived, there were ships that flew like birds," she said, looking up into the blue sky. "They are called airplanes. They take people all over the world through the air."

Mattock was listening with interest. "Do they have wings?"

"They do, but the wings don't move. They have engines for that."

"What's 'engine'?"

Destry wasn't sure how she could explain it with nothing to really compare it to. "I'll ask your dad how to describe that one to you," she said. "But it was really wonderful, I promise."

Mattock grinned at her, and she let the subject drop, at least for the moment, because he seemed to be more interested in their surroundings at this point. They'd reached a street that was full of blacksmiths, and the smell of molten metal was heavy in the air. So was the smell of smoke.

Mattock practically dragged her over to a larger stall that had a few men working in it. Right up front, slung over a rail, was a fine leather saddle on a wooden frame.

Mattock walked right up to it. "There," he said, gesturing to the saddle. "*This* is the surprise."

Destry looked at the saddle, puzzled. "For your father?"

Mattock shrugged. Then he reluctantly shook his head. "For me," he said. "Will you please convince Dada that I need it? I cannot become a warrior if I do not have a proper saddle. Please?"

Destry wasn't happy. She looked at the boy, who was nearly as tall as she was, and folded her arms across her chest.

"So this is the saddle you were talking about last night?" she asked.

He nodded eagerly. "Aye."

Destry was coming to see that she had been used. "And this is why you brought me out here," she said, shaking her head in disappointment. "This wasn't so much a surprise for your father as it was tricking me into buying it for you."

Mattock refused to look guilty. "It will be a surprise for Dada when you buy it for me."

Destry had to snort at the child's logic, self-serving as it was. "Mattock, I'm going to point something out to you, so I want you to listen carefully. Are you listening?"

"Aye, *Mamai.*"

"You lied to me to get me out here," she said. "You lied to me and you manipulated me, and neither one of those things are honorable. Your father would have never done that to me, so why did you think it was acceptable to do that? Can you tell me?"

That wasn't the reaction Mattock had been expecting. "Then you will not tell Dada I need the saddle?"

Destry cocked an eyebrow. "I'm going to tell him that you tricked me to get me out here and then tried to manipulate me. What do you think he is going to say?"

Finally, Mattock was losing his confidence. He was becoming both defensive and remorseful. "I did not trick you," he said. "I convinced you."

"You lied."

"Sometimes men must lie to get what they want."

"Who in the hell told you that?"

Mattock was sliding more into the dark side of remorse now. "I've heard the soldiers say things like that," he said. "I thought... I thought if I told you the truth, you would not come."

"And you would have been right," she said. "What you did was not very nice. Would you have done this to your father?"

Mattock hesitated before shaking his head and lowering his gaze. "Nay, *Mamai.*"

"Then why did you feel as if you could do it to me?"

"I do not know."

Destry didn't want to lose this moment with him, though she was pissed off because he'd lied to her. She didn't remember raising Mattock, or his brothers, so she was still very new at this parenting gig. Therefore, she tried to be rational about it.

"I know we haven't spent a lot of time together, so maybe this was your way of coming to know me, as your mother," she said. "Maybe you thought I'd be easier to trick than your father would be, but I promise you, I'm not easy to trick. I love you and I would like to be a mother you love and respect, but this isn't the way to do it. Do you understand that?"

Mattock nodded, lifting her head to look at her. "Will you punish me?"

Destry shook her head. "Not this time," she said. "I will give you a warning. But if this happens again, I will have to punish you. Is that clear?"

He nodded. "Thank you, *Mamai.*"

Destry let her gaze linger on him for a moment before reaching out to take his hand. "Come on," she said. "We'll go back to the castle, and I'll tell your dad about this amazing saddle you need. Maybe *he'll* buy it for you."

Mattock's face lit up with surprise. "You will?"

"I will. But you'd better not lie to me again. Understood?"

"Aye," the boy said, throwing his arms around her and hugging her. "Thank you, *Mamai!*"

Destry gave the boy a squeeze. But just as he pulled back, he caught sight of something over her shoulder, and his expression went from confusion to surprise to horror very quickly. Puzzled, Destry turned around to see a man with oddly colored dark hair several feet away, heading in her direction. She had no idea who he was until Mattock grabbed her by the arm and pulled her away, very quickly.

"Run," Mattock told her in a panic. "Run back to Cian! *Run!*"

Destry had no idea why she was running and no idea why Mattock was nearly hysterical. She started to run with him, stumbling, but the man with the dark hair intercepted them both. Mattock managed to get out of the way, but Destry tripped on her long cloak, unused to wearing heavy dresses and cloaks with material around her legs. She started to fall, but the man was in front of her, and she caught a glint of metal. She had no idea what it was, or what was going on, until searing pain carved into her midsection as the blade the man was holding plunged right into her belly.

Down she went, into the dirt.

And that was when all hell broke loose.

# CHAPTER NINETEEN

"**S**HE WENT INTO the city," Padraigan told Conor with a twinkle in her eye. "Mattock was dragging her out of the gates."

Conor, who had just come out of the armory, had been looking for his wife when he came across Padraigan near the gatehouse. The white witch was smiling, but Conor wasn't amused.

"Why?" he said. "She should know better than to go into town without an escort. Why didn't you stop them?"

"Because I did not see them until it was too late," Padraigan said. "It has only been a few minutes. They should not be difficult to find."

Conor rolled his eyes. "What in the hell is Matt up to?" he muttered, mostly to himself. "And why take her?"

Padraigan shrugged. "Perhaps he had a certain destination in mind."

"Like what?"

"Like the saddle he spoke of constantly at the meal last night?"

Conor shook his head when he realized what his son had

done. "I've already seen it, and now he takes his mother to get her on his side?" he said. Then he snorted. "He is not going to let that rest, is he?"

"More than likely not."

Conor sighed sharply. "I'll go find them," he said. "I'll save Des from the begging of an eleven-year-old."

Padraigan fought off a smile. "I suspect the fact that she does not spend much time with him might have influenced her decision to go," she said. "Mattock does not usually spend time with his mother because he is always with you."

Conor lifted his eyebrows. "So she went to see this saddle because she wants to spend time with him?"

"Perhaps she is simply eager to be with her son."

Conor shrugged, but he understood what Padraigan was saying. "All right, then," he said. "Care to go see this saddle with me?"

"I would be honored, great lord."

"It's just a saddle."

"To you, perhaps, but not to your son."

He narrowed his eyes at her. "I get it," he said. "You're on his side too."

Padraigan merely grinned. That told Conor all he needed to know.

With a snort, he headed for the gatehouse with Padraigan following.

Auley, who had been in the armory with Conor earlier, saw them crossing the bailey and he ran to catch up with them. "Where are you going?" he asked.

Conor pointed to the gatehouse. "It seems that Mattock has abducted his mother," he said. "I'm going out to find them."

"Abduct her where?"

"To see a certain saddle."

Auley understood. They'd all heard about that damnable saddle last night. Because Padraigan was going with Conor, he tagged along, and the three of them exited the gatehouse and turned in the direction of the avenue of the smithies. Auley ordered the gatehouse closed, as they'd been keeping it secure for the past couple of days, so the soldiers were watching them from the battlements above as they headed toward the town center.

Conor's focus was up ahead, toward the avenue of the smithies, but Padraigan and Auley were walking together, slightly behind him, exchanging sweet glances. Auley was fighting off a smile, trying not to be so obvious about looking at her.

"Great lord, I forgot to tell you that the men on the battlements see ships approaching from the north," he said. "Brone has his sights on them."

Conor was looking at the fork in the road ahead, the one that led to different avenues of different vendors. "Ships come into the river all the time," he said. "They do it every day."

"But not from the north," Auley said. "Usually, the ships come from the south or the east."

"Why do we worry about ships from the north?"

"Because that is the way the Northmen have been known to come," Auley said. "They have taken control of Rathin Island to the north and use it as a point to launch their raids."

Conor looked at him then. "Do we think it's Northmen?"

Auley shrugged. "Difficult to tell," he said. "We'll know when they get closer."

"Then I need to find Des and Matt and bring them back to the safety of the castle."

"That would be wise, great lord."

"Should we tell the villagers and lock down the city?"

"We should know that soon, great lord. The ships are too far out to know."

That seemed to feed some urgency in Conor. His wife and eldest son were in the city, so he wanted to get them back to the castle quickly. Even if the ships turned out to be a false alarm, he wasn't comfortable having them out in the open like this.

He picked his pace up.

Auley and Padraigan followed at a quickened pace as well, though she was nearly skipping to keep up with the men with longer strides. They passed by the well with the women doing their wash and headed into the avenue of the smithies, though their view was blocked slightly by the branches of the big yew tree that grew at the mouth of the street. Branches hung down, and there were people in the way, but Conor walked around them, and a few of them even greeted him pleasantly. He responded in kind.

At one of the smithy stalls, men were calling to him, wanting him to see their wares. He politely begged off, assuring them that he would once he finished his business.

But then there was screaming.

Something was happening.

Startled, Conor snapped his head in the direction of the yelling, but he couldn't see anything other than people scattering. He ran in the direction of the screams, pushing people out of his way, in time to see Mattock leaping onto the back of a man who was bent over something on the dirt. The boy was punching the man in the head, and Conor kicked into a dead run at the sight of his son doing battle with a grown man. Only when he came closer did he see that the "something" in the dirt was Destry.

And she was covered in blood.

Conor didn't ask questions. He didn't even hesitate. He plowed into the man from behind, also plowing into his son, and they all went down in a heap. There was a great deal of commotion and yelling going on, and through it all, Conor could hear Mattock shouting at the man he was still trying to punch.

"You killed her!" he screamed. "Uncle, you killed her! Why did you do that? *Why?*"

*Uncle.*

Conor's mind began to short-circuit. There was only one uncle he knew of, and that was Geric. Geric, the man who had taken his throne. Geric, the man who they had been expecting to return. No one had seen an army yet, but that didn't mean that Geric wasn't here. That didn't mean he wasn't in their midst.

Suddenly, things Padraigan had told him began filling his brain.

*I know there is danger in the mist, but I cannot see it.*

She had meant Geric.

It had been a warning.

Realizing whom he had in his grip, Conor roared with anguish and fury, throwing Geric into a headlock and yanking the man backward, against him. They were still rolling around in the dirt, and he saw the glint of a very nasty-looking dagger. It was covered with blood, which he assumed to be Destry's, which made him go mad. He tightened the headlock on Geric, but his brother was panicking. He slashed at Conor's arms with the blade before finally stabbing him in the right forearm. The shock and pain of the wound was enough to cause Conor to lose his grip, and Geric wormed out of his grasp, throwing himself away from his enraged brother.

The battle was absolute chaos.

Geric could hardly breathe because Conor's grip had been tight. That monstrous brother of his had arms of iron. He tried to leap to his feet to get away from him but couldn't seem to manage it.

Conor, however, was already standing, grabbing at a weapon in the nearest smithy stall. It was a dull sword, waiting to be completed, but it was enough. It was the weapon he needed. Bringing the sword to bear, Conor charged after Geric and his long, razor-sharp dagger.

"Then the last fight is to be between us, is it?" Geric said, trying to taunt him. "Do what you must, big brother. It has been a long time since we have faced off against each other, and this time, I shall emerge the victor."

Conor got a good look at the man who had upended his entire life. The man who had changed his destiny and, with Destry down, quite possibly destroyed everything that mattered to him.

He dared to glance at Destry, who was still on the ground as Padraigan and Auley worked furiously to stop the bleeding. He didn't know if she was dead or alive. All he could see was blood.

Looking back to his brother, all he could feel was rage.

Pure, black rage.

It was strange how a man he'd never seen was oddly familiar to him. It wasn't so much that he actually remembered Geric, but more a feeling in his bones. Something told him that he knew this man. He knew the voice, the eyes. He knew the mind and heart.

And it was all rotten.

"You're a pathetic bastard," he growled. "You're also a dead man. I hope you enjoy pain, because you're about to experience a shitload of it."

He didn't give Geric a chance to respond. He was suddenly charging at him, using every bit of training he'd ever had in ancient hand-to-hand combat. As he attacked his brother with a series of heavy strikes, visions of his life began to pop into his head. As a student, learning everything he could about weapons and ancient warfare. As a graduate, following the Medieval fight clubs around Ireland and even into England, participating in the competitions and learning to use his wits as much as his strength.

He had visions of his office at Trinity College, with all of the weapons on the wall, the knowledge he could use every one of them with skill. Perhaps this was the moment he'd been waiting for, the very moment that everything in his life—his education and training—had been pointing toward.

The moment when he would decide the fate of a kingdom.

But Geric wasn't making it easy. He wasn't as big as Conor was, but he was fast and he was skilled. He also didn't have wounds on his arms and blood streaming all over his body the way Conor did. The wounds weren't particularly bad, but they were bloody. Conor didn't care, however. He chased Geric all over the avenue of the smithies as his brother defended himself.

"You should have stayed in the nether region," Geric said, winded because of all the fighting. "Now, I am going to do what I should have done before—I am going to kill you, you self-righteous whoreson. I hated you as a child and I hate you now. You are going to die, and Ciannachta will be mine once and for all!"

Conor wasn't doing much damage with the dull sword. He

was simply exhausting them both. He came to a halt near the smithy stall with the saddle, watching Geric bend over to catch his breath. When he did that, Conor dared to take his attention away long enough to see a magnificent sword near the anvil. The smithies had been working on it when the trouble started, and it looked as if it was nearly finished. He snapped his fingers at the petrified smithies and pointed to the sword. When they realized what he wanted, they handed it over.

It was everything Conor had hoped for. Razor-sharp and powerful, this was the sword of a king.

He got a good grip on the hilt and took off after Geric again, who was caught off guard by the charge. He tried to get away but ended up stumbling over his own feet, something Conor took advantage of—he grabbed his brother by the hair and plunged the sword straight into Geric's belly. Geric screamed in agony as he went down, with a sword in his stomach and his furious brother right on top of him.

Conor's face was an inch from his. "That's for taking my kingdom, you fucking bastard," he snarled. Then he stood up and pulled out the sword, lifting it above Geric's head. "And this is for whatever you did to my wife. I hope you rot in hell."

With that, he brought the sword down, decapitating his brother in the middle of the street.

As this was going on, he failed to see an old man with a shaved head and shaved eyebrows approaching him from the side. The old man tossed back the hood of his cloak, focusing on Conor as he thrust his hands forward, fingers bent like claws.

"*Fill ar ais nuair a tháinig tú,*" the old man growled. "*Dul ar ais…*"

"*Cuir deireadh le do olc agus reo mar reo an sneachta ar an sliabh!*" Padraigan was on her feet, her voice raised and her hands extended to the bald man. "*Reo go dtí go nglaoidh mé ar na déithe tú a scaoileadh saor!*"

Startled, the old man turned in her direction, but his movements were laborious. He could hardly move. He lifted his hands to her and tried to say a spell that would counter whatever she had done, but he couldn't manage it. His mouth froze, his hands froze, and he stood there like a statue in the middle of the street.

*Freeze until I call upon the gods to release you!*

That had been the gist of Padraigan's spell when she saw Olc go after Conor. The last time they'd met, he had the jump on her, and she wasn't going to let that happen again.

As Olc turned to stone, Padraigan rushed over to Conor and began to pull him away from the body of his dead brother.

"I do not know how long the spell will last," she said, urgency in her tone for nearly the first time since Conor had known her. "You must take your beloved and go!"

"Great lord!"

Another voice filled the air as Conor stumbled over to Destry. He looked up to see Bradaigh running toward him through the dusty street.

"Great lord!" Bradaigh shouted again. "The Northmen are near our shores. We must get everyone into the city!"

Conor wasn't surprised to hear it. The ships that had been sighted to the north were indeed Northmen. Conor had no way of knowing that it was Geric's army, or at least Ranak's army, now returning to Ciannachta to loot and pillage. He had no way of knowing he was about to get it from all sides. Geric's army, as Padraigan had suggested, hadn't come the obvious way. They had used stealth and the element of surprise. There were also two factions—one using Olc's subversive tactics and one simply acting on its own.

Even if Conor had known any of that, it wouldn't have mattered.

His entire life, at the moment, was in chaos.

He fell to his knees beside Destry.

"Oh… God," he breathed, tears coming to his eyes as he looked at her. "Is she dead?"

Auley had a section of his tunic that he'd torn off pressed against Destry's abdominal wound. "Nay, great lord," he said, though he sounded grim. "But we must take her back to the cashel immediately. She needs a physic."

"Nay," Padraigan said. "She will die if we take her back to the cashel."

Both Conor and Auley looked at her. "There is nowhere else to take her," Conor said, his voice trembling with fear. "Where else can I—"

Padraigan cut him off. "You must take her back to the nether realm," she said, grasping at his arm. "You must take her back to the world you have come from. They have the means to heal her. We do not. But we must leave now, because my spell will only hold Olc for so long before he breaks free. And when he breaks free, he will kill you both."

"But—"

"If you love your wife, you will go," Padraigan said. But she could see the utter horror and grief in Conor's eyes, and she softened. "You loved one another so much that you found each other in the nether realm. Your story is not meant to end this way, great lord. Nor is my lady's. This was not something I foresaw, so it is not something that is part of the fight between good and evil. You have killed Geric; now, there is no one else to challenge Ciannachta's throne. We can fight away the Northmen, but you… you will not survive if your lady dies. I know you will not. This was not meant to happen."

Tears spilled out of Conor's eyes and coursed down his cheeks. "I asked you once if you could open the time portal with a spell," he said hoarsely. "Can you do it?"

Padraigan could see how heartbroken he was. "I am Padraigan the White," she murmured. "I am your *litrithe*. I have always loved you and your lady with bonds as strong as any family. Though I should like you to stay and rule Ciannachta, my desire to save your lady is stronger. Mattock will make a fine king, someday. I will see to it. But you… you have done what you came to do. You have made this a kingdom that your son can rule without threat from your brother. Can I open the door to the nether realm? I believe I can. Now it is time to face your greatest battle and save your lady's life."

Conor's lower lip trembled as he closed his eyes and nodded. "Then let's do it," he said. "But I have one request."

"What's that?"

"That I remember who she is," he said. "The last time, we forgot everything. I couldn't stand it if she didn't know me and I didn't know her. Truthfully, I'd rather lose her to death than go through life not knowing her."

Padraigan was full of sympathy. "I will do my best," she said. "But we must leave. There is no more time."

Conor understood. He turned to Auley, who was holding the unconscious Destry against him, and put his hand on the man's shoulder.

"Take care of my sons," he whispered tightly. "I entrust them to you and to Padraigan. Raise them to be fine, strong, and noble. I trust you to do that for me."

Auley was deeply grieved, but he nodded. "I shall, great lord," he said. "I shall make you proud."

Conor was too choked up to reply. He pulled Destry to him and stood as Auley continued to put pressure on the wound. But Auley had to let go as he ran for the nearest wagon that would take them out of the village.

As Conor shifted so he could put pressure on Destry's wound, he caught sight of Mattock a few feet away. The boy was sobbing.

"Dada, I'm sorry," Mattock said. "I did not mean to be wicked. I'm so sorry."

Conor smiled faintly. "You are a fine lad, strong and true," he said. "Your mother and I must leave you, but I want you to know how much we love you. I don't think I'll be back, so this kingdom is yours, and I want you to be an honorable ruler. Be fair and be kind. Show compassion toward your subjects. You've seen how I've ruled over the people and what I've done, so use my example. And always, always treat your brothers kindly. They will need you, Matt, now more than ever. Can you do that?"

Mattock wiped his eyes furiously. "I will," he said. "Why must you go, Dada?"

"I must go to save your mother's life. Do you understand that?"

"Will I see you again?"

Conor shook his head, bending over to kiss the boy on the head. "I love you, lad," he murmured. "Get back to the cashel with Bradaigh and let him command the battle."

"Aye, Dada."

"Learn from him. He will teach you well."

"I will, Papa."

"And buy that saddle when all of this is over. I give you permission."

At that moment, Auley suddenly rushed up in a wagon he'd stolen from a merchant on the next street. The two ponies in harness were quite excited, and there was merchandise falling off the wagon bed, but no one stopped to pick it up. Time was of the essence.

Padraigan leapt into the wagon bed, extending her arms for Destry. Conor laid her carefully in Padraigan's lap and jumped onto the wagon himself. With a yell at the ponies, Auley snapped them into a frenzy and thundered out of the avenue of the smithies, heading toward the western gate of Ciannachta, and out of the castle walls to the green, verdant countryside beyond.

After that… they were free.

# EPILOGUE

S HE COULD HEAR voices.

Voices and footsteps on hard surfaces and somewhere in the distance. Something was beeping.

Destry was fading in and out of consciousness, sleeping on and off, before she finally became lucid.

Her eyes slowly opened.

She was in a room with white walls and a big window to her left. Blinking, she looked around a little more and could see that it was a hospital room. When she tried to move, a shooting pain in her shoulder stopped her.

She gasped.

"Des?"

Aisling was suddenly in her field of vision, looking very concerned. When she realized that Destry's eyes were open, she gasped herself.

"Oh my God," she said, putting her hands on Destry's arm. "You're awake. Holy shit!"

With that, she scooted over to the door and urgently flagged down a nurse. A young woman in scrubs and with braided blonde hair listened to Aisling's excited chatter before pulling a pair of sterile gloves out of the box on the wall as she entered the room.

"So," the nurse said. "You decided to wake up? That's fantastic. How do you feel?"

She had a thick Irish accent. Destry shifted on the bed, trying to figure out where all of the pain was coming from. "I don't know," she mumbled thickly. "What happened?"

"A cave-in," Aisling said anxiously, standing at the bottom of the bed. "Do you remember going to that ancient mound? Running away and not telling me where you were going?"

Destry thought on that, but her mind was full of cobwebs. "Ancient mound?" she repeated. "What mound? Where in the hell are we?"

"Ireland," Aisling said. "Remember we came to Ireland?"

Destry nodded, very weakly. "Of course I do," she said. "Ancient mound… you mean the one in the country? Dowth?"

"That one," Aisling said, coming around the side of the bed as the nurse checked all the monitors. "The one where you heard the voices. You went back there."

"I did?"

Aisling nodded. "Conor found you, but there was a cave-in," she said. "The whole thing just collapsed. We had to dig you out."

The cobwebs were starting to peel away. "Conor," Destry said as if she didn't recognize the name, but suddenly, her eyes widened. "*Conor!* Where is he?"

"He went to get a cup of coffee," Aisling said. "He's been with you every second, Des. Since this whole thing happened, he hasn't left your side. Not even at night. He almost got into a fistfight with the doctor when he tried to kick Conor out on the first night."

"First night?"

"You've been out for about six days."

Destry lay there and tried to settle her whirling mind. Her memory was starting to come back like an avalanche, and she remembered Dowth, the time travel, Padraigan, her boys, and Ciannachta. She remembered every single thing, but here she was in a modern hospital with no memory of how she got here.

Nothing made sense at the moment.

"Six days," she repeated, stunned. "What *are* you talking about? What am I doing here?"

"The cave-in knocked you out," Aisling said. "You had some internal damage. The doctors had to go in and remove your gallbladder. You don't remember any of this? Not even going to the mound?"

Instinctively, Destry put her hand on her belly, feeling the pain from the wound on her right side, about mid-torso.

Right where she had been stabbed.

"Oh, shit," she muttered to herself, closing her eyes as she realized something was off. Something was *very* off. "I don't know what I remember. I've been out for six days?"

"Yes," Aisling said. "That's a long time, but with the surgery and everything, I guess your body had a lot to heal from."

"Christ! Is she awake?"

Destry turned to see Conor standing in the doorway, looking much the same as he did the first time she'd ever seen him—a newsboy cap on his red head, and wearing a sweater and jeans. He had a cup of coffee in his hand, but that ended up on the table as he rushed to the bed, sitting in the chair next to it and putting his arms around Destry.

"Oh my God," he said, kissing her several times. "You're awake. You've been out so long, I was afraid you weren't going to wake up at all."

He was tearing up. Destry put her arms around his neck, as much as she could with the pain on her right side, and held him tightly. "You're here," she said. "Thank God you're here. What in the hell is happening?"

Conor didn't answer her right away. He simply kissed her a few more times, thrilled and relieved, as Aisling watched with surprise from the other side of the bed.

"Um…" Aisling said after witnessing the fifth or sixth kiss. "Like, what's going on here? You guys are *really* happy to see one another, eh?"

Conor started laughing, but Destry wouldn't let him go. She just wanted to kiss him.

"Hey," he whispered between kisses. "Aisling doesn't know about us, so maybe we'd better ease up for now."

Instead of letting him go, Destry turned to her friend. "We're madly in love," she told her. "Couldn't you figure that out when he drove all the way out to Dowth to find me?"

Aisling looked at her strangely for a moment before shaking her head and turning back to the chair she'd been sitting on.

"No offense to Conor, but you think that's a good idea?" she said. "I mean, you were jilted at the altar three weeks ago. You really think you're ready for love so fast?"

Destry looked at Conor, an expression of pure adoration on her face. "I can't remember when I haven't loved him," she said. "I had to come all the way to Ireland just to find my soul mate, but now that I've found him, I'm never leaving him."

Conor grinned and kissed her gently on the cheek as Aisling rolled her eyes and picked up the book she'd been reading.

"Great," she said. "Well, regardless of what you two are going to do with your newfound love, I'm keeping with the itinerary. Once Des is up and moving, the next place we're going to is east of Drogheda, an archaeological dig of an ancient kingdom."

She started flipping through the pages, looking for something in the back section, as Destry remained focused on Conor, her hand on his cheek. She took advantage of the fact that Aisling was occupied with the book to find out what Conor knew of their situation.

"Do you remember what… happened?" she whispered.

He nodded faintly. "You mean a thousand years in the past?

"Yes."

"So you remember too?"

"Yes, but it feels like a dream."

"Can you still speak Gaelic?"

"*Is feidir liom.*" *Yes, I can.*

"Then it was no dream." Conor paused. "Did Aisling tell you what happened when we came back?"

"A cave-in?"

"There was," he said. "Des, I've had six days to figure out what happened, and as near as I can tell, no time passed from the moment I found you in the tunnel at Dowth and the cave-in that expelled me but nearly buried you. According to Aisling, it happened almost immediately after I went in to get you out of the tunnel. But I think the cave-in was caused when Padraigan cast her spell and sent us back."

Destry laid her head back against the pillow. "I don't remember any of that," she said. "I remember some guy attacking me, but after that… nothing. What happened?"

Conor sighed. "A lot," he said. "I'll tell you more when we're alone."

He meant Aisling. Destry understood that, so she nodded.

"But you're okay?"

"I'm fine."

Destry put her hand down to her torso. "Aisling said I had an operation."

He nodded. "You did," he said. "The doctors said the cave-in damaged your abdomen. They said a sharp end of a rock must have punctured you."

"It was a knife."

"I know," he said softly. He was gazing deeply into her bright blue eyes, seeing how bewildered she was. "It *really* happened, Des, all of it. I had to bring you back here—and Padraigan had to cast a spell to send us back through the time portal to save your life. If we'd remained in Ciannachta, you would have died."

Hearing the details of how she ended up here, Destry started to tear up. "Oh, God," she muttered. "I took you away from your destiny."

"That's not true."

"You came back because of me!"

"I came back *for* you."

"What are you two mumbling about over there?" Aisling said.

"Nothing," Destry said, wiping her tears. "What's that book about?"

Aisling evidently didn't think it was too important to pursue what they'd been whispering about. She was looking at the back of the book.

"It's a guidebook for ancient sites," she said. "But it has a lot of history in it. We're supposed to go to the dig at the ancient kingdom at Ciannachta, which was really ancient Drogheda. Ciannachta has one of the biggest archaeological digs in Ireland because it was a city at the center of a tenth-century power struggle."

As soon as Aisling mentioned Ciannachta, she had Destry's attention. Destry had seen their itinerary before they ever came to Ireland, and she remembered the Drogheda dig, but not the Ciannachta name. It suddenly occurred to her that the two were one and the same, with Ciannachta being the ancient name for Drogheda.

She was staring at Aisling with a rather startled look as Conor spoke.

"I know of Ciannachta," he said. "I didn't realize it was on your tour schedule."

Aisling nodded, still reading. "We were supposed to go right after we visited Dowth," she said. Then she lowered the book and looked at Destry. "You know, we were supposed to fly out of here in two days. I had to call the airlines and reschedule until next week because the doctors said you shouldn't fly right now."

Destry shook her head. "You can still go home," she said. "But me... I'm staying."

Aisling looked at Conor, knowing he was the reason for Destry's desire to remain, and shrugged. She turned back to the book.

"Whatever you want to do," she said. "But *I'm* going to finish this tour. It says in the book that Ciannachta was the prelude to Drogheda. The power struggle in the tenth century was between family factions, evidently, but one faction won out, and Ciannachta became a weirdly progressive city with a type of welfare system for its citizens, among other things. The king was called Mattock the Enlightened, and he ruled for about seventy years, making him one of the longest-ruling high kings in Ireland's history. The reason for the archeological dig is because it's one of the most revered cities in Ireland, and the castle is well preserved. They've got enormous kitchens and a big weapons collection. Hey, that's cool. I'd like to see that."

As Aisling continued reading aloud about Ciannachta before moving on to another area they were supposed to visit, Destry turned her head away from her friend and put her hand over her face.

Conor could see that she was sobbing silently, and he knew why.

*Mattock the Enlightened.*

That manipulative, sweet little boy they'd left behind had done something great.

It was astonishing.

"I haven't had the courage to read about Ciannachta since we came back," Conor said quietly, holding her hand and whispering against her fingers. "I've been too concerned about you. Doesn't seem like a coincidence that Aisling is reading about it right now, does it?"

Destry shook her head, still weeping over the success of their eldest boy. "There are no coincidences in our life," she whispered. "Everything that has happened to us has happened for a reason."

Conor kissed her hand as she struggled with her composure. "Padraigan told me that she thought I was the king of prophecy," he said. "As it turns out, it was my son. I guess he just needed me to get the ball rolling."

Destry wiped her eyes. "You did great things, Conor. Don't sell yourself short."

"I set an example, at least," he said. "Before we left, I told Padraigan and Auley to take care of the boys. We know they were in good hands, so I'm really not surprised to hear that he was a good king."

"Maybe Auley and Padraigan finally got married, after all."

"You knew about the romance, did you?"

"I've got eyes, Conor. I could see what was going on."

"I hope they got married, too."

"I miss them all."

"Me too," Conor said. "But most importantly, we fulfilled a destiny. You and I did something that shaped the fate of a kingdom. A country, even. Not everybody can say that."

Destry looked at him, her eyes red and watery, but the expression on her face was one of joy. "I never knew it was my calling," she said. "I feel like every experience in my life lined up for this particular moment in time. But it still seems surreal, you know?"

"I know," he said. Then he slipped a hand onto her tender belly. "Oh, and by the way—the doctor says the pregnancy is fine. He says it's really early, but he doesn't think there was any damage."

Destry chuckled. "I forgot to even ask if I had imagined that."

"You didn't."

"Then how are we going to explain that to Aisling?" she said. "Or to my parents? If this baby goes full term, it'll still look like it's about six weeks early."

Conor shrugged. "We'll cross that bridge when we come to it, I suppose."

"Are we ever going to tell anyone about our adventure?"

"Would they believe us?"

"Probably not," Destry said. "We can use a test subject and see, though."

Conor looked over at Aisling, who was seriously studying

the guidebook. "She'll never believe it."

"Let me try."

"You're going to tell her about time travel, witches, wizards, magic, and Vikings?"

"Now that you say it out loud, it does sound a little strange."

"A little?"

"A *lot*."

Conor chuckled at her, but in the end, he was right. Aisling listened to the wild story of magic, time travel, and Ireland and refused to believe any of it. But she did return to America, and to their mutual friends, with a tale of a great adventure in Ireland and a new love for Destry. A new love that wasn't so new, after all. A love that had been Destry's destiny in this lifetime and many others. Two souls that had found each other once again.

The high king and his queen that not even the nether realm could separate.

Love, for Conor and Etain, was truly immortal.

## ☾ THE END? ☾

Children of Conor and Destry

*(Mattock, Devlin, Slane)*

*Anahera*

*Casey*

*Findlay*

*Kellan*

*Nolan*

*Ronan*

*Torrin*

*Kiara*

# AUTHOR AFTERWORD

I hope you enjoyed the "whole" story of Conor and Destry. I had missed them, so I really enjoyed completing the story. But this is a perfect example of a tale that really wrote itself, because I had intended a different ending, but the story went in such a way that a return to modern times was inevitable and preferable. I think it's so cool for Conor and Destry to look back in the annals of history and see what became of Conor's kingdom and their children.

But we have a few unanswered questions, don't we? I'm well aware, but there was no real way to incorporate the "answers" the way the story ended. The big one—in my mind—is the marriage of Auley and Padraigan. Did he finally convince her to marry him? The answer is yes—they married and raised the three boys as their own. Padraigan, from the ancient Tuatha de Dannan tribe, had to give up her immortality, but love is the greatest reason of all to do that.

What became of Bradaigh and Cara, and even Brone and Fallon (who appeared only briefly)? They simply went on to serve Mattock the Enlightened. Defeated by Padraigan, Olc of the Eye went off to find someone else to manipulate. Being Formorian, he was an immortal creature, but the rule of Mattock the Enlightened saw the decline of the Formorians, at least in that part of Ireland. As Aisling's guidebook said, Ciannachta was a progressive kingdom, moving into a new millennium. No more room for wizards, sorceresses, or fanged dragons that shot out poison spit.

Speaking of fanged dragons, what was that thing that attacked Mattock's pony? It was a prehistoric creature called a Megalania. Basically, a giant monitor lizard, but meaner and deadlier. They did exist (in Australia), but who's to say that some prehistoric creatures didn't survive into the Dark Ages, only to be killed off by ancient man? Anything is possible. As Conor said, there's a grain of truth to every legend.

Oh—and why did Conor and Destry have so many kids? Simple. He's Irish Catholic and she converted. Plus, as she said, they screw like rabbits, so it's probably a miracle they didn't have more. They had a great, big, lovely Irish family.

And with that, I'll leave you with dreams of white witches, sexy Irish warriors, and the beauty of an ancient land that is still ancient in many ways. Thank goodness it's still around to inspire stories like this one!

Hugs,

# Kathryn Le Veque Novels

*Medieval Romance:*

**De Wolfe Pack Series:**
Warwolfe
The Wolfe
Nighthawk
ShadowWolfe
DarkWolfe
A Joyous de Wolfe Christmas
BlackWolfe
Serpent
A Wolfe Among Dragons
Scorpion
StormWolfe
Dark Destroyer
The Lion of the North
Walls of Babylon
The Best Is Yet To Be
BattleWolfe
Castle of Bones

**De Wolfe Pack Generations:**
WolfeHeart
WolfeStrike
WolfeSword
WolfeBlade
WolfeLord
WolfeShield
Nevermore
WolfeAx

**The Executioner Knights:**
By the Unholy Hand
The Mountain Dark
Starless
A Time of End
Winter of Solace
Lord of the Sky
The Splendid Hour
The Whispering Night
Netherworld
Lord of the Shadows
Of Mortal Fury
'Twas the Executioner Knight
Before Christmas
Crimson Shield

**The de Russe Legacy:**
The Falls of Erith
Lord of War: Black Angel
The Iron Knight
Beast
The Dark One: Dark Knight
The White Lord of Wellesbourne
Dark Moon
Dark Steel
A de Russe Christmas Miracle
Dark Warrior

**The de Lohr Dynasty:**
While Angels Slept
Rise of the Defender
Steelheart
Shadowmoor
Silversword
Spectre of the Sword
Unending Love

Archangel
A Blessed de Lohr Christmas

**The Brothers de Lohr:**
The Earl in Winter

**Lords of East Anglia:**
While Angels Slept
Godspeed
Age of Gods and Mortals

**Great Lords of le Bec:**
Great Protector

**House of de Royans:**
Lord of Winter
To the Lady Born
The Centurion

**Lords of Eire:**
Echoes of Ancient Dreams
Blacksword
The Darkland

**Ancient Kings of Anglecynn:**
The Whispering Night
Netherworld

**Battle Lords of de Velt:**
The Dark Lord
Devil's Dominion
Bay of Fear
The Dark Lord's First Christmas
The Dark Spawn
The Dark Conqueror
The Dark Angel

**Reign of the House of de Winter:**
Lespada
Swords and Shields

**De Reyne Domination:**

Guardian of Darkness
The Black Storm
A Cold Wynter's Knight
With Dreams
Master of the Dawn

**House of d'Vant:**
Tender is the Knight (House of d'Vant)
The Red Fury (House of d'Vant)

**The Dragonblade Series:**
Fragments of Grace
Dragonblade
Island of Glass
The Savage Curtain
The Fallen One
The Phantom Bride

**Great Marcher Lords of de Lara**
Dragonblade

**House of St. Hever**
Fragments of Grace
Island of Glass
Queen of Lost Stars

**Lords of Pembury:**
The Savage Curtain

**Lords of Thunder: The de Shera Brotherhood Trilogy**
The Thunder Lord
The Thunder Warrior
The Thunder Knight

**The Great Knights of de Moray:**
Shield of Kronos
The Gorgon

**The House of De Nerra:**

The Promise
The Falls of Erith
Vestiges of Valor
Realm of Angels

**Highland Warriors of Munro:**
The Red Lion
Deep Into Darkness

**The House of de Garr:**
Lord of Light
Realm of Angels

**Saxon Lords of Hage:**
The Crusader
Kingdom Come

**High Warriors of Rohan:**
High Warrior
High King

**The House of Ashbourne:**
Upon a Midnight Dream

**The House of D'Aurilliac:**
Valiant Chaos

**The House of De Dere:**
Of Love and Legend

**St. John and de Gare Clans:**
The Warrior Poet

**The House of de Bretagne:**
The Questing

**The House of Summerlin:**
The Legend

**The Kingdom of Hendocia:**
Kingdom by the Sea

**The BlackChurch Guild: Shadow Knights:**
The Leviathan

*Regency Historical Romance:*
Sin Like Flynn: A Regency
Historical Romance Duet
The Sin Commandments
Georgina and the Red Charger

*Gothic Regency Romance:*
Emma

*Contemporary Romance:*

**Kathlyn Trent/Marcus Burton Series:**
Valley of the Shadow
The Eden Factor
Canyon of the Sphinx

**The American Heroes Anthology Series:**
The Lucius Robe
Fires of Autumn
Evenshade
Sea of Dreams
Purgatory

**Other non-connected Contemporary Romance:**
Lady of Heaven
Darkling, I Listen
In the Dreaming Hour
River's End
The Fountain

**Sons of Poseidon:**
The Immortal Sea

**Pirates of Britannia Series (with**

**Eliza Knight**):
Savage of the Sea by Eliza Knight
Leader of Titans by Kathryn Le

Veque
The Sea Devil by Eliza Knight
Sea Wolfe by Kathryn Le Veque

<u>**Note:**</u> All Kathryn's novels are designed to be read as stand-alones, although many have cross-over characters or cross-over family groups. Novels that are grouped together have related characters or family groups. You will notice that some series have the same books; that is because they are cross-overs. A hero in one book may be the secondary character in another.

There is NO reading order except by chronology, but even in that case, you can still read the books as stand-alones. No novel is connected to another by a cliff hanger, and every book has an HEA.

Series are clearly marked. All series contain the same characters or family groups except the American Heroes Series, which is an anthology with unrelated characters.

For more information, find it in **A Reader's Guide to the Medieval World of Le Veque**.

# ABOUT KATHRYN LE VEQUE

*Bringing the Medieval to Romance*

KATHRYN LE VEQUE is a critically acclaimed, multiple USA TODAY Bestselling author, an Indie Reader bestseller, a charter Amazon All-Star author, and a #1 bestselling, award-winning, multi-published author in Medieval Historical Romance with over 100 published novels.

Kathryn is a multiple award nominee and winner, including the winner of Uncaged Book Reviews Magazine 2017 and 2018 "Raven Award" for Favorite Medieval Romance. Kathryn is also a multiple RONE nominee (InD'Tale Magazine), holding a record for the number of nominations. In 2018, her novel WARWOLFE was the winner in the Romance category of the Book Excellence Award and in 2019, her novel A WOLFE AMONG DRAGONS won the prestigious RONE award for best pre-16th century romance.

Kathryn is considered one of the top Indie authors in the world with over 2M copies in circulation, and her novels have been translated into several languages. Kathryn recently signed with Sourcebooks Casablanca for a Medieval Fight Club series, first published in 2020.

In addition to her own published works, Kathryn is also the President/CEO of Dragonblade Publishing, a boutique publishing house specializing in Historical Romance. Dragonblade's success has seen it rise in the ranks to become Amazon's #1 e-book publisher of Historical Romance (K-Lytics report July 2020).

Kathryn loves to hear from her readers. Please find Kathryn on Facebook at Kathryn Le Veque, Author, or join her on Twitter @kathrynleveque. Sign up for Kathryn's blog at www.kathrynleveque.com for the latest news and sales.

www.ingramcontent.com/pod-product-compliance
Lightning Source LLC
Chambersburg PA
CBHW071209210726
48293CB00002B/348